BOBBY'S GIRL

by

Bernie Morris

Bobby's Girl

Published by Bronwyn Editions in the United Kingdom 2009
Copyright © Bernie Morris

Cover design © Linda Koperski
Photos courtesy of Robert Morris and Linda Koperski

Photographic models: Koi Quittenton and Sam Quittenton
Full parental permission for use of Sam's image obtained from
Jane Quittenton

Printed by
Lightning Source UK
2009

For
Robert Morris (Bobby)
with love

Excerpt from Katharine Keegan's diary:

Dear Bobby,

For all the agony I caused you, may God forgive me,
just like you did.

ACKNOWLEDGEMENTS

To Robert Morris, the perfect role model.

To Koi and Sam, my supermodels

To Jeffrey Palmer for putting up with all this in the beginning.

To Adrian Howe for the "Spinner's Haunt" legend.

To Valerie Freeman and George Foreman for painstaking help with musical dates.

To all the excellent vocalists, musicians and lyricists of the rock 'n roll years, who inspired this story – especially Susan Maughan for the title song.

Everything else in this story has been dredged from the author's imagination. All characters are fictitious and bear no resemblance to any real persons known to the author.

Some of the places mentioned are real, but many no longer exist. However, the underlying emotion is very real, and is based on personal soul-shattering experience.

Innocence, a fleeting thing
Like the blossoms of the spring
Like the pretty butterfly
Dancing now but soon to die.
Not for long that wide-eyed gaze
All too soon those baby days –
are gone.

Chapter One
(1956)

Gene Vincent was singing "Be Bop a Lula" about the time it all began. Not that she was much concerned with such a thing as popular music, but it was there in the background of her awareness, and remained throbbing concurrently with subsequent events, and ever since entwined with the memories.

Katharine Mary Keegan was born and raised in Stepney, East London. East End kids were supposed to be tough, but this one wasn't – not at first.

1956 was a significant year in several ways. It was a time of drastic change. This began around midsummer with the onset of premature adolescence and all the associated problems. It was unexpected – because Katharine (AKA Kate or Kitty) was just ten years old at the time.

As if this were not enough of a shock, her parents then decided to transfer her to another school. St. Michael's was better, so they had heard; better discipline, better teaching. It might even make a lady of their awkward, blundering daughter. It could possibly get her through the damning eleven plus examination. That was their ambition for Kate.

It was a difficult time to change schools. She was a shy kid who did not make friends with ease, and was way behind average with her schoolwork. It was largely due to the strenuous efforts of her new teacher, Miss Benson, that she survived the transition. This heroic woman gave her special personal attention – no mean feat in a class of forty. She encouraged her writing and strove to bring her maths to the required standard. Under her patient guidance, fractions and compound interest slowly began to make sense. Kate always knew that she owed a lot to Miss Benson.

She also met Mary Erika Johnson.

Both shy, awkward loners, they took to each other at once, and quickly discovered, to their mutual delight, that they had been born on the same day, and almost at the same hour. They decided then and there that they were twins, and even tried to dress alike. This was easy enough in school uniform, but it was more difficult to persuade their mothers to buy them similar clothes for out-of-school.

Mary insisted that they looked alike. Kate thought this was wishful thinking; although they both had brown hair in pigtails, hers was a dark, rich brown, whereas Mary's was that lighter colour, unkindly known as "mouse".

They both had blue eyes. But Kate argued again. Mary's were truest, deepest blue, like a pre-dawn sky. Whereas her eyes were not really blue at all – more a dark, bluish kind of grey.

'Airforce blue,' Mary insisted. And so Kate acquiesced.

They both hated being girls and wished they were boys; they longed to have their hair cut short like "George" in Enid Blyton's "Famous Five" but neither set of parents would allow it. And so they had to put up with their pigtails: an ever-present temptation for boys to pull.

Mary and Kate became inseparable, although they could not sit together in class. Mary had to sit near the front due to poor hearing, and Kate had to sit at the back as she was one of the tallest. Her desk-mate was Joe Warner, a fat boy who always had a snot-nose. He constantly copied her work, but she didn't mind this too much. At least he didn't pull her pigtails or put spiders in her desk like some boys would have. She frequently lent him handkerchiefs which his mother never washed and returned, until her mum began to complain about the amount of hankies she lost at school. But anything was better than listening to his sniffles and snorts all day. Aside from that, they got along okay.

Years later, Kate met Joe again at the youth club. He had slimmed down a lot and looked amazingly cool. He told her, among other things, that she had been the only girl in school who had ever been civil to him. She understood finally that loneliness was more widespread than she'd ever imagined.

But every playtime was shared with Mary, and their play was not the usual girlie stuff. They enacted Enid Blyton stories, or favourite historic scenes, invented spooky games and scared themselves silly; but their favourite game was "stone-agers" when they imagined themselves as cave-men. Mary shared Kate's fascination for pre-history.

Then they began to play a more serious game which they called "Operation Escape". This was because of Shelagh Durran who was the female version of the school bully. Years later, Kate could still recall her dreaded face with clarity. Shelagh had thick, ginger-brown hair, coiled into many ringlets which reminded her of sausages. Her eyes were green, slanted, and mocking. She was bigger than the average ten-year-old; not fat, but heftily built. She must have weighed seven stone to Kate's six.

Shelagh had always taken great delight in tormenting Mary. Now she had two of them – quiet girls who wouldn't say "boo" to the proverbial goose. She had even thought up her own pet names for them: Mary-wary and Kitty-witty, obviously more from sarcasm than affection. She revelled in the task of making their lives a misery. She was strong, and could twist an arm behind someone's back until they yelped. She pulled hair much more viciously than the boys ever did – great handfuls of it. Even they (the boys) seemed afraid of her.

With the greatest of ease, Shelagh extorted all their pocket money, which was little enough. Kate got only twopence a day, and Mary got sixpence as her parents were better off. All this was handed over to Shelagh every morning at break-time for "protection" which meant she would beat them up otherwise. Kate only wished she could have seen through her from the start. It would have saved a lot of trouble for herself and Mary.

On one occasion, Shelagh deliberately spilled water on the bench in the art room, just as Kate was about to sit there. When she had done so and discovered herself to be soaking wet, Shelagh promptly wailed to the teacher, 'Please Miss, Katharine's wet herself!' And she managed to sound genuinely disgusted. Kate was ordered from the room in disgrace, accompanied by the derision of the class. That was the most humiliating thing she did, but there were many others. Yet it never occurred to the girls to report Shelagh's misdeeds to a teacher. There was a kind of unwritten law that simply forbade such a thing. To split on a schoolmate was the lowest thing to do. The fact that Shelagh herself did not observe this rule made no difference. Just because she was low didn't mean they had to join her. It was a kind of fierce, unreasoning pride.

There was the time Shelagh ruined Mary's new cardigan. This happened in sewing class. She slyly cut a small piece from Mary's elbow with her scissors, causing a mass of ladders to run straight up the sleeve. Mary was quite distraught when she told Kate about it. Her mum was likely to hit the roof when she got home. 'Shelagh's a puckfig!' she said with vehemence.

'Oh Mary,' Kate feigned horror, 'what would your dad say if he really knew what you meant?'

She grinned. 'He'd probably wash my mouth out with soap. What would your dad say?'

Kate's mind boggled at the thought. 'I bet I wouldn't have a mouth left. I'd still be spitting out teeth.' They lapsed into helpless giggles; and from that day on, Shelagh was referred to as 'Puckfig' – a polite reference to what they really thought.

So that's what they were up against.

Mary and Kate began to slip out of school at lunchtime to avoid Shelagh. This was against the rules, and they'd have been in trouble if they'd been caught, but they considered it worth the risk. They even gave up having school lunch to avoid seeing her in the dining hall. Hunger was the worst part of this idea; and they couldn't use their dinner money to buy food, as this was collected by Miss Benson each Monday morning, which was just as well, else Shelagh would surely have claimed it. They tried to bring extra sandwiches from home for the morning break, without arousing parents' suspicions. These combined with bottles of school milk had to suffice for the day.

Most days they went to the local park. This was about five minutes walk from the rear gate of the school, comprised extensive lawns and gardens, a children's playground, and was situated by the busy River Thames.

They would stand by the waterside railings and watch the little tugs towing barges, while the black oily water made rainbowed slicks along the muddy shore. They loved to see the really big ships which often passed, moving towards Tower Bridge and the Pool of London. These would blow a deafening signal, and the famous bridge would open to allow passage.

Or they might go to the children's playground. Except for a few young mums with toddlers, this would be blissfully deserted on schooldays. As they played on the swings or roundabouts, they would devise elaborate plans for getting rid of Shelagh, none of which they would ever have dared to execute. That's why they called it "Operation Escape".

Although they were heartily ashamed of being so firmly in the power of such a bully, there did not seem to be a way out. If they ganged up on her, she would not hesitate to split on them, then they would be in big trouble – not only at school – their parents would be told. Mary's father was strict, but Kate's stepfather was downright scary. He needed very little excuse to tan her backside with his leather belt. This always happened in the evenings when her mum worked part-time, and the significance of that did not strike her until much later. She just lived in mortal fear of him, and would rather have put up with Shelagh forever than face his anger.

Then came the day when Shelagh was waiting for them at the school gate, wearing a triumphant grin on her freckled face. 'Where have you been?' she wanted to know. 'Tell me, or I'll split!'

Mary was quicker-witted than Kate. She tipped her friend a blue-eyed wink and nudged her to silence. 'We've been to explore the bommies,' she lied.

The bommies were derelict bombed houses, of which there were an abundance in the East End. These were considered unsafe and definitely out of bounds for schoolchildren.

Shelagh's green eyes gleamed wickedly. 'I'm gonna split,' she announced.

Kate summoned courage. 'That's 'cos you wouldn't dare go there. They're haunted, you know.'

'Pah!' she exclaimed. 'There ain't no such thing as ghosts!'

But they could see her pride was rankled. The bell sounded at that moment and she viciously yanked a pigtail from each defiant kid, almost knocking their heads together.

Mary and Kate were on tenterhooks all afternoon, expecting Shelagh to split but, amazingly, she didn't. They both thought she must have something else in mind, and they were right.

School broke out at 4:30pm and Kate had a fairly long walk home. On wintry evenings, she usually made it just before full darkness, which was when her parents expected her. She was naturally dismayed when Shelagh began to walk with her. It was not the bigger girl's usual direction and Kate did not relish the thought of her company.

'Show me these bommies,' Shelagh commanded.

'It'll be dark soon,' Kate protested.

'Who's scared now?' she jeered.

'Okay Shelagh.' And Kitty led her to the eeriest derelict she knew: Spinner's Haunt.

Spinner's Haunt was a particular bombed house which appeared to have been cleaved straight down the middle, and was still attached to the end of an abandoned terrace. It was spooky to see half a house like that. The place whispered of death and destruction, and fired the imagination. Mary and Kate had made up their own story about it, just the way they made up stories about everything.

Mildewed wallpaper still clung to the standing walls, and two black fireplaces resembled open yawning mouths in the fading light.

The staircase was miraculously intact, though it swayed and groaned as if tired of waiting for demolition. The roof was gone, but the one of the adjoining house could be reached from the upper level, via broken brickwork which had formed convenient steps in the rear wall.

Shelagh gripped Kate's arm with a heavy hand. 'Why is it called Spinner's Haunt?'

Kate could see she was scared; the atmosphere was getting to her. 'Spinner was the dog who used to live here,' she lied in a whispering voice. 'He was killed when the house was bombed, along with all of the children. He still comes back to look for them. After dark, if you sit on the roof, you can hear him howling. It's really very sad. Mary and me have heard him.'

'You've sat on the roof?' She looked incredulous and eyed the creaking staircase with apprehension.

'Yeah, you can't hear him otherwise,' Kate reminded.

'Then I'm gonna do it!' she said defiantly. 'I'll show you who's a scaredy-cat.' She glared at Kate, green eyes more feline than she knew. 'You'll have to go first, to show me the way.'

'Okay,' Kate said with less hesitation than she felt. She'd often made this climb before, though never in growing darkness. Still, she was more scared of Shelagh than she was of the dark. Her heart hammered in her chest, but she wasn't going to chicken out now.

She began to climb the creaky staircase. That was the easy bit. Shelagh followed, gripping the bannister for support, careful not to let Kate out of her sight. They reached the upper level, and stood precariously in the remains of a bedroom. 'Mind the hole in the floor,' Kate warned. 'Walk around the edge like me.'

Shelagh nodded, too fearful to notice who was giving the orders. They reached the stepped brickwork. Kate was just as scared as she was, but for a different reason. She wondered if Shelagh would push her off the roof. Was she capable of murder? Or she might do it in a moment of panic. Either way, she didn't trust her one little bit. Alone on a roof with Shelagh was the last place in the world she wanted to be.

She reached the top and stood on a ledge which must have once been part of the chimney stack. Shelagh arrived to join her, panting as much from fear as physical effort. The black-tiled roof of the next house reached about waist level, and stretched before them, resembling a pyramid in the half-light. Stars had begun to wink, and cold wind whistled past their ears.

'You've gotta ride the roof,' Kate wickedly informed.

Shelagh gulped and visibly paled in the starlight. 'Go on then, Kitty-witty,' she taunted. 'You go first.'

There didn't seem to be much choice. Kate hoisted herself to the apex of the sloping roof and sat astride. Then she made her way to the middle, shifting her weight alternately from hands to thighs. The slates were icily cold and damp, like gravestones, she thought. She and Mary, or street mates, usually did this daredevil feat in the summer when the black-tiled roofs were warm. What happens to the blatant nerve of the very young? She did not even think to glance down at the drop to the street below. It never occurred to her that she might fall, unless Shelagh had anything to do with it.

She turned, twisting her body to look back at the other girl. 'Come on, Shelagh,' she coaxed. 'It's good up here.' She could see the bully was petrified, and obviously had no head for heights, yet was determined not to lose face.

Shelagh placed her hands on the crest of the roof, and Kate turned away to hide her grinning face.

Then somewhere not too distant, a dog howled mournfully in the silent night. This could not have been better timed if Kate had arranged it. And it was more than enough for Shelagh. She screamed and fled. Kate heard her frantic footsteps descending the brickwork, and then the staircase. Then all was silent; she'd bottled out.

Kate threw back her head and laughed aloud at the twinkling stars. 'Thanks, Spinner old mate!' she yelled. Serves you right, Puckfig! she thought savagely to Shelagh.

A moment of short-lived glory.

She knew that revenge would be swift and sure.

Chapter Two

The next morning at break time, Katharine was delayed after class by Miss Benson.

The kind teacher wanted to be sure that she understood the fundamentals of the new decimals they were learning. Kate hardly listened to the teacher's patient instruction; she was more concerned about Mary who would be alone and unsuspecting in the playground – and that Shelagh would get her...

Her worst fears were realised as she raced into the yard; then had to force her way through the crowd which had gathered around them. Shelagh had Mary in a fierce throttlehold, twisting her arm behind her back at the same time. The boys in the crowd were cheering her on. They thought it highly amusing to see girls fighting. "Cat fight" they called it.

Something terrible snapped inside Kate's head; something that would save or betray her for the rest of her life – like a fine wire around the edge of swelling rage. Mary was her friend, and her eyes were full of tears – only she could save her. 'Let her go Puckfig!' Her normally quiet voice had become a venomous hiss.

Silence descended as every head turned in her direction and she realised, with a twinge of dismay, that all those listening boys had probably instantly labelled her as a slag. Girls who swore were just that, even when using an obvious coded euphemism, the intention was there. It never occurred to the opposite sex that girls might be only human, the same as they were (or so she thought).

Shelagh released Mary with a sudden push which caused the hapless girl to fall; then turned towards Katharine. Green eyes gleamed expectant triumph. Kate could see Shelagh thought her no problem at all. Mary was pulled to her feet by many willing hands and roughly comforted with awkward pats. She wasn't a slag.

Kate launched herself at Shelagh before the fury had time to abate. Her head rammed into Shelagh's middle and she went down, quite unprepared for such an attack from little old quiet Kitty-witty. Kate followed the other girl's fall, going down with her, straddling her body, grazing both her knees on the rough tarmac of the playground.

The kids shouted encouragement. 'Go Kate! – kill her!' And she was surprised that they seemed to be on her side. She began to beat Shelagh's face with her clenched fists, not even knowing how to use fists. She didn't use her knuckles – just the ends of rolled-up pudgy fingers, like rubber hammers. She hit her as if she were beating a drum.

But it was enough. Shelagh began to cry as her nose bled all down the front of her school blouse. Then two boys pulled Kate off her and held her firmly while she struggled in their grip. Later, she understood that they'd been trying to save her from getting into worse trouble, but at the time she thought of nothing beyond murdering Shelagh – she had hurt her friend. Shelagh got up and staggered away to split to a teacher. Mary was looking at Kate with wonder and gratitude.

One boy grinned wickedly. 'Show us yer knickers again!' he taunted.

Kate blushed furiously, realising she already had.

'Nah, school navy-blues – so boring!' another boy added.

'Leave her alone!' This sharp command came from Jon Daley. He was the biggest boy in school, the toughest – and the nicest. This might seem a rare combination. That was very true of Jon. He was a rare boy whom she'd often admired from a distance. His arm went straight around her shoulders. 'You sorted her out real good,' he said gently. 'S'about time someone did. You was brilliant!'

There was frank admiration in his warm brown eyes. Kate noted his dark glossy hair and short stubby nose with its mild dash of freckles and, most of all, his wonderful smile.

And at that precise moment, Katharine Mary Keegan fell in love with Jon James Daley.

Then the teachers came, cold-eyed and stern. They took her to the headmistress to answer to her crime.

Kate received three strokes of the council cane across each palm and, for the first time ever, she counted herself lucky to be a girl – a boy would have got it on the backside. She had always considered this to be most unfair.

The headmistress was a nun: Sister Marie-Clair. She looked quite old and frail, but wielded that cane with a vengeance. Then Kate had to stand and listen while the nun lectured, holding her stinging palms behind her back and hanging her head in shame. She said all the things Kate expected to hear: Young ladies did not attack other young ladies (she almost laughed at that reference) and they most certainly did not use foul language. She said Kate was an animal and deserved to be expelled, and she promised a letter to her parents.

This was the most ominous threat of all. Kate felt weak with fear at the thought of her dad's anger; but still she did not split on Shelagh. It would have made no difference if she had. She was just as guilty as the other girl.

There was a kind of awed silence when she walked back into class. They all looked at her as if they had never seen her before, but she detected admiration in most of their looks, for no-one liked Shelagh. She was surprised when Miss Benson smiled sympathetically; she'd heard a full account of what had happened from the rest of the class. There was no sign of Shelagh – she must have gone home. Kate was even more pleasantly surprised when she arrived at her desk to find Jon Daley seated in Joe's usual place beside hers. She was immediately conscious of how awful she must look. Her eyes were all puffy from crying and, having lost one ribbon, she had pulled both pigtails loose.

He grinned in that heart-melting way that remained etched in her mind forever. 'I persuaded Joe to swap desks,' he said.

She saw fat Joe looking subdued in the far corner, and she knew persuasion would not have been difficult. All the boys had a very healthy respect for Jon.

He smiled again and said, 'I like your hair like that. It's all wavy, like Mona Lisa.'

She smiled back at him. That was the first compliment she had ever received from a boy. Mary was giving her the upturned thumb from her fist, in what they privately called "the gesture of triumph". Her spirit began to lift. What the hell? Her dad was going to beat her – but he'd probably do it a hundred times more anyway, before she grew up and fled the nest.

Miss Benson rapped her desk for attention.

'Take out your English books...'

As it turned out, no letter ever went home to her parents. Kate never understood why, but suspected that Miss Benson must have had words with the headmistress.

Shelagh never returned to school, so maybe her parents got a letter instead, or her humiliation might have been so great that she begged them to put her in another school. She probably found someone else to pick on – someone smaller and weaker than she was; that's if she hadn't learned her lesson. It proved something to Kate though – something she'd read in an Enid Blyton story (Enid was her childhood heroine). She said that all bullies are cowards; they're really scared inside. That never made sense to Kate at the time she read it, but now it did. Cheers Enid!

Jon agreed with this entirely. He never bullied, although he often got into fights at school. These were always with boys his own age, and never lasted long – he always won. He had that quiet inner strength that didn't need constant assertion – it simply rallied when required. This was a quality she ever after sought in a man, and rarely found. But Jon became the hero in every future story she wrote. Every one of them was woven around his soul.

After that Katharine actually began to enjoy school. She and Mary had no further need to make lunchtime escapes, though they still sometimes did, just for the crack. Jon was her constant companion in class, but never in the playground. At that age, boys were expected to stick with their mates, and girls likewise. But although it was never mentioned, everyone knew of the rapport between them. She was Jon's girl.

They certainly never mentioned love. She was afraid that he would laugh, and he later confessed that he'd feared the same from her. But Kate knew that she loved Jon like she'd never loved anyone or anything before. Puppy-love usually attacks those least able to cope with it.

There was nothing physical about it at that early age. They were young enough to find such things embarrassing. Sometimes their eyes would meet, then hastily separate, afraid the truth might show. It was all the more painful for that.

Elvis was singing "Love me Tender" and, for the first time ever, the words of a love song held special meaning. Kate would turn up the volume control on the old wireless set in the kitchen whenever they played it. If her dad was there, he would turn it down again. 'Rock 'n Roll is mad music,' he would say. 'It'll never catch on.'

Jon and Kate never had proper dates out of school, unless you counted Saturdays when they went swimming or to morning pictures. Mary was never allowed out on Saturday; her mum made her do most of the housework. So these days were spent with Jon, as unobtrusively as possible. He would inform her in advance of where he was likely to be with his mates. Then she would arrange to go there as well with friends from her street. In that way, they spent many a pleasant Saturday morning watching "Flash Gordon" or "Superman" safely inconspicuous in the crowd. Neither of them ever had much money, but these simple pleasures were cheap. Kate would save her twopence a day for a whole week to be able to afford them.

Jon always gave her his wonderful smile as soon as he saw her. She never saw him without welcome in his eyes, except once...

A few times he took her to his house at lunchtime, usually when Mary was off school with a cold or something. There was never anyone at home, and Jon had his own front door key which she thought was awfully grown-up and responsible. On the first occasion, he seemed quite embarrassed and apologised for the mess. 'My mum works,' he explained. 'She has to 'cos my dad died. She don't get much time to tidy up.'

Kate expressed rough childish sympathy, but didn't think the mess was that bad. It was just the usual upheaval left by a hurried family in the morning, which is normally cleared up later by Mum.

There was a rag doll on the floor and several wooden baby blocks. Jon grinned as he picked these up. 'My little sister, Susie. She's only two. She has to stay with a minder while Mum works.'

Kate felt a pang of sorrow. How hard it must be for Jon's mum to be mother and father both.

There was a bowl of chips already prepared and a pot of home-made soup on the gas stove. 'Let's have nosh,' Jon invited. 'I ain't a bad cook for a man.'

He was right. She had to admire the efficient way he prepared the food, and wondered how many other boys his age could have done it.

That was definitely the most romantic meal of her life. No amount of candle-lit dinners in posh restaurants could ever equal the mood. Jon sat opposite her in his mum's shabby, but cosy kitchen and they chatted and laughed like they never could in school. They drowned their golden chips in tomato ketchup (Kate's mum would have had a fit). Then Jon raided the biscuit tin and they dunked these in their tea – another disgusting habit that would never have been allowed at home.

She noticed the photo of a nice-looking man on the sideboard. His smile was just like Jon's. 'Is that your dad?' she asked needlessly.

The sudden pain in his eyes made her wish she hadn't.

'Yeah, I miss him a lot.' He lowered his gaze.

'I'm sorry Jon,' she said helplessly, and reached for his hand.

He continued to hold hers after the first gentle pressure, and she began to tell him about her dad – her stepfather. She'd never told anyone before except Mary.

As she spoke, the fear must have shown in her eyes, for his own suddenly blazed with a rage she had never seen before, and his grip on her hand tightened. 'He beats you?' he asked incredulously.

'With a belt? – But you're just a little girl!' Then his expression changed to a fierce resolve and he said, 'When I grow up – I'll beat him.'

How easily childhood promises are made.

And that was one of the reasons why Katharine Mary Keegan loved Jon James Daley.

Chapter Three

Then came the series of rather shocking incidents which taught Kate several valuable lessons about human nature and the ways of the world. It began with a new boy in school – Warren Craig.

Miss Benson gave them a class briefing the day before his arrival.

He was an American boy (he had to be with a name like that) and a good deal older than them, but was way behind in his schoolwork and would be joining their class while his father was in England. He had been continually shunted to and fro between his divorced parents for the last few years, which explained his faltering education. His father was a rich businessman, but Warren was a problem child. The teacher asked the class to make special allowances for him.

This put their backs up at once. Quite a few of them had problems at home and they didn't need special attention. Jon's was a one-parent family; Kate's stepfather beat the living daylights out of her, and Harpie's mother was divorced. The poor kid had to put up with an endless succession of 'uncles' which probably explained her flighty ways.

Her real name was Doris Harper and she didn't mind a bit being called Harpie, until some bright spark told her it was a kind of bat monster. But by that time, the other kids were so used to the name they just weren't able to stop using it. Anyway, she didn't look a bit like a bat monster. Harpie was the most beautiful girl you could imagine. She made other girls feel like shadows in sunlight. Natural white-blonde hair curled to her shoulders; big baby-blue eyes melted your heart and, even at that tender age, her figure had begun to show stunning promise. She also had a sunny nature. In fact, she was the only one who seemed pleased about the newcomer. As they left the classroom she voiced her enthusiasm, 'Cor! A rich American. I hope he's good looking.'

'There ain't nothing wrong with English boys,' Mary staunchly defended.

Kate agreed whole-heartedly, while Jon smiled and winked at her.

'Well, I wouldn't mind a rich fella for a change.' Harpie announced with a devilish pout.

'Go Harpie!' Kate encouraged.

'Go man go!' Mary added, teasingly.

Harpie beamed at them. She never needed much encouragement where boys were concerned but, if it was given, she fairly lapped it up. She pranced away on long coltish legs, her short pleated skirt swinging with her hips. They all laughed. No-one seriously disliked Harpie; she wasn't a bad kid, and was never bitchy like most beautiful girls. The others mostly laughed at her antics.

But no-one laughed much the next morning – least of all Kate.

Warren Craig arrived at about 10 o'clock, and was duly ushered in by Miss Benson, who had been to the Head's office to collect him. He stared at the class with disdain, as if he were a prize stallion who'd been asked to share a stable with donkeys. They all stared right back at him with varying degrees of amazement.

He wasn't much bigger than most of them – about Jon's height, though stockier built. And he certainly was good-looking, Harpie was very pleased to note. "Too bloody handsome" one kid said later. Warren looked just like the typical American boy they'd seen in films. Sun-blond crew-cut; light blue eyes, the colour of icy winter skies – and just as cold. He had a splendid tan, although it was January; but it was his clothes that were most fascinating. He had probably been excused school uniform due to his short stay, for he wore tight blue jeans, the kind they'd all have loved to own, but no ordinary parents could afford. Most impressive of all was the matching blue denim jacket (bomber style) which topped the jeans over a dazzling white T-shirt. His hands were sunk deep into his pockets, and he glared sullenly.

'This is Warren,' Miss Benson said, a bit uneasily, having sensed the immediate hostility between her class and the new boy.

He was silently christened "rabbit-hole" by most of the brighter wits present, though Jon told Kate later that he could have thought of a more fitting description.

Warren then smiled – surprising everyone, and showing a perfect set of American teeth, startling white against his tan; but his eyes remained cold. 'Hi kids,' he said, and his voice was unexpectedly deep, like a man's.

Return greetings were mumbled half-heartedly, except for Harpie's 'Hi Warren!' brightly determined to atone for the rest of them, and she gave him her most enchanting smile.

'Someone hold her down,' Martin Sykes stage-whispered in the tone of a man betrayed, and they all stifled giggles.

Warren returned Harpie's smile, eyeing her with his first spark of interest. Then his eyes swept the classroom, seeking an empty seat. They finally came to rest on Kate – and stopped.

The icy-blue gaze disturbed her in a way she did not understand. There was something about him that was different from Jon and all the other boys in class – something that whispered around the edges of her mind, like a recent dream that cannot be recalled. It wasn't just his good looks, or his clothes or even his deep voice – it was something much more. And the way he looked at her made her shiver in a fashion that was not entirely unpleasant.

Much later, she understood what it was.

Warren Craig was a man – at least physically so. She later learned that his mental age did not quite match up.

And she was suddenly afraid.

He moved down the gangway between desks, to the back row, towards the empty one in the corner, two paces to her right, and there he seated himself. His eyes flickered over her, and lingered, then they returned to hers and fixed.

She received his silent message as loudly and clearly as if he had shouted. Like the mating song of a bird, Warren was calling her to him. He was giving the most primeval signal of all, and he did not expect to be denied.

Kate's face flamed and her heart pounded.

Jon was not oblivious to all this. She heard his breathing quicken with righteous indignation. He caught her arm and she glanced at him, but he was looking past her at Warren. The boys' eyes locked and she felt the fierce conflict between them, though neither said a word. Ice-blue eyes bored into brown. The challenge was given and taken up – another ritual as old as man himself. War had been declared, and she could almost hear the drums pounding in her head.

The most frightening thing of all was this: something deep inside her wanted to answer Warren. Instinctively, she was drawn to him like a moth to the candle, even though she knew the contact would be fatal. She was the child become woman; she was ahead of Jon in this way.

Warren's eyes returned to hers, and he smiled and winked at her. 'Hi, gorgeous,' he said boldly.

Kate couldn't remember if she replied; she just gripped Jon's hand to reassure herself of his safe presence, ashamed and terrified of the turbulence inside her. She wondered if Jon knew. He must have even understood, for he returned the pressure of her hand and whispered in her ear, 'He's eyeing you up. I'll sort him out later.'

Her fear for Jon only increased the raging storm.

At break-time, Warren deliberately sought Kate out, blissfully ignorant of the golden rule that separated boys from girls in the playground. She was sitting on a wooden bench with Mary when he came and sat right down beside her, ignoring her friend except for a brief smile.

He didn't waste a single moment.

'What's your name?' he wanted to know.

She told him, nervously, as it was no secret, unable to hide her confusion.

He seemed pleased by her obvious agitation. 'I wanna date you, Kate.' His eyes explored her from top to toe. 'You're one swell cute chick.'

His accent seemed very strange, and his slang words were vastly different from theirs, yet she had no trouble understanding him. They were well used to hearing American talk on films and television, yet still it seemed odd to hear a real live person speak that way.

Kate's face flamed at his outspoken compliment, and Mary giggled most unhelpfully. 'I don't go out with boys,' she told him, a little untruthfully. 'I'm too young.'

He shook his head in disagreement. 'You ain't too young. I can see you ain't.' He studied her face for a few moments. 'What about that guy you sit with? Don't you date him?'

'I ain't even allowed out evenings,' she informed evasively (though quite truthfully this time). 'Why don't you ask Harpie? She dates.'

He grinned his perfect American grin. 'I know a million dames like her back home,' (Now that had to be a lie. There just couldn't be a million like Harpie.) 'but you're different. You're special. I want you, baby.'

He certainly didn't believe in beating around the bush. She stared at him silently, quite lost for words.

'I've got plenty of dough.' He produced a wad of notes from his pocket and flicked through them with his thumb. Mary and Kate were wide-eyed with disbelief. They'd never seen so much money all at once in their lives. 'I can take you anywhere you want, buy you anything you want – a new dress, jewellery – anything.'

'I wish Harpie could hear this,' Mary said, grinning wickedly.

'I ain't no gold digger,' Kate told Warren, 'besides, you're too old for me. You scare me.'

His arm around her shoulders was strategically meant to reassure, though it didn't. 'I'm just the right age for you. Can't you see that? I'll show you what a man's for. That young guy you're with – he ain't no use to you.'

Angrily, she shrugged his arm away. 'That's for me to decide, ain't it?'

He seemed quite undeterred by this rejection. Icy eyes still roamed and caressed. 'I'll give you a few days to think about it – I ain't pushy.'

Mary exploded in giggles.

Warren smiled disarmingly, and left them.

Kate couldn't help smiling herself, though her heart pounded wildly with mingled fear and excitement. Warren was certainly a charmer, but still something in his eyes made her afraid.

Both girls watched his lazy, swaggering walk across the playground. Then Jon appeared and met him halfway. They exchanged words with cold, unfriendly faces, glancing just once back in the girls' direction. Kate couldn't help comparing the two of them. Jon was big for his age, but still did not look more than twelve. Warren was no taller than Jon, but was much more man-shaped. He looked at least fifteen – it wasn't a matter of size. She was relieved when they both turned and strode away from each other. They'd obviously reached some kind of uneasy truce.

Jon came towards her with anxious eyes. He looked at her searchingly as he sat down beside her. 'What did he say to you?' he asked.

Kate told him as nearly as she could remember; she could never lie to Jon. His eyes grew increasingly troubled as she spoke. She had never seen him look that way before, and began to hate herself for even listening to Warren.

'You know, what he said to me is right,' he finally said. It is up to you. You gonna think about it?'

'No way, Jon. He's creepy. He scares me.'

Instant relief brightened his face and his arm crept around her, hesitantly. They didn't usually show affection in such a public place, but she sensed his need for reassurance and put her arm around him too.

'Seeya later,' Mary said, sensing their emotion. She skipped away to find Harpie.

'You're my fella,' Kate told Jon, firmly.

'My Kit,' he whispered against her cheek. 'Let me know if he gives you any bovver.'

And that's exactly what she did.

At lunchtime, Harpie was bubbling over when she told them that Warren had asked her out that very same evening. She could hardly contain her excitement. Kate didn't have the heart to tell her he'd asked her first; it didn't seem worth bursting her bubble for. But she couldn't help feeling a bit worried about her – Harpie didn't know a thing about him really. But then, Kate told herself, their crazy friend was used to older boys; she said she went out with them all the time. She should know what to expect.

'I ain't got a thing to wear!' she wailed, despairingly.

'Don't worry 'bout it, Harpie.' Kate soothed. 'You'd look good in a dishcloth.'

She smiled sweetly, as she idly reflected, 'I'll borra stockings from Mum.'

'Have mercy on the poor boy!' Kate joked, and they all giggled.

'I dunno what you see in him,' Mary said, more seriously. 'I hate the way he struts around like Mr Cool. Why don't he ever take his hands outa his pockets?'

'Don't you know nothing?' Harpie shook her blonde head in worldly-wise fashion. 'He does that to make his jeans tighter in front – so we can all see what a big man he is.'

They just squealed with laughter.

But the next morning Kate thought Harpie looked a little subdued. She was puffy-eyed, as if she'd been crying, and there was a bruise on her face that neither friend liked the look of.

They cornered her in the girls' cloakroom for the inevitable sound-out. 'How'd it go?' Kate asked her worriedly. 'Did he do that to your face?'

'No!' she replied, too quickly. 'My uncle was annoyed 'cos I was late home.'

'Where'd you go?' Mary asked next.

Harpie brightened a little. 'We went to Leicester Square to see a film. Then we wandered all over the West End, eating hot-dogs and drinking beer – we went in all the good coffee bars.'

'Beer?' Kate wrinkled her nose in distaste.

'Beer's okay once you get used to the taste,' Harpie informed. 'It makes you feel good. Warren drinks a lot; he smokes fags too – and boy – is he a fast mover!'

They could well believe it.

'Look what he gave me.' She showed them the tiny gold bangle she was wearing.

They both cooed over it. You could see it was real gold. Whatever else Warren might be, he certainly wasn't mean – but somehow Kate didn't feel the least bit envious.

'And this!' Harpie pulled something out from her Teeny-bra.

Mary and Kate both gasped when they saw what it was – a brand-new, crisp, five pound note.

Kate couldn't help feeling it was all too much like a gangster film. A cold shiver travelled down her spine. She was convinced that Warren had bought Harpie's silence.

Chapter Four

Jon wasn't able to walk Kate home from school as often as he would have liked. Except for Fridays or end of term days, he usually picked up his little sister from the minder and took her home before his mum finished work. Kate greatly admired his family loyalty and never expected to replace it, but she knew Jon worried about her on winter evenings. She lived half an hour's walk from the school, that's if she didn't dawdle, and it was usually dark by the time she got home.

And so it happened that two nights later, she was walking down the lonely "Highway" which was her quickest route though not the most desirable – passing the dark and sinister shapes of derelict houses. She wasn't feeling the least bit spooked. Her thoughts were full of Jon, as they usually were, and vague fanciful dreams about their future. That's why she was taken completely by surprise when a strong arm suddenly encircled her body and pulled her into the shadowed doorway of a bombed house.

Kate's little scream of shock was stifled by his firm hand over her mouth. It was Warren. She noticed his handsome young face with relief which she soon realised was premature.

'Don't be scared, baby,' he said. 'I only want a chance to talk alone with you.' He removed the hand from her mouth and retrieved a bottle of beer from his pocket. Several empties were strewn in the doorway around him and she wondered how many he'd had. 'I want to know your answer, babe.' he continued. 'I've given you time to think about it.'

'Ain't you dating Harpie?' she asked stupidly. She knew he wasn't. One night out with him had been enough for her.

'I don't want no dumb blonde,' he said emphatically. 'I told you before, I want you, baby. You're a real English rose.'

'But I'm Jon's girl,' she protested feebly, feeling quite weak at the knees with the closeness of this strange man creature.

'He's no good to you. I know what you need.' He lifted his sweater and placed her hand under it, against his warm chest. 'Touch me, Kate.'

He certainly knew the "go" button. He knew that if he'd touched her he'd have triggered the slap reaction. Warren was shrewder than that; he made her touch him. She felt, for the first time, solid male flesh with his heart pounding beneath it, and was ashamed to realise she was almost lost. There he was – Satan in blue denim – the serpent who offered the sweetest apple to an Eve who was very young and gullible. And the feel of him thrilled her.

'Be my girl,' he said enticingly. 'Drop that other kid. He's just a child.'

But now he'd hit the "stop" button. There was no way Kate could ever do that. She loved Jon, and knew that in a few years he would give her much more than Warren ever could. 'No,' she said decidedly, with a glorious feeling that she'd passed some kind of test with flying colours.

But this enraged him. 'You crazy bitch!' He put one arm around the back of her neck; then, with his free hand, he broke his beer bottle against the crumbling brickwork and held up the jagged remains to her face. 'I don't wanna hurt you,' he said passionately. 'But I'm warning you I can hurt him. I'm stronger and a lot meaner and I'm ruthless. You'd better change your mind real quick.'

The brown jagged glass glowed golden in the light of the streetlamps, just inches from her widened eyes. In that moment, Kate saw Warren exactly how he really was – just a little spoiled brat who couldn't bear not to get his own way. Any attraction she'd felt for him flew straight out of her mind's window. Her first impulse was to bring her knee up hard into his crotch, but she controlled this. For one thing, she didn't really want to do that to him (It really is the worst and lowest thing to do, but then, a boy has to be pretty low to deserve it). Also, with that glass so close to her face, she knew very well what pain reflex could do. She tried to sound calm. 'Okay, Warren. You don't need that glass.'

He smiled his beautiful smile – all sunshine, dimples and poison. 'That's better,' he approved. 'That's how I like my dames – nice and willing. 'He threw the glass behind him into the rubble, where it crashed and tinkled to pieces; then he put both arms around Kate and pulled her closer. 'Just a few kisses, babe. I don't wanna rush you.'

Here, she thought, you'll have to excuse the sarcasm: But wasn't that good of him? Wasn't that just fine and noble? This creep really thought he was being easy on her.

His lips sought hers and she smelled the beer on his breath. She was suddenly more revolted than she had ever been. She didn't have to put up with this! She had a mind of her own, didn't she? Jon would never force her like this; he was worth a dozen of Warren. Her temper flared in several shades of bright glaring red, and she brought her knee up hard and fast into his groin, hardening her heart to the agonized sound he made. Then she ran, as he grovelled in pain. She ran as fast as she was able, and just prayed he would not recover in time to catch her.

She fled with the mindless terror of a hunted animal – there was still quite a distance to cover before she got home, and she was sure he would catch her before then, certain he would be angry enough to kill her. After what seemed an impossibly short time, she heard his footsteps behind her, gaining fast. He was swifter and stronger than she; there was no doubt in her mind that he would get her. She tried to run faster, knowing she could not. Her sides were stitched with pain, every breath rasped in her throat, and her feet seemed hardly aware of the ground they were supposed to touch.

She raced into her home alley, which was flanked with bommies and slum dwellings, and led to the square where she lived – and there she almost collided with Bobby and Adam, two boys from her street. Bobby was about Warren's age, but more suitably sized, and Kate knew he was sweet on her. Adam was a little Jewish kid, even smaller than Kate was, but hard as nails. Bobby was leader of their street gang which was humorously known as the Alley-cats. Adam was his second – five feet of war machine, small but deadly.

Bobby held out his arms to check Kate's headlong flight, and could hardly fail to notice her desperate fear. 'You got trouble kid?'

She nodded, wild-eyed, breathless, and never so glad to see anyone in her life. She dived between these two saviours while they stood before her, waiting. Adam took a bicycle chain from beneath the tattered rag which was supposed to have been his school blazer; his shock of unruly black hair clouding his freckled face, fierce dark eyes sharply alert.

Warren rounded the corner, and stopped in mid-gallop when he saw these two defenders.

'This our street,' Bobby informed in a tone which dared argument. He flicked his fag butt at Warren as he spoke, and a shower of sparks burst all over the American boy. 'We don't want you here. Get lost!'

'Yeah, fuck off!' Adam added with his usual eloquence. He was a man of very few words but tremendous impact.

Warren visibly quailed. Kate could see him eyeing up the two boys, weighing his chances, deciding they weren't much. But still he tried sweet-talk. 'Let me through – it's a free country. I ain't got no quarrel with you guys.'

'Oh no?' Bobby said sceptically. 'But this kitten belongs with us. You quarrel with her – you quarrel with me.' Then he yelled, 'Cats!'

With impeccable response, the others began to appear. Like dark shadows they came, almost like zombies from the ruins – boys and girls both. And Kate's heart cheered to see them. They had been sharing a crafty fag, or snogging – or whatever else kids do in the dark, but they came to the call of their leader; every one determined to defend his own. Silent warriors, ragged but faithful – the Alley-cats. Several of them picked up bricks.

'You see, Yank?' Bobby gloated. 'You're outweighed.'

Warren did see, though he still gave Kate the filthiest look. 'Seeya tomorrow,' he said meaningfully. 'And him.' Then he ran off into the darkness.

Bobby turned and put his arm around Kate's shoulders. Adam put his arm around her waist, which was easier for him to reach. They walked her right up to her front door as if it were some kind of royal ceremony. East End kids were like that – terrific tribal instinct. They protected their own. Bobby had been Kate's friend for almost as long as she could remember, and she supposed she took him a bit for granted. Bobby had always been there. He was confident Kate was going to be his girlfriend some day. He was just waiting for her to get a few years older. (Well, that's what he thought.) He was sure that Jon and she would outgrow each other. That was just kidstuff, he reckoned. 'Don't forget, Kitty,' he said sincerely, 'you ever need me, just whistle.'

'Thanks Bobcat.' (That was his nickname. They used a series of cat names. It was a sort of silly ritual.) 'And thanks, Adam. I really 'preciate your help.'

'Stay cool, Kitty-cat.' (That was Bobby's pet name for her.) Then he kissed her right on the lips, much to her confusion, while Adam chuckled approval.

'Take care,' Bobby further reminded.

Her two rescuers left.

Chapter Five

The next morning, Kate wasn't quite sure what to do. She didn't dare face Warren after what she'd done to him, yet she couldn't just stay off school and leave Jon to face him unprepared. In the end, she got up specially early and tip-toed around getting ready so as not to wake anyone else. She combed her hair loose, as she couldn't manage pigtails without her mum's help. Then she left around sevenish, before anyone else was even up. She avoided The Highway, half afraid that Warren might be waiting there again, and she walked the long distance to Jon's road on the other side of town. She knew he had an early morning paper round and, at 7:45, was rewarded with the sight of him trudging towards her, his paper sack on one shoulder.

'Kit!' he greeted joyfully. 'It ain't my birthday yet.'

'Jon,' she began nervously, 'I gotta talk to you. It's very important.'

'Okay, sweetness,' he sensed her concern at once. 'Come home to breakfast. My mum and Susie's gone by now.'

She went with him gladly. She didn't think she'd ever felt so close to him before. Somehow Jon would make everything all right. Of course he would!

They sat by the blazing fire, eating toast and dripping. And, in between bites, Kate told him what had happened. She left out only the broken glass threat as she didn't want to upset him too much.

Jon listened gravely for the most part, though he laughed when she told him she'd kneed Warren. 'Serves him right!' he said gleefully. 'I'm surprised he could still run.' He was looking at her with fond admiration. 'Right little firecracker, ain't you? I remember the time you done Shelagh Durran over.'

Although she gloried in his praise, she was still worried. 'But he'll be gunning for you now Jon.'

He stroked her hair – he liked it loose. 'Don't you worry 'bout it. I ain't your man for nothing.'

'I know,' she declared with faith. But the niggling anxiety was still there inside. A boy who would threaten a girl with glass – what might he do to Jon?

They left exactly on time to get to school, to arrive just as the bell went. On the way, Kate asked Jon something which had been bothering her. 'Why do you s'pose Warren is even int'rested in me? I'm so much younger than him, and I ain't nearly as pretty as Harpie.'

He smiled at her self doubt, and gripped her hand tighter; then said, 'Don't forget he's small for his age. Girls of fourteen or so prob'ly won't even look at him. Besides...' He smiled wider, '...whatever else Warren might be, he ain't stupid; he knows a good thing when he sees it.'

Kate had to smile back at this loving appraisal, though it didn't really make her feel any less nervous. But it was good to walk the misty cold morning with Jon holding her hand. She wished it could always be that way.

Warren had no chance to say anything before class. He sat in his usual place on Kate's right, and glowered at both of them all through the first lesson. Once she caught him eyeing her loose hair with approval, as she brushed it back from her face. Then he sent her a love-letter (if you could call it that) by way of a paper aeroplane. She crumpled this up as soon as she'd read it, with her face in flames. It was just filth – a lurid description of all the things he would like to do to her, some of which she'd never heard of, nor imagined. It was the most obscene thing she'd ever read. She tried to hide this from Jon, but he took it from her hand, and she watched his face darken with rage as he read it. He half-rose from his seat right then, to smash Warren's grinning face. But Kate laid a restraining hand on his arm. 'Don't let him bait you, Jon. He'd love that.'

He sat down again, realising the truth of this, then whispered just once to the other boy, 'You're dead!'

'No whispering at the back there!' Miss Benson called.

Warren mouthed an obscenity.

Somehow word had got around that there was going to be a fight (funny how it always does). The morning break of fifteen minutes was the logical time, as this was when the teachers had their coffee-break, and the playground was largely unsupervised. A group of girls were staging a slanging match in the library to create a diversion from the real issue – just in case. Fights were always arranged this way. Nothing was planned; no-one was instructed. Everyone knew what to do. The punishment for fighting in school was severe caning, but this did not deter East End kids. If your blood was up, you fought. That was the natural order of things.

Kids gathered around the schoolyard like Romans at the arena, leaving a wide space in the middle for Warren and Jon. Kate's hero removed his blazer and threw it to her. Then he didn't waste a single moment. 'You got any last requests?' he taunted the other boy.

'Motherfucker!' Warren snarled.

All those listening kids gasped with shock. No-one had ever heard a swear like that; it was the all-American kind. East End kids were not averse to swearing when the occasion arose, but never like that. It was the worst thing they'd ever heard.

And it was more than enough for Jon, who thought the world of his mother. He fairly hurled himself at Warren with fists flying.

The American went down at once beneath this furious onslaught, not quite prepared for the "bat from hell" approach. Kate realised she needn't have worried that Jon's strength would not match Warren's. Jon had the kind of strength that was built from frequent fights and hard work. Warren had probably never done a stroke of physical work in his life. The kids began to cheer and shout encouragement. Warren's nose had bled already.

Then suddenly, Jon jumped back as if he had been burned. He sat down hard with the force of his retreat. There was a glistening red slash down his face, and Kate screamed.

The kids gasped again, with horror, when they realised what had happened. 'Cor Blimey!' someone said, to her right.

'Bloody hell!' someone else said, aptly.

Warren had regained his feet and was standing over Jon. There were three inches of steel blade glinting in his hand – a flick-knife!

'You dratsab!' Kate raged at Warren, and would have run at him herself if she had not been forcibly restrained by surrounding kids.

Well, they'd only ever seen them on films before – illegal weapons, and totally horrific. They didn't think people used them in real life. But there was Warren moving towards Jon with that knife in his hand and murder in his eyes. Kate almost fainted with fear.

She would never forget what happened next as long as she lived because, in a way, it was kind of wonderful. Every boy in the playground moved, as if by silent command, pushing girls behind them as they went. One of them pulled Jon to his feet, and they closed in on Warren, forming a tight ring around him. 'Which one of us you gonna knife first?' Joe Warner enquired, testily.

Warren stood, still as a stone, eyeing them all warily. He knew he was beaten. Then two boys jumped on his back, and he fell flat on his face. Joe ran across, and used his great weight to full advantage, stamping on Warren's hand until he released the knife.

Warren howled with pain.

Joe – triumphant, picked up the knife and flicked back the blade, then all those boys moved back again.

'Now get up and fight fair,' Jon said.

Kate suddenly knew what was meant by tribal instinct. It was much stronger than she'd previously thought, especially in the young; and every tribe protected its own. Warren was the outsider – the invader, and he had been given no choice but to fight Jon fairly, the only way the tribe would allow.

Blood from Jon's injured face was all down his shirt by this time, but still he moved in again, and delivered a few swift punches to Warren's head. But the American made no further attempt to defend himself. He just held his damaged hand to his chest while trying to guard his head with the other arm, and there were tears in his eyes. Kate could see that Jon didn't have the heart to hit him any more.

'Finish him off, Jon!' Joe said savagely. 'He woulda killed you.'

'I think you broke his fingers, mate,' Jon pointed out. 'He can't fight no more.'

'We ain't seen him fight yet,' someone jeered.

Then Mr Thorpe, the boys' games master came marching through the crowd, his face dark and angry. 'What's going on here?' he asked needlessly as he stared aghast at the two injured boys. 'You again, Daley?' He glowered at Jon.

Voices from all sides were immediately raised in Jon's defence.

Warren snatched a few words with her, in spite of his pain. They must have been important to him. 'I'm sorry Kate,' he said miserably. 'I know I did everything all wrong. But I really like you – I'm sorry...'

She had to turn abruptly away from him before she slapped his face – this creature who'd hurt Jon. Only later when she'd calmed down, she realised that Warren couldn't be completely bad to have said what he did. He probably craved someone to love him to such an extent, that he went about things in just the manner to achieve the opposite. Like Miss Benson said, he was a problem child. Kate wondered why that made her feel like such a louse.

They were both carted off to hospital, and Sister Marie-Clair phoned up Warren's dad to suggest he collect his son from there. She wanted no juvenile delinquents in her school.

Mr Thorpe was deputy head as well as games master. He spent the whole afternoon interviewing kids, until he was satisfied he'd got the true story. Kate was surprised and a bit alarmed when she was summoned to his office; he usually dealt only with the punishment of boys. Mr Thorpe was young, very fair-minded, and extremely wise. He gave her a searching look while she stood, nervous and flustered before him. 'Katharine,' he said at last. 'Have you ever heard of Helen of Troy?'

'Oh yes, sir,' she said at once (she was always fascinated with ancient history). 'She was a Greek princess who left her prince and ran away with another.'

'And she started a war which lasted twenty years,' he finished for her.

She saw then what he was getting at, and reddened profusely while she defended herself. 'I'm not like that, sir. I never done nothing on purpose. I hope you don't think I enjoyed two boys fighting and getting hurt 'cos of me.' She was close to tears and full of self doubt. Had she encouraged Warren just a little bit? Had she? She wasn't even sure.

'I know it wasn't deliberate,' he soothed. 'I only called you in here to warn you. I'm a man and I can see it very clearly.'

'What?' she asked wretchedly.

'You are very young,' he continued thoughtfully, as if being careful with his words. 'But you already have a certain power over boys – a certain way with you. This will get worse as you grow older. It could be a great advantage to you, or it could be deadly, as with Helen of Troy. She ended up heartbroken. Take care that you never abuse your talents.'

Kate wasn't even sure what he meant. Yet his words struck a chill which reached right down to her soul. She would never forget them. Mr Thorpe was wiser than he knew.

He continued to interview the boys. Joe Warner freely admitted that he'd broken Warren's fingers. He pointed out that there would not have been time to fetch a teacher before the American used the knife again – they'd had to stop him. He gave the weapon to Mr Thorpe, and the police were called at that point. Kate was glad to know that Jon wasn't blamed, nor Joe. Mr Thorpe didn't even cane them. Everyone said they'd done their best in the circumstances.

Jon returned to school with seven stitches in his face, and he wore that scar for the rest of his life. Every time Kate looked at it, she remembered he'd got that for her. It was then that she began to call him "Hero".

So that was the way to learn lessons – from sharp personal experience. But this she thought the greatest lesson of all.

Man is ever a fierce and warlike creature, no matter how civilised he pretends to be. And woman isn't very much different when all's said and done. But a good man always takes care of his own – and the tribe will take care of him.

Always.

44

Chapter Six

Tommy Steele was "Singing the Blues" by this time, but Jon and Kate did not sympathise – they were perfectly happy. In February, he sent her a Valentine. It was the first she had ever received. He simply laid the envelope inside her desk, and it was there when she opened the lid. It was the most romantic, satin-hearted and lacy kind, and the message was very simple, "To Kit, the best girl in the world – my girl". It was unsigned, in keeping with tradition, but she knew Jon's ungainly scrawl at once. She smiled shyly at him, and he smiled back and added a wink. This was his first admission that he felt anything like the same as she did.

The Easter holidays were busy ones, as usual. Kate had to help at home with spring cleaning, or taking the younger kids out of Mum's way. At the time, she was the eldest of four. Her brother, Tony, was still pram-sized, and she wasn't quite trusted with him; but she often took her two little sisters to the park or to the Tower for the afternoon. Yvonne and Liz were aged six and two respectively.

One such occasion, she chanced to meet Jon, and he said he would bring Susie the next time. He often looked after her during the school holidays. This meant his mum did not have to pay so much to the minder. He said Susie would enjoy playing with other little girls, and it would be a perfect excuse to be with Kate.

She was pleased to note that he didn't seem embarrassed any more. He just came right out and said wonderful things like that.

The Tower was one of their favourite haunts – The Tower of London, that is. It was not fifteen minutes walk from where Kate lived, and was a perfect playground for kids.

Susie had not been there before, and stared in awe at the brilliantly dressed beefeaters, and red-coated guards in their busbies, marching up and down. She followed one of the latter, trying to ask him questions. They had to pull her out of the way when he turned, with three fierce stamps, to march back. They tried to explain that the funny man wasn't allowed to speak, but were sure she thought he was some kind of monster who tried to stamp on little girls. She also loved the ravens which were almost as big as she was. 'Chick-chick!' she cried, gleefully, and followed one of these as well, trying to mimic its ungainly walk. They decided the pigeons would be much safer, and all the kids spent a happy half-hour feeding these with the bread they had brought. The birds boldly ate right from the girls' hands until the bread ran out, then sauntered off in disgust.

At that time, great bronze cannon were lined up all along the riverside walk, and kids had a fine time clambering all over them, playing "Pirates" or "Sea Battles". The girls wanted to climb every one. Jon was very careful not to let the little ones fall, and it briefly crossed Kate's mind, what a wonderful father he would make.

They couldn't afford to see the Crown Jewels. It cost ten shillings each. Jon promised that when he left school and got a job, he would take her to see them. Strange, you might think, an East End kid who lived next door to the Tower half her life, when people travel from all over the world to see the Crown Jewels. But life is like that – full of insignificant irony – that which used to be called "Sod's Law".

The Tower is no longer the same. The cannon have been moved back and are ringed with chains. Kids don't climb them now. These days you have to pay just to step inside the Tower gate, which used to be free. The inexorable, heavy tread of time marks everything. And time is a tireless and ruthless traveller.

After Easter, their school transferred to a brand-new building. It was all yellow brick, glass, and blue tiles; the most modern school in London, they were told. It was so new that the rectangular sections of the grass turves could still be seen on the lawns. Inside was all parquet floors and blue painted walls. Even the desks were brand new, and had that lovely rich wood smell, like pencil shavings. They were all duly warned against carving initials or other acts of vandalism. Punishment would be most severe.

Kate was simply happy that Jon still sat next to her. Everyone roughly adopted the position they'd had in the old classroom. And she was relieved that they still had Miss Benson. She'd have hated to change teachers at that stage. She had risen to top of the class in English, and was about third in maths (one behind Jon). Miss Benson said she had high hopes that Kate would pass the eleven plus with distinction. Kate didn't quite share her optimism, but was pleased to note that she said the same about Mary and Jon.

The early summer days passed happily enough, until Jon informed her, about mid-July, that he'd found himself a job for the summer holidays. He seemed enormously pleased about it. 'It's at Morrey's garage,' he told her excitedly. 'The money'll be a big help to Mum. And I won't have to look after Susie no more.'

Kate tried to hide her disappointment. 'But I'll still see you on Saturdays?'

'Er – no,' he said, hesitantly. 'I'll be working Saturdays too. But don't worry, Kit – I'll come round in the evenings...'

She shook her head, sadly. 'I ain't allowed out after tea-time.'

He stared at her, aghast; he'd never realised this before. 'But it's broad daylight till nine o'clock.'

'I know it's daft,' she said helplessly. 'But that's the way it is. I stop in after six o'clock.'

'Roll on September,' he said. 'I'll miss you Kit.'

She turned away from him then, just in case she cried.

She spent a lot of time that summer at Mary's house. Mary was lucky enough to have received a record player for her eleventh birthday and, like Kate, she was a great fan of Elvis. They both agreed that he was God's gift.

'Except for Jon,' Kate added.

'Of course,' Mary agreed with a knowing wink.

Her latest Elvis record was "I wanna be your teddy bear".

On days when Kate had to take the kids out, she was often accompanied by Bobby and his sister Tia. These had been friends since her earliest childhood. Bobby had just left school but had not yet managed to find a job. He didn't seem to mind looking after little kids; he seemed happy to go anywhere with Kate. Tia was a year older than Kate. Her real name was Teresa. But "Tia" had come about due to Bobby's mispronunciation of the name in his toddler days. The name had stuck because it really seemed to suit her. They were great kids – and great company. But nothing compared to Jon in Kate's mind.

September began the final year of primary school. They had discovered rock 'n roll with a vengeance, and frothy coffee, and pony-tails were in full swing. Mary's mum and Kate's allowed this one concession. They both wore pony-tails to school instead of the hated pigtails; but flashy socks were definitely barred. A spate of these socks suddenly appeared at school, in bright, glaring colours: shocking pink, lime green, flame, or electric blue, until the headmistress announced at morning assembly that she wanted to see no more "flashy socks" in her school. School kids were pettishly disciplined then, but it probably didn't do them any harm.

Kate realised, with dismay, that she had outgrown Jon by at least two inches, which often happens at that age. Girls grow madly, and boys seem to hang back a few years.

'It don't matter,' he said. 'I'll be bigger in the end.' He was looking at her admiringly. 'You ain't half getting pretty.'

She blushed with pleasure.

At the Christmas party, Sister Marie-Clair was actually seasonal enough to allow a few pop records (though she drew the line at mistletoe). "Rock Around the Clock" was the favourite of the evening, closely followed by "Jailhouse Rock" and "Whole Lotta Shakin". All the girls danced with each other (when they weren't mobbing Mr Thorpe), anxious to show off their jiving prowess, and their new rock 'n roll skirts. Most of the latter had been borrowed from older sisters, or converted from Mum's old summer dresses (as in Kate's case). The headmistress was not too keen on these, some of which were cut in a full circle, and showed a bit too much leg for her liking when the girls twirled around.

Harpie was actually wearing stockings and suspenders, and was sent out to remove them after the Head had noticed several boys sitting on the floor to get a better view of this wonder. Sister Marie-Clair wasn't as daft as she looked.

Jon's mum had managed to buy him a pair of drainpipe trousers as an early Christmas present. Kate thought he looked like the coolest thing since Elvis, and told him so. He was the only boy with guts enough to ask a girl to dance and, she was pleased to say, that was her. She had never felt so proud as she did at that moment. She'd not even realised that he could dance, and asked him where he had learned.

'Just watched 'em on telly.' he explained; but he was obviously a natural.

As he didn't have to collect Susie, Jon walked her home after the party. He seemed subdued and thoughtful, in spite of the glorious fun they'd just had. He held her hand as faithfully as ever, and softly sang a snatch of "Peggy Sue". Then he said, glumly, 'I wish we was going home together for real. I wish you could come to my house for Christmas – but my mum would think it was funny.'

'Yeah,' Kate sighed, 'so would mine.'

They both knew they were too young to date. There was no getting away from it. Kate wasn't even supposed to talk to boys until she was fourteen. Jon's mum wasn't quite that bad, but even she wouldn't like him "going steady" at the age of eleven. Why had Nature made them feel this way when they weren't old enough? It seemed most unfair.

Jon continued singing, 'If you knew – Peggy Sue, then you'd know why I feel blue – without Peggy...'

It was dark by the time they arrived at her door. Kate's family lived in the top flat of a converted Victorian mansion, which sounded very grand, but was quite slummy really. They huddled inside the porch, in case her dad looked out of the upstairs window and saw them. She knew he wouldn't have been too pleased to see her with a boy, to say the least.

Jon put his arms around her. 'I wish we was older,' he said, sadly. His eyes looked dark and sorrowful in the shadowed porch. He gave her the first of his rare, sweet kisses. 'Merry Christmas, Kit,' he whispered. Then he just ran away from her, almost as if he were afraid of something he might say or do.

She listened to his rapid footsteps until she could hear them no longer. Then she felt the sting of tears, the first of many that she would cry for Jon. The words of that beautiful song persisted in her head, "I love you – Peggy Sue, with a love so rare and true..." and the tears rolled. 'Merry Christmas, Hero,' she whispered – much too late.

She'd just spent the happiest year of her school life, except that was when the wishes and dreams really began.

The holiday was pretty dismal for Kate.

Chapter Seven

January brought intensive preparation for the eleven plus examination. They did practice papers over and over again, and Miss Benson went through their mistakes with meticulous care. Jon's weak point was spelling. He used a dictionary in class, but the teacher warned him he would not be able to do so in the exam. She gave him special tests and lists of words to learn. Kate knew that Jon was tense. His mum really wanted him to get to grammar school because his dad had wanted it. He would feel he had let his dad down if he failed.

It wasn't so bad for Kate. Her parents didn't really expect her to pass. Her dad, especially, thought she was dead thick. She tended to be slow-witted and give that impression – and she had no desire to go to a posh school anyway (class distinction was pretty sharp then). She was sure all the girls there would be snobs, though it wouldn't be too bad if Mary came to the same school. But there weren't any co-ed schools, at least none that her parents would consider. Whatever happened, she wouldn't have Jon beside her any more.

Kate tried hard not to think about that.

The dreaded day finally came, and the atmosphere was hushed and fraught with tension. The normally friendly classroom seemed like a condemned cell and, to many kids, that's exactly what it was. This was the day they were branded for life. Before the advent of the comprehensive school, anything less than grammar education was definitely inferior.

There were three separate papers: Arithmetic, English, and Intelligence. The latter test was like a series of little word games. Kate quite enjoyed that one. The English seemed pretty easy as well. But the Arithmetic was more difficult. There were a couple of devilish problems right at the end – one about a motorcycle overtaking a lorry, and the other about spaces between the rungs of a ladder. It was lucky that these were last, else she might have spent too long mulling over them.

She was worried about Jon. The desks had been separated for the exam, and no-one was allowed to speak or look at another pupil. But she could tell by his sighs, and the long pauses between his pen strokes, that he was having trouble.

At last it was over. Miss Benson gave the order to put pens down, and then collected the final papers. The moment she'd left the room, there was a hubbub of conversation combined with the rumble of moving chairs and desks. Jon slid his furniture back to Kate's with relief. She noticed the sweat on his brow and the weary look in his eyes. Right then, he looked much older than eleven. She wondered if the system ever realised what that exam did to kids.

'I think I flunked it,' he said. Then he smiled and brushed back his quiff of hair. 'But what the hell – I'm glad it's over.' He seized her hand and kissed it, for once oblivious to the rest of the class.

During the Easter holidays, Jon's mum wouldn't allow him to work all the time – only a few days a week. She said he had to have some time off to be with his friends. Kate thought this terribly understanding for a parent. Jon's mum must have been one lovely lady. Kate therefore managed to spend several afternoons with Jon and their little sisters, with the addition of Tony, her little brother, now old enough to be entrusted to her.

Jon was greatly taken with Tony. He had pretend fights with him, and taught him to kick a football in the park. The little boy didn't stop giggling all afternoon.

'I wouldn't have minded a brother,' Jon said, wistfully.

She realised, sadly, that he was thinking of his dad.

'What happened to your real dad?' he suddenly asked.

Kate blushed, painfully, but she couldn't ever lie to Jon. 'My mum had me before she was married,' she explained with her face on fire. 'My dad left her when he found out about me.' She hardly dared to meet his eyes.

'What a dratsab!' he exclaimed. Then hastily added with his hand on her arm, 'I meant him, not you. I hope you don't think that makes any difference to me.'

There was still a deal of shame attached to illegitimacy. She smiled at him, gratefully.

'You ain't had much luck with fathers, have you?' he asked, sympathetically.

'S'pose not.'

He reached for her with his arms for a hug. They were sitting on the grass, while the kids played football around them. She laid a restraining hand on his arm, and rolled her eyes towards Yvonne, her seven-year-old sister, who was quite old enough to notice such things, and might have blabbed to her parents.

He understood at once. 'Okay, Kit. S'long as you know how I feel.'

Elvis was currently singing, "I love you – too much". And she knew exactly how he felt. She loved this boy so hard it hurt.

By the end of May, the exam results had come through. Mary and Kate had both passed with distinction.

Miss Benson was ecstatic. She had twenty-five passes out of forty: a real credit to her patience and concern.

But Jon had not passed.

Kate knew that he was just as intelligent as she was – she had worked beside him for long enough. He had failed on nerves. As she looked at his distraught face, she hated that bloody eleven-plus with a vengeance. How could they do this to him? Wordlessly, she squeezed his arm as he bent his head to fight back tears. 'I let my dad down.' His voice was hoarse with emotion.

'You'll never let him down,' she declared, fiercely. 'You'll be the best man in the world.'

His hand covered hers for a moment. Then he raised his head and said, 'At least my mum won't have to worry 'bout that expensive uniform.'

That was so typical of Jon – always to think of others before himself, and always to look on the bright side.

All school trips, educational or otherwise, were paid for out of the school funds. Parties, treats, and outings were therefore free, or at least seemed so. Every child, however, was expected to bring at least one penny per day towards the school fund for every day he or she attended. This arrangement worked very well. A school trip was a lavish treat, especially for children from poorer families, who would otherwise never have gone anywhere.

They all looked forward to the leavers' outing in early July. They were going to Southend and Thorpe Bay for a day by the sea, and were all saving their pocket money so as to have ample cash. Jon and Kate especially hoped to be able to snatch some time alone together. It would almost be like a date for them and, they further hoped, a day to remember.

As they were walking home, he asked, 'You got a 'kini?'

'Yeah,' she admitted. 'I persuaded Mum to buy it for an early birthday prezzie – but my dad don't know. He'd never let me wear a thing like that.'

'I can't wait to see you in it. Will you wear it for me?'

'Yes, Hero – even if it pours with rain,' she promised.

'That's my girl!' he smiled, wickedly.

'You little letch!' She pinched his cheek, lovingly.

The great day drew nearer with aggravating slowness...

Then, on the Thursday before, Mary went down with mumps.

Kate was quite distraught. Her friend was going to miss the best school-day ever – the most memorable day of their lives. She was slightly cheered when Mary sent her this little note:

Dear Kate,
Don't worry about it. I'll see you lots in the
holidays when Jon is working. Enjoy this chance to have

him all to yourself, and don't do anything I wouldn't do.

Mumps hurts – ouch!

Seeya mate.

Twins forever – love, Mary. xxx

Wasn't that sweet? Mary was like that – just an angel of a girl. Kate showed the note to Jon, and he couldn't help it (bless him) when his grin spread almost to his ears. 'Don't think I'm glad she's ill.' He looked at her, guiltily. 'But this could be our best chance ever to be together before we leave. We'll buy her a special present.' His eyes went all hopeful.

Typical man, you might think – jealous of your friends. But no, Jon wasn't like that. He was never resentful of Mary, nor of Kate's street mates. He had his own mates too. After all, you need them to survive.

She just hugged him. That was always her best reassurance when words failed her. He hugged her back with rough boyish strength that took her breath away. 'I can hardly wait, Kit,' he told her left ear.

Then, on Saturday evening, two days before the trip, Kate's dad caught her chatting to Bobby and Adam on the street corner. Her mum had gone to a ladies' church meeting, and he'd sent her to the local shop to get him some fags. He happened to look out of the window to see what was taking her so long, when he saw her with the Alley-cats. Young people of today might not believe that Kate was literally forbidden to speak to boys – but that's the way it was.

Dad threw up the sash window and roared at her, 'Get in here – you little slag!'

Kate was so scared, she dropped his packet of fags and his change all over the road. Adam bent with her to help pick them up, and she saw the dark, silent rage in his eyes. Then she saw Bobby's fists clench, and thought he might give her dad some verbal, which wouldn't have helped. 'Don't say nothing,' she pleaded through her tears. 'He'll only hit me worse.'

Concern and outrage in Bobby's grey eyes. He thought the world of Kate. But he was a fifteen-year-old kid. What could he do? 'One of these dark nights, I'll do 'im!' he seethed. 'You just gimme the word, kid.'

'Thanks, Bobby and Adam. Seeya!' Then she ran to her door as fast as she could, while they sadly watched her retreat. She knew they really cared – rough kids with hearts of gold. No-one could help her, but still it was good to have friends on her side – and Jon was going to beat her dad too, wasn't he? As soon as he was old enough, he was going to take her away. He'd promised.

Chapter Eight

Sunday morning, Kate surveyed the damage, with dismay, in her wardrobe mirror. The red wheals and bruises were not just confined to her bottom. They extended halfway up her back and some down her thighs. Jon was expecting her to wear her bikini tomorrow. How could she let him see this? It would break his heart. Even her school swimming costume wouldn't hide it all. She'd have to tell him she couldn't go swimming; she could say she had her period – but no, she couldn't lie to Jon. He would know if she even tried. So what could she do?

She cried, intermittently, through the day, and didn't leave the house except to go to church. She couldn't even see Mary because she had mumps. Her mum thought she was upset because her friend couldn't go on the outing. She did her best to cheer Kate up. But the girl seriously considered giving that trip a miss. It was only the thought of Jon's disappointment that stopped her.

Monday dawned with the promise of endless sunshine, but the day was already clouded for Kate. She arrived at school around eight. Both coaches were leaving at eight-thirty. There was one for 4b and one for 4a. Miss Benson was coming with their class and Mr Thorpe with his lot.

Jon greeted her with his face a glory of smiles, looking wonderful in khaki shorts and a white T-shirt. He was already well-tanned. Kate knew he did most of his mum's gardening wearing just shorts.

She'd finally decided to wear sawn-off jeans, which she'd bought from the church jumble sale. These would hide her marks, and she'd still be able to get a bit of sun above the knees. She'd put these on over her bikini pants, though she hadn't bothered with the top. She didn't wear a bra as yet; her size 32a did not justify this. A short-sleeved cotton blouse, which she'd tied at the middle by the tails, topped the sawn-offs.

'You look smashing,' Jon said, admiringly. 'Have you brought it?'

She knew he meant the bikini, and nodded, truthfully. She'd had to bring it. Her mum would have thought it strange otherwise. Mum didn't know about the marks, of course.

He grinned happily, and they boarded the coach together.

Fruit drinks in cartons were provided on the journey, and Jon and Kate snuggled contentedly in a shared seat. She was determined to enjoy as much as possible of the day.

For the benefit of those who had not been to Southend before, Miss Benson explained that the tide would be out when they arrived. She further explained that the sea completely receded from sight at low tide. She said, in view of this, the kids would do better to visit the sea-front shops and the fairground in the morning, and then spend all afternoon on the beach when swimming would be possible.

The class agreed to this whole-heartedly with rising cheers. Kate was gladder than most. This would postpone the terrible moment when Jon would expect to see her in her bikini.

The journey was uneventful, except they had to stop once for Martin Sykes to be sick... (He was unkindly christened Martin Sicks for the rest of the term). They sang some songs, and played a few paper-passing games, such as "Consequences". Miss Benson passed sweets around regularly, and Jon whispered occasional sweet nothings in Kate's ear.

At last they arrived, and spilled out of the coach in excited, happy groups. The teachers gave brief instructions – to report to the beach station if anyone got lost, and not to wander off alone or go anywhere without telling someone else. Forty-odd kids was quite a responsibility for two teachers, come to think of it.

Jon and Kate wandered along the sea front with the main bulk of the crowd. They had a whale of a time eating candy-floss, ice cream, and cockles.

'My mum would have fifty fits,' she told him.

'Don't worry Kit, I won't.' He grinned. 'But if you're sick all over me, I'll make you wash it off.'

'How romantic!' she sighed, humorously.

'I might think so.' He grinned even wider.

That was the mood; happy – light-hearted – silly.

They pooled the money to buy a blue teddy-bear for Mary. She collected teddies – like Elvis. Kate said she didn't think her friend had a blue one. Then they bought rocks and gigantic lollipops for their little sisters and brother, and wandered around several penny arcades, squandering their money. Jon bought her a straw hat with a sticker which read, "Hard luck fellas, I'm his". She bought him one which read, "Kiss me quick or I'll stay a frog forever".

'Well go on then,' he urged.

She kissed him with great exuberance while several kids cheered.

'Am I an 'andsome prince now?' he asked with feigned innocence.

'You already was, you fraud!' she rejoined.

A lady named Connie Francis was singing about "Stupid Cupid" but Kate and Jon didn't share her opinion. They thought Cupid was a real nice bloke – he was an angel.

They wanted to go into the Kursaal, the main amusement park, but the teachers didn't think this a very good idea.

'It's too expensive for kids your age,' Mr Thorpe said. 'All your money would be gone in five minutes.'

'But there's a big dipper!' Harpie wailed in protest.

Miss Benson said that none of her kids were going on that horrendous contraption, and Joe Warner cheekily asked if she'd swallowed a dictionary. She laughed along with the kids. Everyone was in holiday mood.

It was finally decided to go to the Peter Pan Playground until lunchtime. This was smaller and less expensive than the Kursaal and the rides were not so "horrendous".

They liked the dodgems best, as kids usually do. Jon and Kate had repeated goes on these until Miss Benson told them to get out and let someone else have a turn. Then they sampled the helter-skelter, the horse carousel, and the rifle range. Jon proved to be a crack shot, demolishing three metal ducks straight off. He won a white, fluffy teddy-bear which he promptly gave to Kate.

'You should give that to Susie,' she protested.

'I want you to have it,' he insisted. 'I ain't never give you a present before.'

They'd long agreed that they would not buy each other presents. For one thing neither of them could afford it, and there was also the problem of explaining to parents where things came from – but this was different.

'You can pretend you won it,' he pointed out.

'Of course,' she agreed. 'I'll love it forever. Thanks, Hero.'

Then they discovered the haunted house and shrieked and giggled their way through its spooky corridors several times.

'The ghost train would've been better,' Jon observed.

'Why? This is good fun.'

'You'd grab me harder if the frights was worse,' he said, mischievously.

'Sex mad, that's your trouble,' she joked.

At lunchtime, they all trooped into a likely-looking restaurant for fish and chips or, at least, partially trooped, as there wasn't room for everyone. The rest of them congregated outside. They fairly bought the place out, and all agreed they were the best fish and chips they had ever tasted. The teachers paid for the lot out of the school fund allowance.

'High tea at five,' Miss Benson announced. 'The tables are already booked, so none of you had better get lost or be late.'

They then made their way towards Thorpe Bay which had a better beach. There were inevitable wisecracks about the name, such as, 'No wonder Mr Thorpe likes this beach.' – 'Do you think he owns it?' – 'Yeah, his millionaire granny left it to him.'

But Kate began to feel rather apprehensive.

The sea had miraculously returned and sparkled magnificently towards infinity, in varying shades of turquoise and blue. The sun was blazing in the mirrored blue of the sky. Sandier beach here, and they were able to discard their plimsolls without hobbling over stones. Although it was a Monday, there were quite a few holidaymakers on the beach, and they walked a fair way towards Shoeburyness before discovering one deserted enough to contain them all.

Miss Benson instructed them again: they could go for walks or explore cliff paths, so long as it was in pairs or groups. They were free to swim within the range of marker buoys, once again, in pairs. They were all to be ready to leave for tea by 4:45.

Then they were free.

Jon and Kate walked on further until they found a little sheltered cove with an overhanging cliff. 'We can pretend we're on a desert island,' he said.

'I wish we was,' she said dreamily.

'Forever,' he added.

Kate should have been deliriously happy. She was more alone with Jon than she had ever been, in this beautiful place like their own little paradise. Yet this was the moment she'd been dreading; this was when she'd either lie to him or refuse his simple request. She didn't want to do either – but how could she let him see the awful truth?

He sat on the sand and removed his T-shirt, then looked up at her with shining eyes. 'You gonna let me watch, sweetness?' he asked, trustingly.

She nodded, with her hands on the ties of her blouse. This much would be all right, so long as she kept her back away from him. She had no qualms about undressing in front of Jon, even though she hadn't ever before. He was her love and she felt completely natural with him.

She admired his beautiful, tanned torso as she loosened her blouse. Jon was not scrawny as boys often are. He was pleasingly shaped and covered in firm, supple flesh, though showing no man-sized muscle as yet. She thought how Jon had to do all the work for his mother which his dad would have done if he had lived. He chopped wood, carried coal, did the gardening, painted and decorated, and even lugged home the shopping. Jon already worked as hard as some men did. Kate was sure that made him as strong, or even stronger than she was. At eleven, she was already taller than her mother, and she would reach her full height of 5' 8" by the age of thirteen.

She pulled off her blouse and dropped it to the sand.

His eyes widened with delight; he had expected to see her bikini top already on. Then they filled up with adoration. 'Ain't you the sweetest thing?' he said.

'But I ain't grown nothing yet,' she protested. 'Fat Joe's got more'n me.'

'But Joe's ain't sweet.' he insisted. 'That's diff'rent.'

She was pleased by his obvious adoration; it matched hers for him. She rummaged in her beach-bag for her bikini top, then began to put it on. It was a blue cotton, polka-dot affair, and she had trouble with the back fastening. She wasn't used to wearing a bra.

'You need a hand?' He was halfway to his feet.

'No!' she said, hastily. 'You stay there. I can manage.'

He sat down again, looking a little subdued. She thought he really wanted to touch her. She managed to fasten the top round the back, then hesitated, and stood, looking at him uncertainly. This was the moment of truth.

'Come on, Kit,' he encouraged. 'Take those off.' His eyes indicated the sawn-offs. 'Don't be shy.'

'I ain't shy.' But her voice hardly made a whisper. Her hand moved to the top button, then froze and refused to move further.

'What's the matter?' Doubt crossed his face for the first time. 'Don't you want me look at you? Is that it?'

'Yes Jon – I mean no – I mean...' Her voice trailed off as both questions confused in her head.

He looked hurt then – hurt and dismayed. He stood up and began to remove his own shorts. His eyes deserted her. 'It looks like you don't trust me. That hurts y'know. This is me and I'm your man. I ain't just anyone.' He dropped the shorts and kicked them away. She could see he was working up to anger.

'Please Jon, don't get upset...'

His eyes returned to hers and blazed with an emotion unknown to her. 'Do you think I'm just a letch? Some dirty old man? D'you think I'm like Warren? Is that what you think?'

'No Jon, please listen...' She was almost ready to tell the truth. It was unbearable to see him thinking all the wrong things.

But Jon was past listening. He pulled off his underpants and she was relieved to see that he had his swim trunks already on. 'See – I'm not ashamed–' His voice shook with emotion. 'I ain't got nothing to hide from you. This is all I am, and I'm for you. If you don't want me, you'd better say so now.'

He was a fine and beautiful sight. She could hardly wrench her eyes away from him. She just wanted to run to him and hold him, and that was the moment she should have. But then she became worried for a different reason. 'Jon, if Mr Thorpe hears you and walks over here – he'll cane you.'

'Fuck Mr Thorpe! This is important to me. Can't you see that!'

It was the first time he had ever sworn at her for real. She looked down at the sand to hide her tears.

Jon turned his back on her, still angry. 'I can see you don't wanna look at me either. S'pect I'm not good enough for you. I bet you wish I was Warren!' He began to tighten the front lace of the trunks. His hands were shaking.

'Jon, don't say that...' He wasn't giving her a chance – he was just going off his head.

Then he looked at her again and the hurt was back in his eyes. 'I thought you understood.' His voice had quietened. 'I thought you felt the same as me. To me, you are a precious and wonderful creature – you are my girl. I can hardly believe it's true. You are like an impossible dream. Sometimes I think I will never have you. I'm so scared that something will happen to spoil it all – that you'll be snatched away from me.'

Her tears spilled onto the sand, making tiny craters which dried almost at once. Jon had a way of putting his heart into a string of words that could make you cry. He was a natural poet, in spite of his cockney accent. He never used long or fancy words; he didn't need to. After all, it's not the words themselves which matter – it's the way that you use them. In a much later time, she often used his words. They always remained stored up in her head.

Then she looked back at him through her tears, and she could feel her own temper rising. How could he think all those wrong things? How could he say she didn't feel the same? Why couldn't he see that something was wrong?

'Take them off!' he ordered.

'NO!' Her rage erupted with all its usual blind, fickle fury. 'Just WHO do you think you are? How DARE you speak to me like that? You don't own me, y'know! You won't even listen – you won't give me a chance to explain! How can you be so hateful to me? Well, I hate you too – Jon Daley!'

He just stared at her, stunned into silence, and the pain in his eyes was more than she could bear. Why did lovers always say the exact opposite of what they really meant when they fought? Was it like the pain reflex that she'd learned about earlier? When something hurts beyond endurance, you just have to lash back.

He said, in a choked voice, 'So that's it then...' Then he pushed past her, almost knocking her over. He just ran down the beach and into the sighing surf. He didn't look back once as he swam away from her with fast, furious strokes.

She watched through a veil of tears until he was out of sight.

'Oh Jon,' she whispered. 'I never meant it, Hero.'

She went over in her mind what had just happened, and could hardly believe it had happened so fast, so out of control – she'd actually rowed with Jon. She didn't understand then that they were just too young to cope with such colossal emotion. How could she have told him she hated him? How could she have said that when she loved him more than her life?

But Jon would come back; he would forgive her when he had calmed down. He had to come back – all his clothes were here. She decided she would tell him the truth when he did. She should have done that in the first place.

She removed the sawn-offs and sat down to wait, then folded all his clothes into a neat pile, picking up his T-shirt last, and burying her face in it for a moment. It smelled like Jon; sweet warm man smell – delicious to her. How she missed him...

It seemed like a long time passed. The shouts of the other kids drifted in Kate's direction, mingling with the shrill cries of seagulls, making her feel lonelier than ever. She managed to discern some of the things they were saying:

'The water's smashing! Where's Joe?'

'He's akip over there on his back.'

'He'll get cooked like a lobster – turn 'im over!'

'Okay. Who's gonna drive the crane?'

Then howls of laughter.

Kate thought she could hear Jon's voice among the others. So – he didn't want to come back. He didn't want to be with her. How could she blame him? Maybe he would never speak to her again.

She decided to go for a swim, even though Miss Benson had said only in pairs. She didn't want to join the others; she wanted no-one to see her misery.

The water was cold at first and took her breath away. Yet Jon had run straight in, unfeeling, uncaring. Once she had begun to swim, it seemed warmer and the salt water was soothing to her ravaged back. She frequently glanced towards the beach, to see if he had returned, but the little cove remained dismally empty. Her tears mingled with the sea. She felt she could have cried that same vast amount, if she'd stayed there long enough.

Kate returned to the beach after half an hour or so. It seemed chilly now, in spite of the fierce sun. She was covered in goose-pimples and shivered uncontrollably. She loosened her pony-tail to let her hair dry, then took the white teddy-bear out of her bag, just to hold it. After spreading her towel, she lay down on her back, so as not to disturb any passers-by with the sight of her ugly red wheals. Her hair was all mussed-up in the sand, but she didn't care. She just lay there while the sun tried in vain to warm her, and she held the white, fluffy bear. She closed her eyes, but that didn't stop the tears

– they rolled down to her ears, then dried in the heat. Jon had left her; he didn't want to know her, and it was her own fault. He thought she hated him, and she just wished she was dead.

It seemed like forever that she lay there.

A sudden, loud wolf-whistle startled her despondency. She opened her eyes to view the whistler, shading them with her hand. It was Joe Warner. Poor Joe – he looked like Buddha in his swim-trunks. His belly bulged over them and his breasts were twice the size of hers. The other kids ragged him rotten about his weight. But Joe couldn't help it – he was still a nice kid. Kate thought it very daring for him to wolf-whistle. He didn't usually have much truck with girls. Not much wonder, she thought sadly, as she looked at the two and eight of him. But she suspected that he knew he wouldn't get a mouthful of abuse from her.

'You look smashing, Kate,' he said, eyeing her appreciatively.

She sat up, carefully keeping her back out of sight. 'Thanks Joe, but I don't feel it,' she replied, miserably.

'You had a barny with Jon?' he asked. 'He's over here with us lot. He's acting the fool, but I can tell he's upset.'

She felt another rush of tears. 'Go away, Joe! There ain't nothing you can do. Leave me alone!'

He looked so forlorn and helpless. 'Sorry, Kate. I never meant to upset you.' He muttered to himself as he lumbered away, 'Jon's an Iriot. Wot an Iriot!'

Now she'd gone and been mean to Joe, but she just couldn't sit there and cry in front of him, could she? She just hoped he understood. She lay down again.

A little later, Harpie hopped over the adjoining beach fence, lithe and graceful as a gazelle, and sat down beside her. She looked absolutely stunning in a white bikini, and she really filled out the top, unlike Kate, who could see the blonde girl was worried as she sat up to greet her.

Harpie hardly knew where to begin. 'Is it true, Kitty?' She finally did.

'What?' Kate asked in a very small voice, dreading her answer.

'Jon...' She avoided the other girl's eyes. 'He's been chasing me for the last two hours. He says you and him are finished.'

Kate's heart dropped like a stone from a tall building, and her skin seemed to freeze and tighten around her. She didn't dare speak, in case she howled.

'I don't believe it,' Harpie continued, her baby-blue eyes full of concern. 'Everyone knows how it is with you two. It's sorta rare and special. It couldn't be finished just like that.' She searched the other girl's face, worriedly. 'Tell me about it, Kate.'

Kate was disturbed to think that everyone knew. Jon and she had always supposed that their deepest feelings were well hidden. But then, she reckoned, a thing like that might just make itself obvious. People were not so blind or insensitive as they imagined. She took a deep breath and told Harpie about the quarrel, fighting back tears as she went. She told her the awful things she'd said to Jon. 'But I never meant it!' She almost sobbed the words. 'Surely he knows that?' Then Kate told her the real reason behind it, and turned to show the other girl her back, while she wiped her eyes with the ears of the fluffy bear.

'Oh, Kate...' Harpie's voice hushed with sympathy. 'That's awful – that's much worse than my uncle.'

Kate turned back to her as she stood up. 'D'you want me to tell him?' the blonde girl asked.

'No Harpie.' Kate shook her head. 'If he says we're finished, then that's it. He must mean it.'

Harpie walked away with her head hung sadly. Her long blonde hair whipped in the sea breeze.

Kate turned over to lie on her front, laid her head on her folded arms and cried all over again. She and Jon were finished; they really were.

Then there was a heavy thud beside her and flying sand spattered her back, 'Kit?' It was his voice – Jon's voice, full of love and concern, yet she didn't dare to turn and face him. She dreaded what he might say – he might have come to tell her...

There was a hot splash on her back, then another – Jon's tears. Then his hand was caressing her across every ugly red mark, gently – and sending tingles of fire all through her. 'Why didn't you just tell me?' he asked. 'Jesus, Kit! I never knew how bad he hit you. And it's on the skin – the bare skin!'

She dared to turn and look at him. His eyes were horrified and still wet with tears. 'I'll kill him!' he vowed, passionately. 'Someday I swear I'll kill him. I'll make it up to you, sweetness, somehow I will.' He lowered his eyes. 'That's if you want me – if you don't still hate me.'

Instinctively, she reached for him and just held him as close as she could. 'I'm sorry, Hero. I never meant to say that.' She couldn't express what she really wanted to say. No kind of words seemed adequate.

But it seemed to suffice, for he smiled and put fierce boyish kisses all over her face. 'Promise you'll always tell me the truth in future – about anything.'

'I promise.'

'I don't want us ever to quarrel again. It was hell!'

'Even chasing Harpie?' she wickedly reminded.

He had the grace to blush. 'Guilty as charged. You can slap my face if you want. But I only done it to take my mind off you – and it never worked.'

'I don't wanna slap your face.'

They gazed at each other, as if with new discovery.

'Where'd you spring from just now?' she suddenly remembered to ask.

'Heaven,' he said flippantly.

'That's what I thought,' she said with equal flippancy.

'I was up on the cliff,' he informed more seriously. 'I heard everything you said to Harpie. I cried, Kate.'

'I know.'

His eyes were caressing her all over – real cave-man style. Jon was growing up. She shivered with delight and said, 'Jon, when you touched me just now – it was wonderful.'

He visibly glowed. 'I was dead scared really, but I just couldn't help it. I often wanted to touch you before but never dared.' He moved closer. 'D'you want some more, darlin'?'

'Oh yes, Hero,' she whispered, almost in awe.

He put one arm around her, and tentatively slipped his free hand inside her bikini top. His fingertips teased one nipple to tightness, and she was unprepared for the shockwaves of pleasure which hit her. Then he did the same to the other nipple – and it happened all over again.

'Jon!' She gripped his shoulders with innocent joy.

'Kit,' he said, softly and wisely. 'We gotta be very careful from now on. I'm finding you too good to leave alone.' Then he pulled her close and they lay down together on the warm sand. His sun-hot skin was pressed firmly against hers; that was the most glorious thing of all. They just stayed there and cuddled and whispered until it was time to go. For them, it was still the age of innocence. And that was the closest Kate ever got to her Jon.

Two kids in a fairytale dreamland?

They could have been. Kate never knew for sure.

But she did know this:

Once upon a time, a boy loved a girl – and it was the sweetest thing. It was the sweetest thing in the whole world.

It really was.

Oh, yes it was.

A white, tear-soaked teddy-bear lay in the sand – forgotten.

Excerpt from Kate's future diary:

"In my house, to this very day, in the bottom of a deep drawer, wrapped in a plastic bag to guard against time and dust – lies a white, fluffy, toy bear. It has blue glass eyes. Sometimes I take this out of its wrapper, just to hold it, and remember... And that is all that remains in this world – of the sweetest thing."

Chapter Nine

The remainder of summer term was a frantic time. Kate could hardly bear the thought that she would soon be losing Jon, and she knew he felt the same. They spent every spare moment together. There were afternoon school activities, such as swimming or tennis, which they both joined. Or she would watch him at football practice, and he would watch her at netball, then they would walk home together. Jon was let off collecting Susie for these last few weeks of term, as he would soon be working all summer (again). Kate felt that she was neglecting Mary, but her friend didn't seem to mind; she understood – Mary always did. Kate still spent Sunday afternoons with her, as Jon's mum liked him home on Sundays.

Mary and Kate realised with dismay that their parents preferred different schools for them. Kate was going to a convent school in Southwark – Mary to one in Victoria. It was bad enough losing Jon, but unthinkable to lose Mary as well. Kate begged and pleaded with her parents, but they would not relent. She cried every night for a week.

She had to go with her mum to a posh shop to buy her new uniform. It was an awful flower-pot colour which they called "London Tan". She hated it. And the summer dress was green stripes – urkk! That lot cost her mum over a hundred quid, which was five weeks of her dad's wages. She hardly felt worth the expense, but her mum was so proud of her. Kate tried to look happy for her sake, though she was more fed-up than she'd ever been.

Jon was going to the local "young thuggery training school". That was the reputation it had. But Kate knew he could hold his own anywhere and, at least, he'd be top of the class there. He didn't even need much uniform – just a few pairs of long trousers and a school tie. He didn't seem to mind too much any more; his mum had been very sympathetic (bless her) and he seemed almost relieved.

A few days before the end of term, Jon said he wanted special words with Kate. They walked to Spinner's Haunt so that they could be entirely alone. They sat on slabs of fallen brickwork, shielded by clumps of tall, purple willowherb, with the scent of wild buddleia in their nostrils and bees droning round their ears, while the afternoon sun relentlessly baked.

Jon looked at her, long and hard, and she could see the glint of tears in his eyes. He took her hand and held it very tightly. Her heart beat fast with sudden conviction. Jon was saying goodbye. How could he?

He lifted her hand to his face and held it there a moment. Then he said, 'Y'know Kit, we're really too young for all this malarkey.'

She nodded dumbly, her heart too full for words.

'But I don't want you to think I don't care...' he tried to continue.

Kate's face must have shown her distress, for he squeezed his eyes shut, then opened them with a new look of fierce resolve. 'Hell! I'm gonna start again. I'm gonna tell you the truth, like I ain't never before...' He moved closer and held her by the shoulders. His eyes were sad, but full of love. 'I love you, Kit. D'you believe me?'

'Yes, Jon.' Her heart began to pound.

'Would you marry me tomorrow, if it was possible?'

'I'd marry you this very minute. Y'know I would.'

'Oh, Kit...' He hugged her tightly. 'I'm so glad you said that.' Then he released her and looked desolate again. 'We gotta cool it, darlin', at least for a while.'

Her heart plummeted. 'Why Jon?'

'Cos there ain't no time left when I can see you. I'm working in the holidays, right?'

'Right,' she agreed miserably, 'including Saturdays.'

'The money helps my mum, and the experience is good for me. I'm gonna be a wiz motor mechanic. It'll be better for us in the end, if I'm skilled.'

'I know, Hero.'

'But you ain't allowed out in the evenings, or even to be seen with a boy.'

'No, Jon.' She was feeling more wretched every moment.

'How long 'til you are?'

'Two years – when I'm fourteen,' she said glumly. That seemed like a lifetime to her.

'Then we'll make that our first real date – on your fourteenth birthday. We'll go to Thorpe Bay again – back to that same beach. Would you like that, Kit?'

'Yeah,' she almost sobbed.

He pulled up his shirt and tried to dry her tears with the tails, though they flowed too fast by this time. She put her hands on the bare flesh of his waist, loving the firm feel of his body.

He said, 'That's the other reason why we must cool it.'

'What is?'

He took a deep breath, as if to gain strength. 'Remember that day on the beach – when we touched?'

'How could I forget?'

'Well, the feelings I got were just magic – wonderful – it's hard to describe.'

'Me too, Jon.'

'I wanted to go on – to touch you more. I was afraid of what I might do.'

'But I didn't mind – I loved it.' She gave her innocent assurance.

'That's the trouble, Kit. Our feelings are too intense for our age. They're gonna get worse – stronger, the more often we see each other – I don't want nothing bad to happen between us.'

'But Jon, how can those feelings be bad? It's right and good that we should want to touch. It's part of loving.'

'I know, sweetness.' He slid his hands under her loose summer blouse and caressed her as he spoke. 'Don't think I don't want to touch you, but don't you see where it might lead?'

She'd closed her eyes to savour his magical touch. 'I think I get your drift.' (The tingles of fire were back.)

'I dreamed about you, Kit, after that day on the beach. It was the most delicious thing that ever happened to me.'

She opened her eyes to stare at him in wonder. 'You mean – a wet dream? You did that?' She hadn't thought him old enough. Although

Jon was almost twelve and big for his age, she didn't think that happened to boys until they were thirteen or fourteen.

'Yes, Kit. I told you – the feelings get stronger all the time.'

'I think that's great, Jon. It means you're nearly a man.'

'And it means I could make you pregnant.'

She was silently stunned. They'd said they wouldn't do that thing, not for years.

He went on, 'I don't know how much longer I could keep my hands off you when we're together like this. What would happen if you got pregnant at twelve, or thirteen, or even fourteen? I still wouldn't have the power to protect you from your dad, nor the money to take care of you.'

She realised then how wise and sensible he was trying to be, and how much he truly cared.

'I've only got three years to do in school,' he continued. 'Then I'll leave and get my apprenticeship. The garage has already promised – but I still won't have much money 'til I'm over twenty.' He looked suddenly defeated.

Kate gripped his shoulders. 'I'll get a good job when I'm sixteen. I've got to stay in school that long to take GCEs. My dad had to sign a form to say so. But then I'll help you through your apprenticeship. We'll be able to afford to get married if we don't have babies 'til you're through.'

His smile was pure relief. 'Oh darlin', I love you so much. I don't know how I'll stand it – being away from you for so long.'

'You've convinced me, Hero. It's the only way we're gonna survive. Please kiss me.' She pulled him closer.

He did so, gently at first, though his lips lingered, wanting more. Then suddenly he was kissing her with all the passion of a man. Indescribable desire surged through her like nothing she'd ever known, as she clung to him in desperation. This was even better than touching, and she knew he felt it too. His arms tightened around her and his body pressed close. How could she ever let him go? This wonderful creature and the magic between them – it was the sweetest thing she had ever known.

He released her, breathing fast, and Kate could see he was as shaken as she was. 'I know what that "killer" means now,' he said, 'when he sings "Great balls of fire". Y'see, Kit?'

She could see only too well. 'Yes, Jon,' she said weakly, still clinging to him.

'Tell me you love me, just once,' he begged.

Kate was instantly ashamed that she had never done so before. 'I love you, Jon Daley,' she said. 'I love you so much it kills me. I love you more than anything in the world, and I'll love you forever. Howzat, Hero?'

'It's fantastic!' He pulled her back to him. 'It's so good to hear you say it at last.' Then he kissed her again with full-grown passion. 'You're for me,' he said, still holding her. 'You're my girl forever.' He loosened his collar. 'And the way you are making me feel – I think I'd better take you home, right now.'

Buddy Holly sang, "Rave on that crazy feeling" and the web of dreams was tightly woven.

On the last day of school, Jon looked at her, brown eyes bright with unshed tears, and he said helplessly, 'I might see you in church sometimes.'

'Yeah you might,' she said, without much hope.

'Don't forget me, Kit.'

Her hero – how could she ever?

That first term at the new grammar school was hell.

Kate didn't make any friends except for the three girls who'd come from her old school, and she thought these only tolerated her morose presence because they felt sorry for her. They all knew what was wrong, of course, and tried to advise her to forget him. She knew they thought Jon had just ditched her, and she let them think that. It was easier than explaining all the ins and outs. But she didn't join in their out-of-school activities, nor their eager conversations about boys and pop-stars. All she did was think about Jon. It was unbelievable how much she missed him. Sometimes, she would turn to her left in class, expecting to find him there. Her schoolwork went right down. She was almost bottom of the class, and every night she cried.

Her mum naturally noticed her loss of weight and appetite, and she put it down to female problems, although Kate had actually been menstruating for almost two years. Mum said it was that, coupled with the strain of the new school, and not to worry, she would soon get over it. Dear Mum, she tried to be sympathetic, but how could Kate have confided in her? How could any mother be expected to understand that a twelve-year-old girl could be hopelessly in love? She would have laughed and Kate wouldn't have blamed her. She'd have laughed herself if it had been someone else and not her. She began to think of that song again, "Stupid Cupid". Maybe Connie Francis was right. This situation certainly didn't seem very sensible. Dreary days and tearful nights succeeded each other mercilessly until the Christmas holidays.

On the last day of term, Kate walked home, feeling more desolate than usual. She was thinking of the previous Christmas holiday when Jon had walked her home. He'd been sad then – they both had, but at least they'd been together. Five months since she'd seen him. It might as well have been a million years.

She'd got out of school early as she'd skipped the Christmas party. She just wasn't in the festive mood. It was still daylight when she turned into the south alley, and a thin December fog was drifting down. Kate realised, with annoyance, that her feet had unconsciously carried her there. She usually avoided this route and approached the square from the other side, ashamed to be seen in her hideous school uniform by any of the gang. Perhaps no-one would see her in the fog. Of course they wouldn't, she reminded herself. She was early. They would all still be in school or at work.

But she'd reckoned without Bobby who was unemployed again. He kept walking out of jobs when the bosses told him to get his hair cut. He was getting to be a right little rebel. Even as Kate remembered this, his tall, rangy figure loomed towards her out of the mist. She hastily removed her school hat: a ghastly St. Trinian's effort, and stuffed it into her satchel. Feeling decidedly foolish, she said, 'Hello Bobby,' as casually as possible, half expecting him to laugh at her weirdo gear (which she privately called her clown outfit).

He didn't laugh. He just stood there with his hands in the pockets of his tatty old leather jacket, and gave her a long sweeping glance from head to toe – a real cave-man look. Bobby was particularly good at those. She was sure he did it just to make her blush; he was a relentless tease. Then his eyes returned to her face, and he smiled and winked in his usual roguish fashion. 'Hello, Kitty-cat. I was hoping to see you today. I got something for you.'

'Oh yeah?' she said with thinly-veiled suspicion. 'If it's another one of your all-year-round Christmas kisses, then I'm on the run, Bobcat.'

He smiled wider. 'I mean something apart from that. You'll get that anyway for the privilege.' Then he produced a white envelope from inside his jacket and handed it to her.

It was blotched all over with his grubby fingerprints, but she could see it was unopened. In the centre was one word, unmistakeably scrawled, "Kit". She recognised that wonderful scrawl at once – Jon's writing. It was from him! Her heart flipped a double-take. He hadn't forgotten her – he'd sent her a card. 'Thanks, Bobby,' she remembered to whisper through her daze. 'Where'd you get this?'

'He was here last night,' Bobby informed. 'He was scared to put that through your letterbox, in case your dad found it. I told him I'd give you it.'

'He was here last night? How does he look, Bobby?' Kate was unable to contain her excitement.

He sighed wearily. 'He looks to me – just like a little short-assed bloke. You still sweet on him?'

'Like honey.' She was eyeing the envelope avariciously, yet reluctant to open it in front of Bobby.

'I sorta hoped... I mean – I thought... maybe you and me some day...' He looked confused, unusual for him.

'Don't be daft, Bobcat! By the time I'm old enough for you, you'll be old, square and married.' (Bobby was sixteen at this time, and that seems awfully old when you're twelve.)

'Oh yeah?...' He kicked a tin can with such force that it shot right down the alley, clanging everywhere, and scattering a flock of starlings which were winter-feeding on discarded fish and chips.

'Don't get wild mate,' she said with a tinge of alarm.

He looked back at her – calm grey eyes belying his agitation; fair hair flopped over his forehead, a little too long, shading his eyes. 'I am wild about you, Kitty. Always have been. I can't help it – yet here I am deliv'ring love-letters for another bloke just to make you happy. I must be barmy.'

'Why'd you do it then, crazy-man?'

He shrugged. 'Jon's a good kid. I wouldn't lay one on him – and besides, I'd do anything for you – anything in the world. You're my dream-baby. I'd swing for you, darlin'.'

Kate was staggered by this valiant declaration. He had never been so outspoken before, but then, he usually had Adam with him, his Shadowcat. She looked at him a bit guiltily. 'Thanks Bobby,' (she always seemed to be saying that) 'you're a great mate.'

'Don't that deserve a Christmas kiss then?' he asked hopefully. 'I'm prepared to chase you if ness.' He added his own brand of wicked chivalry.

She couldn't help smiling. 'Okay Bob, but keep it clean.'

He grinned delightedly, then gave her a massive bear-hug which took her breath away and almost lifted her off her feet. Kate couldn't deny that she liked Bobby. He'd been her friend and protector for almost as long as she could remember, and she supposed she took his affection for granted. Bobby was always there. He was a good mate and fun to be with; he had the kind of strength that made a girl feel safe, and he wasn't bad looking either. He was all of those things, yet still he could not compare with Jon. To Kate's mind, no-one could.

He kissed her sweet and gentle, and didn't even try to get sloppy –
he knew she wouldn't like it. Still holding her, he then said, 'If that
letter's bad news, and if you need cheering up – just open your
mouth and yell very loud for me.'

'Will do, Bob,' she promised. But she knew it wouldn't be bad
news, not from Jon.

Bobby let her go and stood aside for her to pass. 'Merry
Christmas, darlin'. And don't forget...' He placed his hand over his
heart. 'This man's for you.'

Kate thought that was sort of sweet, but still couldn't resist her
parting jibe. She moved to a fairly safe distance, then turned to yell
at him, 'Go and eat rats, Bobcat!'

He grinned and blew her a defiant kiss. 'Okay, Teeny-tits!' Then
he growled like a tiger. 'I'm coming to getcha!' and broke into a run
towards her.

She just fled with her face flaming. Bobby knew how to get his
own back. He was a man you couldn't put down; no-one could, or so
she thought then.

As soon as she got indoors, and Mum muttered an absent greeting
like, 'Hello, you're early.' Kate locked herself in the bathroom to
read Jon's card.

'Is it that urgent?' her mum yelled, thinking she needed a
desperate leak.

'Yeah, it's cold out!' she called back, as she tore open her precious
envelope. It was a pretty Christmas card, all glittery with reindeer.
But it was the message inside which she was anxious to read. This is
how it went:

Dear Kit, my sweet,

I must see you. I can't stand it any more not seeing you. Why haven't you been to
my church? Have you forgot I said I'd see you there? Or don't you want to see me?
If that is true then please write back and give the letter to Bobby. I'll come and see
him again in a few days. If you do still want to see me – if you still love me, then

please come to St. Michael's on Christmas day. We can talk after. I miss you so
much Kit, and I love you more than ever. The dreams are worse too.
Please destroy this card as soon as you've read it. I would hate your dad to find
it. I wouldn't have written it if I wasn't desperate.
Your loving man,
Jon. xxx

Can you imagine how she felt? All this time she'd been thinking he'd forgotten her, when in fact he'd been hoping to see her in church every Sunday. Her poor Hero – no wonder he thought she didn't love him. But at the same time, Kate felt gloriously happy, like a great weight had been lifted from her chest. Jon still loved her. He wanted to see her. He did. He did!

Her mum called to ask if she was all right. She called back, yes, she had something in her eye. That was sort-of true – it was tears of regret and joy. She was determined not to destroy Jon's lovely card. She stuffed it down the front of her dress until she reached the comparative safety of her bedroom (a converted cupboard). Then she hid it inside a Beano Annual, along with the Valentine and birthday cards he'd sent her. And, for the first time in two years, she just couldn't wait for Christmas day.

Kate played this record incessantly,

Love-letters straight from your heart
keep us so near when we're apart.
I'm not alone in the night – when I can have all the love you write.
I memorise every line – and I kiss the name that you sign.
And darling then, I read again right from the start –
Love-letters straight from your heart.
Nat King Cole. 1957

On Christmas morning, the weather was mild, though Kate wouldn't have cared if there had been six feet of snow. She didn't remember what presents she got, and was much too excited to eat breakfast. She told her mum she was going to St. Michael's church to see some old friends from school. Mum looked at her a little strangely. It was half-an-hour's walk to St. Michael's; the local church was much nearer, and Kate didn't usually put in that kind of effort where religion was concerned. But Mum just said to hurry back; she would need help with the Christmas dinner. Kate said "Okay" feeling thoroughly dishonest. She wasn't going to hurry back if she could help it.

She left on time for the 10 o'clock Mass. Jon had forgotten to mention which one he would attend and, as there were three, she'd opted for the middle one, hoping he would do the same. She wondered what she would do if his mum were with him. She told herself to stop worrying; at least she would see him whatever happened.

She couldn't help thinking of Lonnie Donegan's song words: "Sweet sixteen goes to church just to see the boys..." Kate thought that was very appropriate except, in this case, it was sweet twelve, and there was only one boy she wanted to see.

The church was crowded and she was unable to locate him at first. She squeezed herself into a back pew, trying to swallow her disappointment. He was here somewhere – he had to be.

Then, when everyone sat down for the sermon, she saw him. He had remained standing a little longer than all the rest, so that she would see him. Kate did likewise, and his face lit up with pure joy when he saw her. He blew her a kiss, right there in church, quite oblivious to the disapproving look he got from the old lady beside him.

That must have been the longest Mass in the history of the world.

Outside, on the church steps, he just seized her hand and looked at her as if he couldn't believe she was real. 'I thought you'd forgot me,' he said.

'I thought the same about you.'

'Never,' he simply assured, though his eyes spoke volumes more.

She noted how fine he was growing. By this time he was tall as she was and his shoulders were broader. The new Elvis hairstyle really suited him, and there was a slight husky edge to his voice. Jon was only twelve, but he looked at least fifteen. He was a man already, her Jon.

'Let's get outa here,' he said, 'so's I can tell you how beautiful you are.'

Hand in hand, they weaved their way through groups of gossiping ladies in best Sunday hats. Kate's hair was combed loose, the way he liked it, and she wore a white beret. When they got down the road a bit, she said, 'Why couldn't you tell me outside the church, Jon?' though she'd already guessed.

He grinned. 'Because you're bloody gorgeous!' Then he kissed her before she could argue.

Now Jon wasn't a boy who swore all the time. He didn't even swear a lot. None of them swore every other word like some people today. But whenever he stressed a word in that particularly, emphatic way, she knew it was to express his most heartfelt emotion. That's what a swear really is – man's most profound expression. But like everything else, if it is overdone or used to excess, it loses its value and becomes cheap and sordid.

As they still clung together joyfully, Kate said, 'I'm sure God wouldn't have minded. He knows how you feel. I bet Jesus had a few good swears that time he lost his rag in the temple.'

He chuckled at the thought. 'You could be right. He was half human after all.'

'Yeah, half cave-man,' she agreed. Ever since the Warren episode, they'd had this theory that all people are really cave-men, deep inside, and she still reckoned they were right.

He was looking at her as if she were beautiful scenery or something. 'Are you still my girl?' he asked, wistfully.

'You bet!' she assured.

'D'you still wanna marry me?'

'After dinner be all right?'

He laughed, happiness brimming right up to his eyes. Then he grabbed her hand again. 'You don't have to go home just yet?' It was a plea, not a demand.

'I oughta, but I won't.'

So they ran all the way to the park, still holding hands and laughing. Her beret blew away twice in the wind and, in the end, he put it in his pocket.

'My lady's favour,' he said.

'Yours, Sir Jon,' she agreed.

'It's all muddy now anyway. Your mum would blow a gasket.'

'Whassat?'

'Engine talk – boring stuff for girls.'

That was their usual sort of inane conversation when they were together. They were just giddy with joy.

They reached the park which was closed on Christmas day, as expected. But Jon knew where there was a missing bar in the railings. They squeezed through this space, then ploughed their way through loads of bushes.

'Real jungle stuff,' he commented.

'Yeah, cave-man. Sure you don't wanna swing in the trees?'

'The kids' swings'll do.'

And so they went to the children's playground and had goes on everything, just like little kids. They were amazed at how small the equipment seemed now that they were so much bigger. And there they got down to some serious talking.

Jon began: 'I've decided I can't stand not to see you for another year and a half. I'll go nuts. I'll have to leave it up to you to fight me off if I get outa control. Promise you will, Kit?'

'I promise, Hero.' She knew this was important to him; it had to be if he'd given up seeing her for five months because of it.

'We can meet like this on Sundays,' he continued thoughtfully. 'Got any more ideas?'

Kate thought hard. She still wasn't allowed out evenings, and he had to stay home the best part of Sunday, 'There's the library,' she finally suggested. 'My mum knows I read a lot. I usually go two evenings a week, and sometimes I take ages choosing books.'

'Great idea, Kit!' His eyes lit with excitement. 'I like reading too. And I wouldn't care if I didn't. I'm gonna join the library.'

That's how the secret plans were made.

The way they carried on you'd have thought they were a couple of grown-ups having an illicit affair. But if Kate's dad ever found out about Jon, not only would he have half-killed her, he would have probably gone round to his house and given Jon's poor mum a load of bovver. They just couldn't risk that.

So that's the way it had to be – top secret.

Chapter Ten

Kate's mum said: at the age of fourteen she would be allowed out evenings, so long as she was home at a reasonable hour. She would also be allowed to go out with boys, providing they were nice boys, not like "those yobs down the alley". Kate knew she was referring to Bobby and the gang. As far as her mum was concerned, they were riff-raff or scum or, in her dad's opinion, "not worth a light". Bobby, in particular, worried her mum. She could see he had eyes on Kate; he made no effort to hide it. Whenever she happened to pass him by with her mum in tow, always the sweeping appraisal and the lecherous wink. Mum would say, loudly enough for him to hear, 'Don't ever have anything to do with that creature. You're too good for the likes of him.'

Kate would always look back at him and smile, if she was able to without Mum seeing, to show that she didn't share her opinion, though he knew that perfectly well, as she shortly discovered.

On one such occasion, Kate's mum saw her looking back at Bobby. She didn't say anything right then, but when they got down the road a bit, she suddenly turned and slapped her daughter's head.

'Ouch!' Kate exclaimed, more surprised than hurt. 'Whassat for!'

Mum looked absolutely furious. 'Nice girls DON'T look at boys that way!'

'What way?' Kate stupidly asked.

'You know very what way well!' She was so mad, she was getting her words mixed up. That was a bad sign; she was really fuming. 'I saw how you were looking at that bloke, and you better not let me catch you doing it again!'

'I— I...' Kate's argument trailed off. She wanted to say that Bobby wasn't a bloke – not just any bloke. He was her friend and he was a nice boy. But this would only have further incriminated her.

'I don't want to hear any more cheek!' Mum stated, emphatically.

That shut Kate up like a clam. Any form of verbal self-defence was regarded as "cheek" and would be reported to her dad. Cheek to parents was a cardinal sin in those days.

But her mum's words had greater effect than she knew. "Nice girls don't look at boys that way".
What way? she wondered.
Nice girls don't look at boys...
Nice girls don't...
Kate worried about it all the way home. So she wasn't a nice girl. Could be she wasn't good enough for a nice boy like Jon. Maybe she was going to grow up bad. But she didn't feel bad – it couldn't be wrong just to look at Bobby. All the other girls did. And she was his special friend – he said so. How could any girl help looking at him anyway? He was fine looking.
Nice girls don't.

Later that evening, Kate looked at all the pin-up pics on her bedroom wall: Elvis, Cliff Richard, and Rick Nelson. They were all gorgeous. She thought she liked Cliff Richard the best – he was sort of like Jon. Was it bad to like pop stars? Her mum didn't seem to mind those. That was really just the same as looking at boys, wasn't it? Should she take them all down? Maybe she should ask Jon first. He was wise for his age; he would know the truth. But no – how could she ask him a thing like that? He might think she went around staring at other boys all the time, and that wasn't true, was it? She couldn't picture any boy's face clearly except Jon's and Bobby's, and maybe Adam's or Joe's. Did that make her a bad girl?
Mary wouldn't be much help either. She was just as dumb as Kate was about those sort of things. She didn't even know the obvious things like, you don't belittle a boy in front of his mates – you mustn't show him up that way 'cos male pride is fierce. Kate had to tell Mary these things, which came natural to her. So what could she do?

She finally decided to ask Bobby himself. He wouldn't mind. He might tease her a bit, but he would tell her. He was older than Jon or Mary and far more worldly-wise. Bobby would surely know if nice girls don't.

She would never have guessed what he said.

Saturday, she got up early, and went to get her dad's morning paper before he woke up. This would be a good time to see Bobby. She knew he wasn't one to lie in bed when there was life to get on with. The weather was damp, but fairly warm. She pulled on a sweater over her jeans, then loped down the alley.

The ground was wet with recent rain. Congealed mud had settled in all the cracks and dips of the alley flagstones. This reminded her of school-dinner gravy – sort of lumpy with bits in, and she jumped over every squidgy-looking place. She saw Bobby lounging in his own doorway with Adam, and her heart sank a little; she'd hoped to find him alone – her question was important.

'Hey, look at that!' Bobby said as she skipped towards them. 'Don't she bounce nice?'

Kate stopped in mid-gallop, immediately conscious of her thin sweater and no bra.

Bobby's grin almost reached his ears. 'I hope you're looking for me, darlin', 'cos I think you just found me.'

Adam's expression was fiendish too. She wished he would go away. Not that she disliked him – she knew he was a good bloke. He was Bobby's best friend, so how could he be anything else? But his fierce eyes always unnerved her a bit. They seemed to bore right through her.

She managed to stammer through her blushes, 'I – I am looking for you, Bobby. I – I wanna ask you something important.'

He grinned so wide you'd have thought his jaw would fall off. 'Ask away, sweetness. This man knows everything.'

'I–' Her voice sounded thin and peevish even to herself. 'I wanted to talk to you alone, Bobby.'

'Ain't it my lucky day, darlin'?' To Adam he said, 'Fade out, Shadow.' (Shadowcat was Adam's nickname.)

Adam said, 'You should ask me, little girl – not him. The Shadow knows it all.' His grin was still fiendish, but the intensity of his dark-eyed gaze was making Kate more nervous than ever. She shook her head, dumbly.

'I know what's on your mind,' he insisted. 'The Shadow knows.'

'Get lost!' Bobby told him. 'You trying to steal my bird?'

'Who me?' Adam's dark eyes widened and assumed the innocence of a bush-baby. But he began to move away, silent as a cat on his crepe-soled boots.

'Seeya, sweetness!' he told Kate with a lecherous wink. Then he moved fast to avoid Bobby's well-aimed kick at his backside. They said there was no man faster than the Shadowcat, and Kate learned the truth of this much later.

But she knew they didn't mean it. Bobby and Adam were very close friends – closer than a lot of brothers she knew. They were worse than Mary and her.

'I'll git you later,' Bobby promised Adam's fast-moving shape.

'Bobby,' Kate said, 'I ain't your bird. You know I don't like that word. I ain't no feathered creature. I'm just a girl, Bobby, and I'm your friend. I need your wise head.'

She knew this pleased him by the way his eyes sparkled over his grin. 'What's up then, darlin'?' He sat on the doorstep and patted the space beside him to indicate that she should join him. 'Come and tell Bobby your trouble.'

Kate sat down beside him, gladly. She was so lucky to have Bobby. He fulfilled the role of father, big brother, friend and confidant better than anyone else ever could. He was like her guardian angel.

'Bobby,' she began at once, 'the other day, when you saw me with my mum, she slapped me and she said, "Nice girls don't look at boys that way". What did she mean, Bobby? What way was I looking at you?'

He didn't reply at once; he seemed to be too busy grinning. Indeed, his grin was threatening to split his face. 'Oh, Jesus!' he exclaimed. 'Now I've really heard it all.' He continued his silent grinning and then she noticed, with dismay, that he was actually shaking with suppressed laughter. It was the kind of helpless mirth that takes your breath away. He just couldn't speak with the force of it. Her Bobcat, her old mate – he was laughing at her!

Kate's face flushed with colourful indignation, and she began to get up to run away. 'I shoulda known better,' she told him hotly, 'than to ask a clown like you anything serious!'

He laid a restraining hand on her arm as his laughter finally escaped. 'Please don't go. Hee hee – har har! I'm gonna tell you. Hoo hoo – hee! I'm gonna answer your question – hee hee har! – in a minute – hee hee – I promise.'

She remained sitting beside him. Curiosity overcame her indignation.

'Bobby,' she pleaded, 'this kid needs your help.'

He then made a determined effort to be serious, even though the tears rolled down his cheeks and the corners of his mouth still twitched, still trying to laugh. 'Kitty-cat, you're really killing me,' he said.

'Why Bobby? What's so funny? Please tell me.'

'I'm sorry I laughed,' he said, still grinning, 'I never meant to upset you, Kitty. You know I think the world of you – and I really wanna help.'

'Okay, Bobcat. I forgive you. Please go on.'

'You look at me with them big-baby eyes and you ask me that. That's what I found so funny darlin'. You was looking at me just the same way that you asked about.'

'What way, Bobby?' She gripped his shoulder. 'Please tell me. It's important to me.'

'Kate, I'm nuts about you. And I know that don't mean nothin' to you right now – you're very young and confused.'

'I ain't confused. Get on with it, Bobby. Please!'

He smiled at her impatience. 'When you look at me with them big, beautiful eyes, they say to me, "Hey man, I think you're fine. Come a little closer".'

'What?' She was appalled. 'My eyes say that!'

'Yeah, kid, they really do. And don't think that I don't like the way you look at me – I love it. But I understand that you're just too young to control it. I realise it's just a primitive thing; like your little mate, Jon would say – it's a cave-man look.'

'Bobby, you're amazing me,' she said, wonderingly. 'I never knew girls did things like that, 'specially without even knowing. Does that mean I'm a bad girl, Bob? Like my mum said?'

'She never meant that you are a bad girl. She never explained enough. Square people often do that – they leave you wonderin'. She was tryin' to warn you that boys might think you are bad if you look at them that way. You see, Kitty-cat, there's a lotta blokes in this world who don't think about nothin' 'cept the deep raging fire in their pants. A boy like that would take that look as encouragement. You gotta be careful, my darlin'.'

Well – wasn't he just wonderful? Her great big, teasy-weasy, gorgeous, impossible Bobcat. She saw with terrifying clarity exactly where she'd gone wrong with Warren. Bobby explained things so well; she'd been right to come to him. She hugged him, impulsively. 'Thanks, Bobby. I'm glad you don't think I'm bad.'

He hugged her back fiercely. 'You ain't no bad girl. You're the loveliest girl I know, and you can give me big-baby eyes any time.'

Adam re-appeared with his usual suddenness, as if he'd just teleported, and with her dad's newspaper. How had he known she intended getting one?

'Put that little girl down!' he scolded. 'She's jailbait!' (He was all of sixteen years old himself.)

Bobby released her, and jumped up to beat Adam's grinning head. The smaller boy barely had time to hand Kate the newspaper before it rolled with him into the mud. She left the two of them, scuffling playfully, and getting their clothes filthy in the process. Boys! Why did they always act like little kids, no matter how old they got?

So, her mum had been right when she'd said, "Nice girls don't". They certainly didn't go around making eyes at every boy. But then,

Mum hadn't known that Bobby wasn't just any-old boy – he was her friend.

"Big-baby eyes" he called it. She smiled at the thought. A big baby? Was that how he thought of her? She couldn't really blame him for that; he was much older than she was. Kate didn't mind Bobby thinking her a baby. He looked after her very well and was always willing to help.

Bobby was always there.

But she was still peeved that her mum thought wrong things about him. This was most unjust. Mum didn't know Bobby like Kate did; she'd never even spoken to him. She knew only that he wore a battered old leather jacket, which instantly labelled him the arch-villain of London. And his hair was too long. She couldn't see the heart of gold that beat beneath this rough exterior. This taught Kate well, never to judge a book by the cover.

But, she told herself, her mum didn't have any real cause for concern about Bobby. Kate had no intention of ever taking up with him, much as she liked him. Jon was her fella, and there was no way she would ever two-time him. She was quite sure her mum would approve of Jon when the time came. He was a good Catholic boy from a nice family. How could she not?

Chapter Eleven

Kate and Jon decided to make Tuesdays and Thursdays the evenings for their library visits, as this would break up the week nicely without long gaps of unbearable separation. And, of course, there were still Sunday mornings after church. If the weather was bad, they would go to the coffee bar; otherwise they went to the park.

Jon would wait for her down the alley. He became quite chummy with Bobby and the gang. Then, as early as she could get away – sometimes 5 o'clock, sometimes 5:30, Kate would run down the alley to meet him, and they would walk to the library together.

They discovered much mutual interest in the books they read. Kate got him hooked on sci-fi, and he got her into sword 'n sorcery, which was the kind of stuff she would eventually write. They swapped books after they'd read them, so that they could discuss the shared content. But their greatest avid interest was pre-history, that is, cave-men, and they couldn't seem to find enough books on this subject to satisfy their lust for knowledge.

'I wish we was cave-men,' Jon said, wistfully. 'Then we wouldn't be having all this bovver.'

'How'd you mean, Hero?'

'I mean we could just get mated. No-one would stop us or tell us we was too young. If our bodies was old enough – then we'd be old enough, just like nature intended.'

'Would you really club me over the head and drag me off by the barnet?'

'Nah, I'd just do this...' And he made a deep, lusty growl in his throat which made her laugh, as it always did.

The librarian gave a fierce "Shhh!" and frowned, warningly.

They quietened down at once, as they had no desire to get barred from the library – it was their haven.

The librarian seemed to be getting used to them. One evening, she actually greeted them, 'Hello, Hero and Kit,' with a knowing smirk.

Kate blushed and giggled. But they were a bit disconcerted to think she'd heard what they called each other and strove to whisper more quietly after that. They nick-named the librarian Big Ears, not that hers were, but she flapped them exceedingly well. She was a small, prim-looking woman with short, dark hair which curled forwards onto her cheeks (twenties style) and she wore large, owlish-type glasses. Although she shushed them with dutiful regularity, Kate was sure she was quite sympathetic, and actually looked forward to their visits (Ah, it's Thursday – episode six of the Hero and Kit saga). They probably brightened her evening overtime, for she always seemed to be watching them whenever they looked her way.

One time, Kate caught her taking a sneaky bite from a large cheese sandwich which she'd had hidden under the counter. She flushed guiltily when she saw the girl looking (maybe she wasn't supposed to eat during overtime), but Kate just smiled and turned away.

'These cave-men get everywhere,' Jon whispered, humorously.

Kate knew what he meant. Some of the most unlikely people turn out to be quite human after all.

They began to do their homework together. This was an even better excuse for Kate to stay longer at the library. She'd told her mum it was easier to concentrate in the quiet, away from the younger kids, which was perfectly true, and Mum had agreed it was a good idea.

Kate was astonished at the simple stuff that Jon was given to do. Most of it was not even up to Miss Benson's standard. He agreed; he found it so easy it was boring, and he was top of the class without even trying. But he became quite interested in her geometry and algebra, and she was able to teach him some. This convinced her, more than ever, that Jon was being deprived of the education he deserved, and she told him so.

'It really don't matter,' he said. 'I'm only gonna be a grease-monkey.'

But Kate couldn't help feeling resentful about it. Jon had an intelligent mind and was being treated like a moron. He said he could always go to night school later on, and get a few GCEs. Kate thought that a very good idea. She was more settled in school now that she was seeing Jon regularly, and was determined to do well, so that she could get a good job and help him through his apprenticeship. They intended to get married as soon as Kate left school, if her parents gave their consent.

'We might have a few problems there,' she told him, worriedly.

'We'll worry about them when the time comes,' he said, wisely. 'We can always elope to Gretna Green,' he added with a grin. 'Then I'll take you home to my house. Your dad won't be able to do a thing about it.'

And so the dreams grew stronger.

Kate began to go Saturday swimming again with the gang, though Jon could no longer join them, as he was working. She was allowed out on Saturdays, providing she did her allotted chores, and she could choose whether to do these in the morning or afternoon. They had outgrown the Saturday morning pictures, but swimming was still a great pleasure. Her mum never knew she went with the Alley-cats; she thought they were mates from school – but Kate knew who her real friends were.

She was amazed at the change in Bobby since the last time she'd seen him in swim-trunks. He wasn't scrawny any more, though he'd grown taller. He was getting muscle in all the right places – and it was beautiful to see. It made her feel all fluttery inside just to look at him. She kept trying to avert her eyes, but it was difficult. This disturbed her more than a little; it was much worse than "big-baby eyes" – she was ogling the man! But she was Jon's girl. How could she look at another boy that way? Then she noticed that all the other girls were looking at Bobby just the same, and finally decided it must be sheer female instinct. She couldn't help it any more than Jon could help looking at Harpie.

But Bobby had seen her hapless admiration and deliberately flexed all his muscles for her. 'D'you like it kid?' he asked, teasingly.

'Yeah, I reckon I do.' (It never occurred to Kate to be anything other than totally honest with a boy. She hadn't learned any coyness or feminine wiles. She had no need of such things with Jon.)

His cheeky grin spread earwise and he held out his arms. 'C'mere then, darlin'.'

'No!' she told him, furiously. 'You don't half fancy yourself, Bobby.'

'Wrong!' He pointed an accusing finger. 'I fancy you, Kitty-cat. I can't help appreciatin' your appreciatin'. I'm only human.'

Kate was lazily floating the width of the pool on her back, looking up at him as he stood on the side. 'Don't you ever give up, Bobcat? You know I'm spoke for. I'm good as engaged.'

His expression was suddenly fierce. 'On the day that you marry that bloke, that's if you ever really do and I don't believe it for a minute – I promise I'll give up. But until then, I never will! Never – never – never!'

Then he dived from the side, breaking water like a depth charge. He streaked towards her like a torpedo. Kate was so taken by surprise, that she had no time to get out of his way. She screamed as he grabbed her around the waist, then pulled her under to a swirl of bubbles and a roaring in her ears. He held her tightly and swam with her a few seconds, then rose gently to the surface without relaxing his hold. 'Mmmm,' he said, pressing her closer against him, 'you feel good.'

She struggled, then raged at him when she had drawn breath, 'Let me go! I HATE you, Bobby!'

'I know you don't mean that.' He released her and flicked her in the face with her wet pony-tail. 'You need me to look after you when Jon ain't around.'

'Who says so?' Still livid, Kate was treading water, slowly backing away from him.

'I do,' he said, firmly. 'And so does he.'

'What..?' She wasn't sure she'd heard right.

'Jon asked me to look out for you when he can't be here – but he never needed to ask. Ain't I always done exactly that?'

Kate was speechless for a moment. It was true. Bobby had always been her friend and protector and, if Jon trusted him that much, (she knew he was no mean judge) then Bobby must be one hell of a good bloke, even better than she'd thought. She was suddenly contrite. 'I'm sorry I shouted at you, Bob, but you did scare me.'

He grinned as if it didn't matter a bit. 'Jon knows the best man will win – and I never meant to scare you. I thought you'd be ready for that.' He chuckled. 'You know what a clown I am.'

'Yeah,' she agreed.

Dear Bobby, she shot him down in flames so many times, and always he came back for more, still smiling. She almost believed his advances were a joke – for whoever looks deep in the eyes of a clown? It took a long, long time for her to discover that it was no joke to him, no joke at all – not ever.

Mary had a boyfriend by this time. His name was Mark and he was fifteen. Unlike Kate, Mary was allowed to go out with him, providing all the usual providings. Kate couldn't help feeling envious of her friend's freedom. Why was she lumbered with the squarest parents in the world? Mark even went to tea at Mary's flat every other Sunday. Because of this, Kate reduced her own visits to once a fortnight.

In the summer term, there was going to be a school trip to the Tate Gallery. They would spend the morning there, then be free for the rest of the day. Kate was idly telling Jon about this, one evening in the library, when he suddenly said, 'I'll skip school that afternoon. We can have a few hours together.' His face glowed with excitement.

Kate was a bit dubious. 'Won't you get into trouble at school?'

'I'll say I'm going to the dentist. I've never done it before. They shouldn't mind.'

Another doubt surfaced. 'I'll be in school uniform. It's absolutely hideous.'

'Mine ain't exactly a rave,' he pointed out. 'And anyway, who cares? To me you'd look good in a sack.'

And so it was decided.

Big-Ears was living up to her name. She sighed and began to hum "Teenager in love".

'Shhh!' Jon and Kate said, both at once.

Chapter Twelve

Kate really didn't remember much about that trip to the Tate Gallery. Only that the teacher's voice droned on and on, the other girls twittered like sparrows, and an endless array of paintings swam before her eyes. She'd never been much of a one for paintings, unless you counted animation drawing which she'd often tried herself. And she didn't think any of the ones she saw were a patch on the cave-man art she'd seen in library books. Painted on cave walls, using coloured earth and animal fat, these had survived for thousands of years. Bison, antelope, and horses – the standard of art was amazing, and they didn't even have brushes, just used twigs or something in their own ingenious way.

They were finally released around two-ish, which was quite a bit later than she'd told Jon. Kate worried that he might not still be there, as they walked along Millbank towards Lambeth Bridge. Those who lived that side of the river drifted off. Some of the rest were going back to school just to collect books and things. She walked along with these until they came to the corner of Lambeth Bridge, and there he was, still waiting.

His school shirt was dazzling white against his early summer tan. It was open at the collar and his tie was stuffed into his pocket. His jacket was thrown over one shoulder – and his smile was wonderful.

Dolores Hutchings voiced an opinion, as usual. She was (supposedly) a Lady's daughter, and spoke with a really affected Queen's English accent, the kind that always made Kate cringe, as well as an infuriating lisp which she didn't suppose the girl could help. 'Ith that your boyfwend, Kathwin? I thay, ithn't he thweet? What a thyame about that nathty thcar on hith fathe – quate thpoilth him, doethn't it?'

This was said loudly enough for Jon to hear and Kate saw the colour rise to his face. She knew he was still conscious of that scar, in spite of her frequent reassurance. Trust Hutchings to open her big north and south, she thought, angrily. 'Shut-up, Hutchings!' Kate told her.

Dolores turned to Kate with wide-eyed contempt. 'Are you tor-king to me?' as if she couldn't believe it.

'Only long enough to say, shut your face,' Kate retorted, 'before I fill it with knuckles.'

The posh girl's eyes were round as blue marbles and her mouth was a perfect capital "O". Kate didn't think she could believe her ears. She was usually quiet in school and kept to herself a lot. But no-one slanged down her Jon, no-one in the world. The Queen herself would have got the same. She turned away from Dolores and walked towards Jon (he was grinning by this time). She took his arm with pride, and he relieved her of her heavy satchel. As they walked away, Kate heard Dolores say, 'How or-fully common!' She never spoke to her again, but Kate was sure she spoke lots about her.

Dolores thought she was such a fine lady. But Kate's mum had told her years ago that it's bad manners to make personal remarks about other people, especially if they can hear. Jon had already given her his definition of a lady, and she entirely agreed with him:

"A lady is a female person who has the grace to consider the feelings of others before her own, at all times, and in all places. It has nothing to do with fine clothes or posh accent, or how much money her father's got. And it don't even matter if she never observes the finer points of unnecessary etiquette. None of these things have anything to do with it unless they conflict with the first rule. In other words, it depends who she's with. A lady is naturally born and cannot be moulded or trained to be anything else. She is a girl that any man would be proud to have by his side."

Jon always said that Kate was a natural lady. She didn't feel that this was quite deserved, but still she loved to hear him say it.

They continued to follow the river while the other girls crossed the Lambeth Bridge. When they were all safely out of sight, he turned to kiss her, then said, 'Still my little fire-bomb, ain't you?'

'Can't help it, Hero.'

He was studying her face, lovingly. Then he touched the scar on his own. 'This makes me look ugly, don't it?'

'Nothing could ever make you look ugly to me,' she said, passionately. 'To me, your face is the finest sight in the world, and I love it like I love every bit of you.'

He hugged her. 'I'm so lucky I got you.'

She ran her finger down the length of his scar. It made a very gradual curve down his right cheek, paler than the rest of his tanned skin, and slightly puckered at the edges where his face had grown around it. Then she kissed all down this blemish to further reassure him that it held no revulsion for her.

'Cor!' he exclaimed. 'That's just my face. I can't wait 'til you make love to all of me.'

She laughed and held him around the waist. 'Let's walk before you get too excited.'

He put his free arm around her shoulders. Her satchel and his jacket were hefted on his other shoulder. Kate was glad she had left her blazer in school – it was too hot to wear it. They made very slow progress, as they continually stopped to cuddle or talk, or just to watch the river. Big Ben struck three as they drew near Westminster.

Jon rolled up his shirt-sleeves, as he was still hot. She noticed the increase of dark hair growth on his arms, and caressed this, enjoying the soft, tickly feel of it.

'It's on my legs too,' he informed wickedly.

Kate realised with a pang that she had not seen all of him since that day on the beach, and he'd grown an awful lot since then. 'I wish I could see how fine you're growing,' she told him.

'I wish the same about you.' He gave her the cave-man look, causing violent tremors in her stomach. 'You know, that dress ain't so hideous. It shows you off real nice.'

She looked down at the green-striped, summer dress with distaste. It was fitted to the waist and belted, with a slightly flared skirt.

'It's a bit like a nurse's dress,' he further approved. Then he grinned mischievously. 'You could always take it off if you don't like it.'

'Oh yeah, in the middle of Victoria Embankment.'

'We could go to Hyde Park and sunbathe.'

'We're walking the wrong way,' she pointed out.

'We could get a bus back.' He grinned wider. 'We could even go swimming in the Turpentine.'

She giggled at this deliberate misnomer. 'We ain't got our swimming gear.'

'Who needs it?' he asked, naughtily.

'You mean – swim naked?'

'Wouldn't you like to – with me? Or just crawl into some bushes and snuggle up a bit and–'

'Jon!' she interrupted. 'I don't think that's a very good idea.' Her heart was racing. Much as it hurt to refuse him anything, she knew she had to – this time.

'Good girl!' He smiled reassurance. 'I wasn't serious, I just had to see what you'd say'

'Oh, you–! She slapped his shoulder with feigned annoyance.

'One more thing,' he said, still smiling.

'Yeah?'

'If I got down on my knees and begged, would you do it then?'

Kate blushed guiltily. 'Yeah, I would. I'm sorry Jon. I ain't a bit strong really where you're concerned. You'd only have to beg once.'

'S'okay,' he spoke soothingly. 'That's good too. I promise you now, I'll never beg. I don't expect you to do it all. I gotta do my bit.'

They stopped to cuddle again.

One of the things Kate loved most about Jon was the way he talked to her. They just never seemed to run out of things to talk about, and they could talk about anything – even the most intimate things, without reserve or embarrassment. That's the way it was supposed to be, he told her – the natural way. She never knew where Jon got his wisdom from. It seemed vast beyond his years.

The City was fairly peaceful at that time of day. Most of its milling workforce being safely entombed in their office blocks. There was not the same volume of traffic on the roads in those days. Driving was yet to become the ordeal it is now. An occasional pleasure cruiser chugged along the river, filled with holidaymakers, mostly tourists. Many of these waved to the boy and girl, and they waved back. Kate always remembered that afternoon as one of the most wonderful ever spent. It stood out in her memory, clear and shining, one of those golden days that poets write about – everyone has them in their lives.

They eventually found a small café, and nestled themselves in a quiet corner to while away the City rush-hour. Kate told Jon she wasn't expected home at any particular time. Her mum thought the school trip was in the afternoon and she'd been unsure of its duration. She always hated lying to her mum, and so did he, but they agreed it was necessary for their survival. They would explain it all to them someday, when they were old enough to be accepted. Kate didn't have the same qualms about her dad, however; she'd have lied to him till the Devil took her home. That was different.

'Got any more cave-man stories?' she asked Jon over the frothy coffee.

'Yeah, I got a real silly one just for you.'

'Thanks a bundle,' she said, smiling.

Jon had begun this series of cave-man stories during their library visits. He made them up straight out of his head, sometimes on the spur of the moment, and Kate found them hilarious. They were silly kind-of comic book humour; sometimes he even drew cartoon characters to go with them – but it was the way he told them that was so funny. He managed to keep a perfectly straight face throughout the whole thing, no matter how outrageous the story got. Jon was a natural clown, and she just loved to hear him.

'Proceed, story-man,' she encouraged.

He smiled and took a swig of his coffee, then began: 'Long ago, in prehistoric times, there lived a man...'

'You don't say!' She always constantly interrupted him, but he never minded. It just seemed to make the story funnier.

'Yeah, I just did. This little bloke was a cave-man named Ogo.'

'Good name,' she approved.

'But Ogo was unhappy...'

'Aww!' she sympathised.

'Because he was madly in love with this cave-girl named Ono.'

'Oh no!' She giggled.

'Exactly. Ono was the dishiest girl in the whole tribe and all the young men wanted her for a mate. She never knew which one to choose, and hardly noticed Ogo, so he thought.'

(Sympathetic attention from Kate.)

'All the blokes in the tribe began to bring her presents, each one trying to outdo the others – so she soon became the richest girl as well as the dishiest.'

'What sorta presents?'

'Furs mostly, and food, fruit and flowers, bone necklaces, things carved of wood, pretty rocks they dug up–'

'Diamonds?'

'Yeah, they mighta been diamonds. Cave-men never knew the difference. They was just pretty rocks to them.'

Kate nodded; she was getting well into this story.

'Ogo tried hard to think of a present he could give Ono that would outshine all the other blokes'. Thinking was hard work for a cave-man. He very soon got a headache. So he went to the back of his cave and began to beat his drum.'

'When he had a headache?' This didn't seem very sensible.

'Yeah. Drumming is soothing to a cave-man – like rock 'n roll music is to us. (Jon stated this as if it were a proven fact.) Ogo closed his eyes and drummed madly and, as he drummed, his headache went away – then he began to think again. It was such a bovver, he hated thinking. Ogo stopped drumming and scratched his shaggy, black mane of hair, and two prehistoric nits fell out.'

'Prehistoric nits! Oh boy, you kill me.' She giggled, helplessly.

'These prehistoric nits were far superior to any nits known today – they were fatter, juicier and greedier. This was because cave-man's shaggy, black mane was far superior to modern hair. (Jon remained perfectly poker-faced as he spouted this nonsense.) They landed on the floor of the cave, laid on their backs, wiggling their legs, and gasping for hair.'

'Gasping for hair?' Kate hooted. 'That's brilliant, Jon!'

'Ogo was in a rotten mood by this time and, instead of picking up the poor creatures and putting them back, like any civilised cave-man, he got his club and batted them both. Bat – Bat! No more nits.'

'What a brute!' She was really getting into the spirit of things. 'What was his club made of, Jon?'

'It was a gigantic bone – a mammoth bone,' he informed.

'Cor! Them nits musta made holes in the floor.'

'They did.' They both laughed this time, and Jon took several moments to compose his features before he continued. 'Then he had it.'

'What?'

'His brilliant idea. He danced all around the cave, batting everything in sight, which was mostly rocks, and he finally beat his own chest with the club and he roared. His mother looked up from her rush-weaving and said in a "seen it all before" kind of voice, "Shut-up Ogo, and stop wrecking the furniture!"

Delighted laughter from Kate. Then she asked, 'What was the idea?'

'He decided to get Ono a brontosor-ass.' (Jon said it just like that.)

Kate simply howled at that one. 'Oh Jon, you iriot! How d'you do it? Why did the bronto have a sore arse?'

'Because...' he said solemnly, 'the deep, forest lake in which this brontosor-ass lurked, had a very rocky, gravelly bottom.'

More helpless mirth from Kate. Jon was really excelling himself. 'Why didn't he move to a new lake then?'

'Because a brontosor-ass had a very small brain, and he just hadn't thought of that.'

'Got an answer for everything, ain't you?'

'An author's s'posed to anticipate questions.'

'Yeah, you're doing great. Carry on.'

'Ogo set off at once with his massive club and hiked through the forest until he came to the swampy bit. He knew the exact lake where Brontosor-ass lurked.'

'How did he know?'

Jon sighed with mock weariness. 'Cos it was perfect residential territory for a brontosor-ass...'

'Oh.' She was impressed until he said,

'And it was the only lake that Ogo knew of.'

This inane statement induced a fit of giggles which Kate didn't seem able to stop. Jon grinned while he waited, then said, 'Normal service will be resumed when the audience has recovered her sanity.'

She struggled to regain her composure. 'Okay Jon, carry on. I'm listening.'

'Ogo reached the lake and found no sign of Brontosor-ass, which meant it was asleep at the bottom. His next problem was how to make the creature come up so he could bat it...'

'Hold on, hold on, story-man.'

'Yeah?'

'How could a man kill a gianormous creature like Brontosor-ass, with just a club?'

'Ah, you ain't been listening. I told you the bronto had a very small brain. That meant he also had a very small skull – no problem for a mammoth bone. All Ogo had to do was reach the head.'

'How could he do that?'

'Well, he was quite brainy for a cave-man.'

'Oh yeah? Prove it.'

'He climbed this tree which was laden with prehistoric fruit.'

'What did he do with his club while he climbed?'

'Er – stuffed it down the back of his kilt.'

'Bit uncomfortable, weren't it?'

'Can you think of anything better? Who's telling this story anyway?'

She knew his grumble wasn't really annoyed. But that was one up for her – he hadn't been prepared for that question. 'Proceed, story-man,' she encouraged again.

'Ogo climbed the tree and began to throw fruit into the water. Brontosor-ass woke up and thought it was his birthday 'cos someone was feeding him. He ate all the fruit, then poked his head up, hoping for more.'

'He was vegetarian then?'

'Yeah, and not a bit dangerous unless he trod or sat on you – then he was extremely dangerous. So there he was, lurking magnificently in his beautiful, blue-green, shimmering skin.'

'How d'you know it was blue-green?'

'I don't. This is pure fiction.'

'You're so convincing, I nearly forgot.'

'So Ogo looked at Brontosor-ass and thought about all the sexy gear that Ono could make from that blue-green, shimmery skin: skirts... dresses... cloaks... She might even make something for him. There would still be enough for a tent for two when the tribe went travelling, and it would also be waterproof. He also thought of all the delicious food they'd have at the wedding feast: roast brontosor-ass... bronto sandwiches... bronto pies... and bronto burgers. Ono would surely value this present more than any other. No man had ever dared before to hunt the monstrous brontosor-ass. This would make him the greatest hero of all.'

Kate realised at this point that several other people in the café were listening.

Jon hadn't noticed. He continued. 'Ogo's next problem was to make the creature turn away from him, so that he could safely attack. He picked another fruit and threw this to the far side of the lake.

Brontosor-ass immediately turned towards this proffered treat. The neck of the creature was long and slender compared to its massive, hulking body. Ogo gritted his teeth, gripped his club, and leaped...'

There was an expectant hush in the café, cups poised in mid-air – all eyes turned towards Jon. Kate's heart swelled with pride.

'Ogo landed safely astride the neck of Brontosor-ass, just as if he were riding a horse, and he gripped with his knees just the same. He raised his great club just as the creature began to buck and thrash, trying to throw him off. Ogo knew he couldn't hold his position for long – the monster's skin was slippery and its movements were fierce. In desperation, he swung his club towards the small skull.

Brontosor-ass bellowed mournfully, and it was like thunder inside a mountain. Ogo was almost deafened by the terrible sound. The prehistoric nits tried to desert and ran down Ogo's back, took one look at the raging lake, and ran back again to hide, trembling, in the thick, black hair. The brontosor-ass' mighty tail whipped and lashed, and the water looked like Ogo's mother's soup. He wished he'd never thought of this brilliant idea. Then the mammoth bone crashed into the brontosaurean skull with a terrific crack which scared all the animals and birds in the whole forest, the prehistoric nits most of all. Several of these jumped into the lake and drowned themselves. There was an eerie sort of silence...'

Jon paused for effect and became aware for the first time of his extended audience. He coloured slightly, but Kate knew he was too far gone into his story to stop now. 'Go on, Jon,' she urged.

'The great long neck began to sway and Ogo knew it was only a matter of seconds before it went crashing through the trees, taking him with it. He began to slide frantically downwards towards the brontosaurean humped back. He reached this comparative safety only just in time, as the great neck fell through the forest, demolishing several trees, and finally landing with a terrible thud, which shook the ground like an earthquake, and almost threw Ogo into the lake. He clung in fright for a few moments, but all was still. The birds in the trees began to sing again, a bit nervously at first, and the prehistoric nits began to itch.

Ogo was filled with wild elation. He stood up on the back of his conquered prey and jumped up and down in delight, while he whooped with joy. He threw his club into the air, and it narrowly missed his own head on the way down. Then he slipped on the shimmery skin and fell, head first, into the lake, thereby taking his first bath in ages. The prehistoric nits shivered and drowned.

When Ogo surfaced and found he was still alive, much to his surprise, he saw Ono standing on the muddy shore, staring at him with an awed kind of wonder. She looked fantastically beautiful in a necklace of bear's teeth and a real mink skirt. Ogo nearly drowned himself as he gasped with delight and took in a great mouthful of water. He then decided this was a most inopportune moment to die, and struck out against the water to reach her. He found he was quite able to do this and swam for the shore, then hauled himself out of the lake and stood, looking down at her, feeling a bit daft, all dripping wet and everything. "Look what I've brought you Ono." he said.

She looked at the brontosor-ass and then back to Ogo. She actually rather fancied him, and thought it was quite funny that he'd gone to all this trouble. She'd heard the commotion he'd caused in the forest, and had come to make sure he was all right. Just to tease him, she said, "Okay, Clever-dick, now let's seeya carry it home for me."

Poor Ogo. He realised he hadn't been so clever after all. There was no way he could get the mighty brontosor-ass back to Cave Town; he hadn't even thought of that before. Roaring with frustration, he charged towards a tree trunk and butted this with his great head. One of the prehistoric fruits fell straight down on him with a loud "plop". It was soft and red, like a giant tomato, and Ogo just stood there while pulpy gunge dripped all down his face and neck.

Ono laughed so hard that she cried.

About then, Ogo decided to give up women forever and become a cave-monk.

But when she was able to speak, Ono said, "Ogo, I ain't never met a man who could make me laugh like you do. Yours is definitely the best present of all." Then she pushed him back into the lake, and jumped in after him to help clean him up.

Ogo was the happiest cave-man in the world...'

There was a sudden round of applause from the surrounding tables.

Jon blushed to the roots of his hair. He'd never had an audience before except for Kate.

A smart city gent stood up to leave, retrieving his bowler and umbrella. He smiled at both of them. 'You should be on the stage, son,' he said to Jon.

'You see?' Kate enthused. 'It ain't just me. They all loved you – you should think about serious writing, Jon.'

'Nah,' he protested. 'I only do it for you. I wanna work with cars. If I done writing all the time, I'd get bored. What about you – you're the serious writer?'

'Only poems,' she reminded. 'I can't write stories.'

'Well – maybe I'll help you someday. Got any new ones?'

At that time, Kate wrote really way-out poetry – wild protest stuff, mostly. Jon always read this avidly. "Primitive" he called it. She delved into her school dress pockets for the inevitable scraps of paper, and she read him some. She was glad that the other occupants of the café had withdrawn their attention.

'That's great!' he praised when she had finished. 'Will you copy them out for me?'

Kate assured him that she would.

People had begun to drift out of the small café. The City was on its way home. They had the place almost to themselves, though they knew their wonderful afternoon was nearly over; they would have to go soon.

Jon got up to get their last two coffees and, on his way back, he put a tanner in the juke box. The Big Bopper sang "Chantilly Lace" and Jon sang right along with him.

Kate was still not quite used to his new, deep voice. Although not gravelly like the Big Bopper's, it was noticeably deeper when he sang:

> Chantilly lace an' a purty face
> An' a pony-tail hanging down.
> Got a wiggle when she walks
> An' a giggle when she talks
> An' it makes the world go round.
> There ain't nothing in the world like a big-eyed girl
> Makes me act so funny – makes me spend my money
> Makes me feel real loose like a long-necked goose
> Like a girl.
> Baby, that's what I like!

She gave him fervent attention while he sang, noting every facial expression, and every loving look. What a wonderful kid he was; so many talents, he was unbelievable. Kate was sure that even if she hadn't been madly in love with him, she would still have thought so. She knew she didn't deserve him. Jon was just too good to be true.

They ended up on Waterloo Bridge, and watched the setting sun over Westminster. The City was peaceful again; its throbbing workforce had deserted. The cool evening breeze was welcome after the day's heat, and the fiery light of the dying sun roseated the black water of the Thames.

They were late; they had lingered too long, reluctant to part. Kate had decided to tell her mum she'd been straight to the library from school. Mum would still be annoyed, but Kate considered that well worth spending some extra time with Jon.

'I will always remember today,' he said. 'For the rest of my life, it will stand out in my mem'ry, and this place will be special to us – sort of magical.'

'Likewise, Hero.' She was too choked up for further comment.

Then, for the first time that day, he treated her to several of his fiercely-sweet, passionate kisses.

And the magic increased.

Chapter Thirteen

But the most wonderful day of Kate's life was yet to come. This was her thirteenth birthday, which happened to fall on a Sunday.

She and Jon had got into the habit of meeting outside the church beforehand, so that they could sit together. He held her hand all the way through the Mass and, afterwards, when they walked down the aisle together, he whispered, 'One day, we'll be doing this for real.'

She squeezed his hand and returned his smile.

Outside, he said, 'Come to Chico's. I got a special present for you, as it's your birthday, darlin'.'

Kate could tell he was really excited about it, and went with him gladly, holding his arm all the way. She no longer cared what people at the church thought. She was almost old enough to go out with boys, and certainly looked it.

Chico's was the coffee bar they usually went to on Sundays, as it was the nearest one that was open. Jon ordered two of their favourite frothy coffees and they sat in a cosy booth for two. The place was deserted except for two boys in leather jackets who were hanging around the juke box.

They spooned far too much brown sugar into their coffee, and Jon gave a strangely shy sort of smile while they stirred. She returned the same and gazed at his face, drinking in every detail, almost as if she knew how much she would need this memory. The way the shining dark hair fell across his forehead; wide brown eyes with tiny golden flecks if you looked close; sprinkled freckles across his nose, which was not so short and squat as it used to be; the tender, loving mouth that smiled so readily; and the scar down his right cheek – he'd got that fighting for her. His was not a truly handsome face, but it was the finest sight in the world to Kate. (That's when you know you are in love, when a face becomes the most beautiful thing there is.)

He put down his spoon and reached inside his jacket. He brought out a small green box like a cube. 'Do you still love me?' His eyes searched, deeply.

'Of course. How can you ask?'

'Then I hope you'll accept this.'

She took the box from him and opened it with trembling hands. It contained a beautiful gold ring, set with three tiny diamonds. She gasped, 'Oh Jon!' Further words eluded her. She just gazed at the tiny miracle sparkling in the soft light.

He was watching her face closely, studying her reaction. 'I'll get you another one later,' he said. 'One of your own choice, when I'm earning more – but it would mean a lot to me if you wore this one right now. It's time you had something to show that you're my girl.'

Kate was moved almost to tears. 'It's beautiful, Jon. How did you afford it?'

'My mum gave it to me – it was hers from my dad. She said it was only to be given to my special girl. That's you, ain't it?' He removed the ring from the box and lifted her hand. 'It might not fit – let's see.' Then he placed it on her third finger, and she was relieved that it did just fit. He twisted it a little, testing the size. 'It might need enlarging if you grow more,' he said, thoughtfully. 'Let me know if it does, and promise that you'll return it if you ever change your mind about me.'

'I won't never change my mind,' she told him, firmly. 'But I promise, my darlin'.'

He still held her hand in his, admiring the sparkle of the ring, as if he couldn't believe it. Then a sudden sound of applause startled them both. They looked up to see the two boys in leather jackets grinning at them. They had obviously witnessed the entire romantic scene.

'Another good man goes to his doom,' one bloke said, humorously.

'And another pretty girl skips the scene,' the other one said.

'Congratulations, kids. We'll play you a song. What'll it be?'

They smiled back at their friendly faces, but Kate couldn't think of any particular song. There were so many good ones in Chico's juke box.

Jon chose for her: Teenager in Love.

The first boy gave them the "gesture of triumph" and they both grinned and winked. Then the second kid stuck a tanner in the juke box, pressed the selector button, and Marty Wilde sang in his soft, sexy voice,

One day I feel so happy
Next day I feel so sad
I guess I'll learn to take
The good with the bad...

Kate always kept that record – and the song never failed to remind her of that magical moment when all the world was pure gold.

'Nuts to Bobby!' Jon said, grinning. Then his eyes filled with emotion as the song ended. 'Don't never forget that you are mine.' He spoke the words that would haunt her forever; then grabbed her hand. 'Let's get outa here.'

They ran all the way to the park, hand in hand, drunk with happiness. They sat close together in the middle of a grassy lawn, where they had often sat before. The park was still pleasantly deserted; it was too early for most Sunday people. Then they talked – they talked all their dreams.

Jon said, 'Morrey at the garage says I've learned so much already, I'll be able to do my apprenticeship in three years. That means I'll be earning good money by the time I'm eighteen. I'm already saving for us, sweetness.'

'That's great, Hero,' she encouraged.

'Only one more year, Kit. Then we can date properly. No more sneaking and hiding – I can hardly wait!'

'I love you, Jon Daley,' she announced.

'I love you , Katharine Daley,' he returned.

'I'm not that yet,' she protested.

'To me, you are,' he placed his hand over his heart, 'in here.' Then he began his wild, urgent kisses, and Kate hardly managed to contain her own fierce desire. She felt she'd have given herself right then if he had asked, but he did not – always the hero. She would never forget the heat of his body through his soft, cotton shirt, nor the way he held her so tightly against the full length of him, and the hard urgent maleness of him pressed so close. He almost moaned his wanting to her, and she felt every measure of his agony when he said, 'Kit, sometimes I need you so bad.'

Incredible as it might seem, that wonderful day began the gradual disintegration of all Kate's hopes and dreams.

She showed her ring to Mary that very afternoon. Her friend was just as happy and wildly enthusiastic as she was. 'It's so romantic,' she said, dreamily. 'I always knew he was for you. What a shame you can't tell your mum and dad, Kitty.'

Kate shrugged helplessly. 'Even if they wasn't so strict, they'd still think thirteen is too young to get engaged.'

'Yeah, you're right,' she agreed. 'My mum and dad would too.'

The next day, Kate showed off Jon's ring to all her schoolmates and, after school, to the Alley-cats. They all exclaimed over it and voiced their congratulations. Bobby's sister Tia looked particularly envious. She was about a year older than Kate, and had quite a thing going for Adam by this time. She married him eventually; she turned out lucky in the end.

But Kate was unprepared for Bobby's reaction. He made no disparaging comment at first – just took her hand in his and stared at the ring while a series of unfathomable emotions flickered through his eyes. Then he looked at her happy, glowing face and said, 'Congratulations!' as if he was forcing out the word. He then added, 'You're just kids!' in a tone that was almost angry. He turned, without another word, and walked into the darkened doorway of a bommie.

Kate couldn't help feeling a bit annoyed with him, though she understood he was jealous. He'd sort of clouded her happiness. She felt somehow deflated. It wasn't as if Bobby didn't know how she felt about Jon – she'd always been perfectly honest with him.

Then Adam gave her a strange look, sort of accusing – his fierce, dark eyes bored into hers for a moment before he turned and followed Bobby.

Kate felt as if she had the plague or something. Did being engaged make you an alien? Did you lose all your friends? Even Tia was looking worriedly after Adam, though she did not follow.

Kate went home. She still had to explain to her mum. She had other things on her mind besides disturbed Alley-cats.

She'd been thinking hard all day about how to explain to her mum. She wasn't going to take off Jon's ring and hide it – no way! She told her it was just a cheap imitation, that she was taking care of it for a girl in school who didn't want her parents to know she was engaged. She wasn't sure if her mum really swallowed this explanation, but she seemed to; she asked no further questions. She probably thought it was just a silly teenage fancy – in typical square fashion.

The following afternoon, walking home from school, Kate was surprised to see Adam waiting on Tower Bridge. Leaning nonchalantly against the ornamental black stonework, he managed to look as if he was there by accident, but Kate knew this could not be so – the Shadowcat did nothing by accident. Even among the milling crowd of the rush hour, she noticed him from a fair distance. He stood out like an eagle amongst starlings, and it wasn't a matter of size. Adam was still quite small for seventeen – maybe an inch shorter than she was. But what he lacked in size, he made up for in quality. He seemed to radiate an invisible power. She hardly knew what to call it. More than strength or masculinity, it was like the gentle thrum of a fine engine, ready to roar into life at the right touch of a pedal. Adam was definitely all man.

He straightened up as she drew near and she eyed him with fascination and a little apprehension – he still made her feel nervous. A fine, dark fuzz showed on his upper lip and lower face.

Adam would have to start shaving soon if he didn't want to look like the chief rabbi. He wore frayed jeans and his suede boots had seen better days. The usual leather jacket was absent in the afternoon heat, and his black T-shirt would have been quite presentable if you could have ignored the roughly painted "Ban the Bomb" symbol which scarred the front and back in glaring white. The silver Star of David, which he always wore, gleamed at his throat. A wide, studded belt did nothing to keep up his jeans, which were tight enough, and he wore a similarly-studded, leather wristband. But most impressive of all was his near-black eye. The swollen redness on the cheekbone, which almost closed the left one, was just turning purplish. This bloke might as well have had Warrior tattooed on his forehead.

Kate strove to keep her cool as his fierce, dark eyes caught hers, though she felt like a proper twit in her awful school uniform. 'Watcher mate,' she gave the expected friendly greeting. 'What you doing here?'

'Hya sexy,' he returned, his tone belying the fierce eyes. 'I was waiting for you.'

'Waiting for me?' Kate was startled enough to forget her self-consciousness. 'How d'you know which way I walk home?' she asked, warily.

He grinned in his devilish way. 'The Shadowcat knows it all,' he said calmly.

Kate was prepared to accept that. It was common knowledge that Adam knew most things about everyone, though he never said much. 'Okay mate, why you waiting for me?' She eyed him, suspiciously.

'I wanna talk,' he said shortly.

Adam wanted to talk? She could hardly believe her ears. She already knew he was a man of very few words. So it must be something important.

At that moment, a group of girls from her school passed by, on the other side of the road. They whispered excitedly to each other when they saw her with Adam. She could just imagine them saying, "How does she get all the cool blokes?" Kate sighed. They would be bitchy, but still jealous. It would be all over the school tomorrow that she was queen of Stepney gangland, or something equally stupid. Adam was so obviously what he was.

He noticed her sigh. 'You 'shamed to be seen with me?' he enquired.

'No, Adam,' she told him, honestly. 'I'm proud.'

He gave her his real smile then. She had rarely seen it before. Adam's smile totally transformed his face. Girls often asked him, "Why don't you do that more often?" He always told them, "It shatters the image." And that was true. When Adam smiled, deep grooves appeared in his cheeks in the most disarming way. He became just a cute little fella that any girl would love to cuddle; the warrior disappeared.

He took her arm, just as if he owned it, and led her to the curved walkway around the base of one of the bridge towers. Here was a little more space from the rushing crowd, and a bit more quiet. Adam had been chewing gum and he suddenly spat a great wad of this, with tremendous force, towards the flock of wheeling gulls which surrounded the bridge. This missile narrowly missed one bird, which squawked and veered off erratically in fright.

'No need to scare the wildlife,' she told him, querulously.

He looked at her and shook his head, as if puzzled. 'You're a strange one,' he said. 'You care about them dumb birds, screamin' and shittin' everywhere – but you don't care about Bobby.'

'How can you say that?' She felt genuine resentment. 'Course I care. I'm very fond of Bobby.'

'Then why'd you rub his nose in it?' he asked accusingly.

Naturally, she knew what he meant, though she hadn't thought of it that way. Her face flamed with guilt which she didn't feel was deserved. 'I ain't never lied to Bobby,' she protested. 'He always knew how I felt about Jon, right from the start. I can't help how he feels.'

'I know you never meant it, kid.' He patted her shoulder. 'You're just too young to see what you're doing.'

'No I ain't— ' she began to argue.

'Hear me first,' he insisted. 'I wanna tell you what happened last night.'

'Okay Shadow.' She gave him his title. 'I'm listening.'

Dark eyes confirmed his seriousness and commanded her attention. 'Last night, just when you left and I followed Bob into the bommie, I was only just in time. He was gonna put his fist through a brick wall.'

'My God!' Kate was suitably horrified. 'How did you stop him, Adam?'

He grinned briefly, and pointed to his injured eye. 'I got in his way.' Then he stopped grinning and his eyes were fierce once more, as he almost hissed at her. 'He would've broken his knuckles, maybe even his wrist. Even after that, I had to wrestle him away from that wall and hit him a few times before he calmed down.'

Her horror was growing every moment. Did Bobby really feel that bad about her? Had she hurt him that much just by telling she was engaged? How many times before had she hurt him unknowingly? She could hardly bear it. She clung to Adam's arm as he spoke, wanting to know the rest, yet dreading to hear it. He seemed to sense her emotion, for he patted the hand which gripped him as he continued: 'Then I told him, "Easy mate. Don't give up yet. You ain't gotta give up. King Alley-cat don't give up that easy. She ain't married yet. There's bombs of time to wait."'

'You told him that?' She didn't think that was wise.

'Yeah, I did.' The dark-eyed gaze never wavered. 'What was I s'posed to tell him?'

'I dunno,' she said, miserably. 'What happened then, Adam?'

He grinned again. 'I told him sorry I hit him. He said sorry he hit me. We went to my house to get cleaned up. Then we went down the boozer and got pissed roaring drunk.' His grin turned rueful. 'We never went to work today. My head still feels like it was kicked.'

Kate was very close to tears. 'And all this was my fault?'

His eyes were suddenly gentler than she'd ever seen them. 'Hey, don't get upset.' His arm went around her shoulders. 'I never told all that to make you feel bad. I just thought it was time you knew the whole story. 'Cos Bobby won't tell you.'

She was staggered by this unexpected gentleness from Adam, and began to realise that no-one really knew this little bloke, except maybe Bobby and Tia, those he allowed to know him. Like an iceberg, he was nine-tenths submerged. And the way he had helped Bobby, like no-one else could have... She said, 'Bobby is lucky to have a friend like you, Adam.'

He smiled his real smile again. They leaned companionably with their elbows on the stone parapet, and absently watched the black, swirling water below. Kate was surprised at the good and relaxed feeling she got, just to be in his company. Of course, he was an old friend, yet she'd never really spoken with him alone before, so why did she feel that she always had?

He seemed to voice her thoughts. 'Friends is for caring. I'm your friend too. Don't forget that. That's why I'm here. I knew you'd understand why I gotta ask you – please Kitty, try not to freak him out that bad again.'

'Oh Adam,' she let the tears roll this time. It was useless trying to hold them back. 'I never knew. I never realised how bad he felt. I always thought he was just messing about.'

Seeing her tears, he took her satchel from her, and set it down gently on the ground. Then he put both his arms around her while he spoke. 'He acts the fool so you won't guess. He don't wanna bovver you with his trouble. But I tell you, kid, this is killing him. He's got it real bad for you.'

'What can I do, Adam?' she asked, wretchedly. 'If I'm cool to him, he'll feel bad, and if I'm sweet to him, he'll get false hope. Maybe I should just avoid him.'

He looked back into her face and those night-dark eyes were deadly serious. 'Don't do that. He likes to think you need him to look after you. Just act natural, like you always do – but try to avoid anything like last night.'

'Will do, Shadow. Thanks a million.' She found her hanky and wiped her eyes.

'What for?' He looked surprised.

'For putting me wise, and just being a great bloke.'

He smiled again, like a burst of sunlight through cloud. 'You know, you're a real sweet lady. I understand now why Bobby always says so.'

'Stop embarrassing me!' She slapped his shoulder, and they laughed together. Adam was a real nice kid. Kate wondered why she'd ever felt scared of him before.

'Y'know,' he said, more seriously, 'you could end up being my sister. I'd like that.'

'How d'ya mean, Adam?' Kate was puzzled.

'I'm gonna marry Tia,' he enlightened. 'If you married Bobby, we'd all be one happy family.'

'That's a sweet thought, Shadow, but I ain't marrying anyone but Jon.'

'We'll see.' He grinned, knowingly.

She could tell he didn't believe it. No-one believed that she and Jon would survive the test of time. Well, we'll show 'em, she thought fiercely. We'll show the whole world. She retrieved her satchel, and they began to walk the length of the bridge. 'I'll walk you home a little way,' he said. 'Then I'll fade out. I don't want Bobby to see me with you. He mustn't know we've talked. Don't tell him, will ya, kid?'

'No, Adam.' She wasn't quite that daft.

His arm slid neatly around her waist, which disturbed her a little. Suppose they did meet Bobby or Tia – what would they think? 'Cool it, mate!' She tried to push his arm away.

He looked quite offended, and stubbornly refused to move his arm. 'When this man walks a girl, he does it right,' he said adamantly. 'You walk with me – I hold you. It's the way of the Shadowcat.'

She could see it was no use arguing with him. His iron will was hard as his fist. 'Okay, Shad,' she told him. 'I'm still proud.'

His smile would have melted the heart of a waxwork. She began to understand why Tia was head-over-heels in love with this boy. 'You really gonna marry Tia?' she asked.

'Oh yeah, that's my baby.' He almost predicted future song words.

'I'm real glad for you, Adam,' she told him, honestly. 'But she's a Christian. I always thought Jews couldn't marry Christians.'

'"Couldn't" is a filthy word to me,' he said.

'What about your mum and dad – won't they object?'

'I don't give a fuck! Sorry, Kitty. I mean I don't care what they think. It's my life, not theirs.'

She understood his fierce feeling with perfect clarity. Adam had what her mum would have called "a foul mouth". In fact, he was the only boy she knew who didn't tone down his language when she was around (or so she thought). But this didn't bother Kate. She recognised it as just another form of teenage rebellion; like smoking and drinking, when you knew you were too young; like running off to Gretna Green to get married without your parents' consent; like getting pregnant in your teens. It was a sign of the times. They were the first generation to seriously rebel against the world as they found it. They – the squares had almost destroyed the world – their world, with the bloodiest war in history. They had released the A bomb. And they, the new generation showed their resentment and disapproval in whatever way they could. They wanted to live. They wanted to show them they were adult and independent. Maybe they went over the top in their efforts, and so defeated themselves. But Kate believed that they laid the foundation for all future generations. The young would be heard; their opinion mattered; they were the future citizens. Rock 'n roll music voiced the general feeling most effectively, which was why they all loved it so. Every young person between the ages of ten and twenty related to the message of rock 'n roll. "This is how we feel, you old squares! This is how life should be! – just love and rock music". Oh yes, Adam swore like a trooper, and he never cared who heard him, but Kate didn't mind – she admired him all the more. Parents didn't have the right to control your adult life. It was bad enough when you were a kid. Adam and Tia were very much like Jon and her, prepared to face the opposition when the time came.

Her thoughts turned to Bobby again, and his fierce and savage emotion.

'Adam?' she sought his worldly wisdom.

'Yes, darlin'?' His arm tightened with reassurance. He was hers for the length of the bridge, his arm told her.

'Why do boys do violent things like that when they're upset? Like Bobby, I mean.'

'Well...' His eyes grew thoughtful. '...don't forget we don't cry so easy as girls – and grief has to come out somehow. If it stays locked inside you, it's poison.'

So clear and logical. Kate understood perfectly, and never forgot his first gem of wisdom. Boy! This man was cool. She looked at him with near disbelief: the Adam she'd never known before, a jewel of many facets. He returned her look with deep, dark eyes. She could swear they were almost black; she couldn't distinguish iris from pupil – powerful eyes that could search your soul. Somehow they didn't unnerve her any more. She was sure Jesus himself must have had eyes just like that.

Suddenly, he stopped walking, and she had to stop with him. His dark gaze swept over her – all over, then came right back to her eyes – a cave-man look. Kate strove to control the surge of delight which tingled through her. But he seemed to sense her reaction at once, though she hadn't made it obvious as far as she knew. His fiendish grin reappeared. 'You liked that, didn't you?'

She was still too naive to lie to a man. 'There'd be something wrong with me if I didn't.'

A wild sparkle danced in his eyes, which she hadn't noticed before. He put his hands on her hips, and his voice lowered to a husky whisper, 'You're real cute, Kitty. D'you fancy a shag?'

She just froze with shock for a moment. Was this the same boy whom she'd thought to be so fine a moment ago? Bobby's best friend? Tia's love? How could he have said a thing like that? How could he?

Then her reaction was pure fiery instinct and so was his. 'You dirty little git!' She lashed at him, wildly, without even thinking, and the edge of her hand caught him across the ribs. He tensed, automatically to rebuff her attack and her hand hit rock-solid muscle, or so it seemed. She yelped with pain and retreated from him, holding her bruised hand with the other.

Dark eyes immediately filled with concern. 'Silly girl,' he said. 'That was a dumbcat thing to do. I thought you'd just slap my face.' He took her hand though she struggled to release it; then he rubbed and soothed away the pain, just like she was a little kid and he was her mother. 'I was only kidding,' he said, as he rubbed. 'I wanted to see your reaction – your face was almost worth it, but I never meant to hurt you.'

She just stared at him, fighting back tears, not knowing what to say.

'I'd never expect that from you,' he went on. 'Please believe me, sweetness. Don't you know Bobby would kill me? I was just joking.'

'I don't like your jokes much,' she told him, tearfully.

'I'm sorry, darlin'.' His eyes were so full of remorse, she just had to forgive him.

'S'okay, Shadow,' she said. 'I really must learn to control my temper.'

'There's lotsa fire in you,' he said. 'I like that, and so does Bobby.'

He was one great heap of surprises. One moment a fiend, next an angel. She wondered what he would do for an encore. He held both her hands in his as he asked the next question. 'Would you object to a Jewboy as a brother?'

'Oh no Shad,' she hastened to reassure. 'When I look at you, I can understand why Jesus chose to be a Jew. I reckon he even looked something like you.'

His smile was pure magic. 'That's beautiful!' he said. 'That deserves a kiss.' His lips found hers and effectively stopped any objection she might have had. How different from Bobby – who usually asked if he could kiss her. This boy just told her she deserved it – and did it. Kate wasn't sure if she should be honoured or outraged; he was doing her head in. But she couldn't deny that he excited her. He was unbelievably sexy. His mouth was gentle on hers, though he tried at once to coax her lips apart with his tongue; he expected a real kiss. But she refused to give it, although he was tempting. Jon was the only boy she really kissed. That was for him alone.

He broke away and looked into her eyes, almost bewildered. 'Ain't I man enough for you to kiss me?' he wanted to know.

'Adam, you're more man than I'd know what to do with,' she told him, truthfully. 'But I don't snog just anyone.'

'I ain't just anyone,' he protested. 'I'm your friend – remember? A kiss ain't no big deal between friends.'

'Even Bobby don't get real kisses from me,' she explained. 'How could I give more to you than him?'

He looked convinced. 'Ain't you the Lady? That's perfectly right. You're a real nice bird. Jon is lucky. I only wish Bobby was.'

'I think Tia is lucky too. I hope she knows it.'

His smile was back. 'She does.' He made no pretence at false modesty, but she noticed the way his eyes softened when he spoke of her. 'She knows the whole story – every inch of the Shadowcat, and she still loves me. Ain't that amazing?'

'I don't think it's all that amazing,' she told him. His smile was shining on. He put his arm right back around her waist, like it was home territory, and they walked again in comfortable silence. After a few minutes, she asked him, 'Ain't you 'shamed to be seen with a schoolgirl?'

'No way,' he assured. 'I'm proud,' returning the compliment she'd given him earlier. 'I sorta like schoolgirls.' His grin was fiendish again, and the black eyes sparkled and roamed.

'Stay cool boy,' she said, nervously. He was like a jumping firecracker. You never knew which direction he'd go off next. They'd almost reached the end of the bridge, and she said, 'It never took me so long to cross the river before.'

'You glad or sorry?' he asked.

'I'm real glad,' she said, positively. 'It's been good talking to you. Why don't you talk much, Adam? I'm sorry you never did before.'

'The Shadow talks when there is something to say,' he said solemnly. 'Any other kind of talk is waste.'

'You're an amazing bloke,' she told him.

'I'm the Shadowcat (as if that explained everything), and if you ever wanna talk again, about anything – problems – Jon – Bobby – school... Remember I'm your friend, and your Shadow too – just like I'm Bobby's.'

'Thanks, Adam.' She felt justly honoured. He didn't have much truck with anyone except Bobby or Tia. Now it seemed he was admitting her to the circle of light beyond the Shadow, as if she were special in some way.

They'd reached East Smithfield, which was the turn-off for the Highway, right by the Royal Mint building, and there he was going to leave her. Kate felt lonely at the thought. He turned to face her and took her hands again. His were rough and calloused, not large, about the same size as Jon's, and they felt strangely good, wrapped around hers, almost familiar. She looked at his bare, sun-browned hands. No knuckleduster rings on Adam. He always maintained that only poofs wore those things, and it was a dirty way to fight.

She looked back to those wonderful dark eyes, and tightened her grip on his hands. 'I wish you really was my brother,' she said.

His hands responded at once with gentle pressure. 'But I am. I just told you. I am your brother 'cos that's how I see it. Bobby is the King and you are the Lady – if I'm his brother, I gotta be yours.'

'No...' she began to argue. He would insist on pairing her off with Bobby.

'You can't change what the Shadowcat knows, 'cos he always knows the truth. The Shadow knows the things that he feels are right. He knows it all. He sees only light or darkness, no shades of grey between. There ain't no misty dawns nor dusky twilights. There is only night or day, or right and wrong. No ifs, buts or maybes – only truth or lies. The Shadowcat knows.'

She stared at him with something close to awe. It seemed impossible for a tough, alley kid to have made such a profound speech, almost like poetry. His eyes looked magical – glowing with bright conviction. If he'd announced he was the prophet Isaiah at that very moment, she thought she'd have believed him.

'Okay mate, you're my brother.' She gave up without further dispute.

He grinned in the old, wicked way, instantly transforming to tough guy, then rummaged in his pocket and brought out a battered fag packet. He found this to contain just one cigarette, slightly squashed. 'Sorry I'm such a pauper,' he said. 'D'you wanna share?'

Kate knew there was no need for him to be a pauper. His family were actually better off than most in their street, for they owned the local small shop. She also knew that Adam refused to help himself to cigarettes he could not afford from his father's stock, on principle. When his wages ran out, he was skint like the rest of the kids.

'S'okay mate, I don't smoke,' she reminded. But she thought it was nice that he would have shared his last fag with her. He searched his pockets again, with the cigarette between his lips, while he still grinned which made him look more devilish than ever, almost comically so. She couldn't help smiling. He realised he didn't have any matches and voiced his frustration. 'Oh fuck!'

Her giggles exploded. He removed the cigarette from his mouth and stuck it behind his ear, glared at her for a moment, and then smiled – transmutation – devil to angel. 'It don't matter,' he said. 'I'll be home in five minutes. I gotta go now Kitty, back to shadowland.'

She sobered at once. This might be the last time she'd see the real Adam. He might never feel the need to talk as he had done this afternoon. He would be remote and taciturn once more – the warrior. 'I'll miss you,' she said without even thinking.

'Already?' His delight was evident. 'You've only known me five minutes. And there ain't no need to miss me – I'm your Shadow, any time you need me.' He hugged her then, and put his face against hers. The soft down on his cheek caressed her skin and his breath was warm in her ear. 'Don't forget what I told you, about Bobby. If you see him on the way home – act natural.'

Kate looked back into those dark, secret eyes, unbelievably gentle right now. 'Shadowcat,' she said, 'thank you, mate.'

Kate always liked to remember Adam the way he looked right then, in the full fire of his youth. As she watched him moving towards Tower Hill, taking the long way home, his easy loping stride was almost feline; the sleek and powerful movements put her in mind of a panther, and she knew he made no sound when he walked. The Shadowcat lived up to his name.

She was thoughtful as she walked the rest of the way home. Why did Adam hide his light in Bobby's shadow? He had plenty of it; could easily have been street leader himself. Though not as big nor as well-built as Bobby, Adam was fast. Everyone knew his speed was matchless, and his shading skill was unsurpassed. It was said he could spend an entire evening with the Hellcats, (the nearest rival street gang) without them ever knowing he was there, and he could tell you everything they said and did. Yet he was content to be Bobby's second. He must have preferred to use his talents that way.

And why didn't the other girls seem to like Adam? They were all over Bobby. There were five in the Alley-cat gang, apart from Tia. They ragged him all the time or made snide remarks about him, not that he ever seemed to notice or care. Couldn't they see how attractive he was? Were they prejudiced because he was Jewish? No, that couldn't be it – two of the girls, Ruth and Anne, were Jewish themselves. Then they must be afraid of his unapproachable manner. She wondered how Tia had got through to him. How had she, herself? It must be Adam who knew the people he wanted – he approached them. She felt even further honoured. The Shadowcat liked her.

What could she do about Bobby? How could she carry on rejecting him? How could she not? She decided to be as nice to him as possible. It was Tuesday – library evening with Jon. She was already late; she began to hurry.

Several years later, Adam confessed to Kate that he had known that very afternoon that something was wrong. Exactly what had not been clear to him, but his mind had been sorely troubled. During his poetic speech, he had wanted to tell her so much more, but had not dared. The Shadow knows it all, but he cannot always tell. Some things are better left untold. The prophet suffered his knowledge in silence – he did that for her.

Kate met Bobby as she turned into the south alley. He was cleaning his mum's front window and had removed his shirt in the afternoon heat. Sweat glistened on his golden-brown body. She noticed the slight ripple of muscle as he moved. Bobby was going to be a very big man.

He turned at her approach, but there was wariness in his smile. 'Hello, Kitty-cat,' he gave his usual greeting. There were bruises on his face and a few more on his body. Adam had put those there – little hammerfist, but she knew it had been with good reason.

She wasn't sure what to say to Bobby, knowing what she did, but she tried to sound just as if nothing had happened. 'You've been fighting again?'

He grinned, ruefully. 'Yeah, me and Adam got pissed up last night. Bashed a few Hellcats on the way home.'

He was lying to spare her feelings and she was determined to consider his for once. She tutted disapprovingly. 'I wish you wouldn't fight so much. One of these days you'll get hurt real bad.' She touched the bruised side of his face as she said this.

He caught the hand that touched him and his fingers closed around it. She was glad it was the right hand and not the one wearing Jon's ring. 'Would you care?' His eyes searched hers.

'Yes Bobcat,' she told him in all truth. 'I would cry.'

He threw down his window-cloth and she dropped her satchel at the same time, knowing his intent. He pulled her close and held her, fiercely, and she hugged him right back. Just this once, she would not reject him in any way – he needed this small comfort. 'Kitty-cat...' he whispered. And that one word conveyed all the misery he felt – all the hopeless, longing things he couldn't ever say in case he complicated her life. He trembled with the force of his repressed emotion, and she almost wept. How could she have failed to see it before? This boy loved her. He always had.

Her eyes just managed to peep over Bobby's shoulder, and she saw Adam moving down the alley on swift, silent, cat's feet. He had reached home almost as fast as she had. He gave her a conspiratorial wink, then disappeared into his dad's shop without a sound – the perfect shadow.

Bobby released her after several moments. He smiled, seeming much better for her reassurance of affection. 'Seeya later when Jon comes,' he simply said.

Kate patted his bare shoulder. 'Yeah, seeya Bob.' Then she deliberately swept her gaze across his golden-tanned torso. 'You look smashing like that,' she told him wickedly. 'Like Adonis.'

His smile of pure delight was her reward.

Chapter Fourteen

But later that evening, when Kate ran down the alley to meet Jon, he wasn't there. She thought he was just a bit late, and waited a while, chatting amiably with the gang. Bobby seemed completely back to his usual jocular self. He tutted with feigned disapproval at Jon's lateness. 'Look at that. He gets a ring on your finger, then starts slacking off. Don't that prove you'd be better off with me, kid?'

She gave him a few friendly slaps for his cheek, and all the kids laughed. Then she caught a look in Adam's eyes that she had never seen before. It was there and gone so fast, she thought she must have imagined it. Only later, she remembered the look she had seen and wondered about it. It seemed improbable, impossible, and utterly alien to the Shadowcat, but just for the barest instant, those dark eyes had shown naked fear.

Kate finally decided to carry on to the library, thinking to see Jon there. But he didn't show up that evening, nor on the Thursday evening. He had always told her not to worry if anything like that should happen. If he got ill, or if his mum or his sister did, he would be unable to get a message to her. There was a summer flu virus going around, and she thought that's probably what it was.

The pity was that Jon was going away on holiday for two weeks, beginning the next weekend, when school ended. His mum had been saving hard to take her kids away to the sea, and Jon could hardly disappoint her by saying he didn't want to go. So Kate didn't expect to see him for those two weeks. She was a bit disgruntled that there was no postcard from him. She knew he could have sent it to Bobby's house.

Then, as luck would have it, she had to go away for two weeks with her own family. They went to Thorpe Bay. The place reminded her so much of Jon, she could hardly stand it, and just counted the days until they got home again.

And that's why it was at least five weeks before she began to seriously worry.

He wasn't at church the next Sunday morning. That's when she began to think he must be avoiding her for some reason. Jon had never missed a single Sunday since that Christmas day when they'd got back together. Kate cried all the way home and Bobby met her as she turned into the alley. He dried her tears with his own hanky and she knew he was feeling for her.

'What's he playing at?' he asked angrily. 'I'd like to bust his head for treating you like this!'

'Don't you DARE ever lay a finger on Jon!' she told him, much too sharply. 'Or I'll never speak to you again and I'll hate you forever!'

He looked startled by her sudden ferocity and she hated herself for the hurt that appeared in his eyes. But he just patted her shoulder, awkwardly. 'I'll let you know the very minute I see him. I'd never hold out on you, Kitty-cat.'

'I know that, Bob.' She was heartily ashamed of her flare-up, but that was nothing new – that's how Bobby usually made her feel.

He then asked hesitantly, 'Wanna come down the Lane with me? I'll buy you sasp'rilla and chestnuts – and you can play with all them puppy-dogs and kittens. You need cheering up, my darlin'.'

He meant, of course, Petticoat Lane, the East End Sunday market. She'd often been there with her mum or dad, and any other time she'd have thought it a real treat to go with Bobby. But she just felt too miserable to summon the enthusiasm. She would only spoil his Sunday. 'Thanks, Bobcat,' she said, sincerely. 'But I don't think that's a good idea. We'd be sure to meet nosy neighbours who would tell my dad I was with a boy.'

'P'raps you're right,' he said with obvious disappointment.

Oh yes. That was one sweet man.

Jon didn't show up at the library on Tuesday. Kate returned the books she had without bothering to choose more. She wouldn't come again for a while – it was too painful.

Big-Ears had not failed to notice his absence. 'Hello Kit,' she said brightly. 'Where's Hero these days?'

Kate knew then that he hadn't been to the library at all in the past six weeks. She mumbled something mundane, but tried to convey the message.

'Never mind, dear.' Big Ears was trying to be kind. 'There's plenty more fish in the sea.'

Kate ran straight out of there with tears threatening to burst. She didn't want anyone else. Jon was irreplaceable. No-one could ever understand how deeply she loved him, nor how lonely she felt without him. Once again, she cried all the way home.

The weeks wore on towards Christmas and Kate tried to tell herself that Jon must have a very good reason for not seeing her. Maybe the physical side of things was getting too much for him again. She blushed, guiltily, as she recalled that it had almost been too much for her the last time they'd been together. She wasn't very good at fighting him off, and he would be determined not to get them into trouble. But at least he could have written to let her know that. He knew he could trust Bobby with his letters.

Or his family might have moved, and he couldn't get to see Bobby. At that time, families were constantly being moved out of the Smoke to the surrounding suburbs – part of the slum clearance and massive rebuilding schedule since the war. There again, Jon would have let her know before he went. He could have changed his mind about her and him and just didn't have the nerve to say so, but somehow she couldn't believe that of him – not her Jon, so strong and faithful. He simply wasn't like that.

Mary was the only one to whom Kate poured out her heartache and she really tried her best to help. 'Maybe he's testing you,' she said, thoughtfully. 'Or he might feel it's too risky to keep seeing you with the physical stuff between you. P'raps he wants to wait out the year 'til you're fourteen and you can date properly. That could be why he gave you the ring when he did – as a token of trust.'

Yes, Kate thought. That sounded like Jon. He always wanted to do things properly. She would be worthy of his trust. Funny how the human mind will snatch at anything, like a drowning man at the straw, when the plain truth is just too awful to bear.

Christmas came, and there was no card from Jon. He had never missed before in the three years she had known him. Bobby gave her a card, along with his inevitable Christmas kiss, and she tried to look happy for his sake; she didn't want to be crying on his shoulder all the time. His card read, "Merry Christmas, Kitty-cat. Remember I'm always here for you. xxx".

Kate put this keepsake away along with all of Jon's. It still wouldn't do for her dad to find a card from a boy.

And that was the worst Christmas ever.

Chapter Fifteen

Then came the night when Kate almost got her come-uppance for walking the lonely Highway – the night she met a really bad boy. This one made Warren look like an angry baby.

She had often been warned against walking The Highway after dark. It was about a mile stretch which ran alongside the dockyards and was fringed with bommies on the other side. Hardly anyone lived there any more and it was deserted at night. It was rare even to see a passing car. She'd heard that people were often attacked and robbed on The Highway, as if in keeping with old English tradition, but she didn't personally know anyone who had been; it was just hearsay – and besides, who would bother to attack little old Kate? She had nothing worth stealing. So went her reasoning. She ignored all the warnings from parents, teachers and even friends. She liked the solitude of The Highway. It was a perfect place for thinking and dreaming, and Kate spent much of her time lost in thought – too much for her own good.

It was about mid January and Kate decided to visit the library again. Reading might help to take her mind off her constant depression.

Bobby cornered her in the alley, seeing she was going out alone. 'Where you going Kitty – let me come with you?' he said, all in one breath.

'Only the library. You'd be dead bored,' she told him.

'I wouldn't be dead bored, not nowhere with you – besides, I don't like you walking home alone.'

She had to smile at his earnestness, but still she said, 'Cool it, Bob. I'm a big girl now. I don't need you holding my hand every minute.'

'I wish you did.' He sighed defeatedly; then in a fiercer tone, 'You hurry home – you hear me?'

'Now you sound like my dad.' She left him with that parting shot.

Kate spent a long time browsing in the library, and managed to get one book on each of sci-fi, sword 'n sorcery, and pre-history. All of these made her feel closer to Jon. She walked home slowly, with the now-familiar sorrow weighing in her chest like a cannonball. Only six months left to wait, she thought with forced optimism. She still believed Jon would turn up on her fourteenth birthday. That was the day they'd fixed for their first proper date, and she had faith in him – she trusted him. She just couldn't do anything else.

It was a clear, cold night with brilliant stars and a mild frost just turning silver. Ugly cranes reared their heads above the dockyard walls – metallic dinosaurs eerily frozen against the starlit sky. Kate was about halfway home and, as usual, distracted by such fanciful thoughts, when suddenly a shadowy form detached itself from the darkness of a derelict doorway and stepped out in front of her, causing a moment of heart-stopping shock.

'You got a light, darlin'?' the shadowy form said.

The lamplight revealed that he was leather-jacketed, hair sleek with brilliantine, taller than she was, and well-built like Bobby. The voice was gentle with no hint of malice. It seemed an innocent request. Kate wasn't too scared just then. 'No, sorry, I don't smoke,' she replied; then noticed he wasn't even holding a cigarette.

'Well, never mind,' the gentle voice soothed, 'you're a bit tasty. You need a smart bloke to walk you home?'

Then she got the first inkling of danger. 'S'okay,' she said, nervously, 'I ain't got far to go.' She side-stepped to try and walk round him, but he moved right along with her, effectively blocking her path.

With sick dismay, Kate realised this man wasn't going to let her pass. The light fell across his face as he moved, and she sort of froze with terror, like a scared rabbit, for she'd recognised him at once. Bobby had pointed him out to her from a distance – and he had warned. This was Steve Ringman, leader of the Hellcats who lived a few streets down from their alley, and he was a thoroughly nasty piece of work. Kate couldn't imagine what he wanted with her, but she was sure it would not be pleasant.

Even as she thought this, two more Hellcats loomed out of the shadows. They grabbed her by the arms, causing her to drop her satchel. This was it; the Hellcats had got her – she was well and truly got.

Kate didn't remember much about the other two boys, except one had sandy hair, and they held her arms tightly enough to bruise. She just watched Ringman's face, fearfully. He looked enormously pleased with his catch (her) though she couldn't think why. He stroked his chin, thoughtfully, as he looked her over, and she noted, with alarm, the row of gleaming knuckleduster rings on his right-hand fingers. This bloke lived up to his name. He was studying her face, carefully, as if trying to remember. At that moment, he didn't even look dangerous, had an innocent, almost choir-boyish expression. Bobby and Adam both looked twice as mean as Ringman did – but Kate knew better. By this time she'd learned not to judge by outward appearance.

'I know you,' he finally said. 'You're Atwell's bird.' (Atwell was Bobby's surname.)

'No–' She began to deny this.

Then he hit her, with stunning precision, right in the mouth – with no provocation that she could understand. For the first time in her life, she knew the deadly hardness of a male fist (Even her dad had never done that). She bit her tongue and tasted blood, and she thought her own teeth cut her lip, for that bled as well. She remembered crazily thinking that she was lucky he hadn't used his knuckle-dustered hand. Stunned and dizzy with pain, only the strong grip of the other two prevented her from falling, and her denial ended in a sort of whimper. She just stared at Ringman with horrified disbelief. He looked so human.

'Don't argue with me again, kid,' he said. 'I don't like it!' (As if she needed telling.) Then he picked up her satchel and tipped the contents on the ground, rummaged through the side pocket, then threw it away in disgust having found nothing of value. He looked back at her, angrily. 'I know Atwell's working now. I bet he buys you lotsa things.'

Kate didn't dare answer this in case she said the wrong thing. She continued to stare at him in silent, trembling fear.

'We'll see,' he said, then began to search her with unnecessary thoroughness. He undid her duffle coat and ran his hands all over her while she squirmed with humiliation, but was still helpless in the relentless grip of those other two who were laughing and egging him on, and she was much too scared to scream; no-one would have heard her anyway. She began to cry, helplessly.

'Whatsa matter, darlin'?' he asked, mockingly. 'Ain't I as pretty as Bobby?'

The other two laughed louder at this dubious humour. Then Ringman searched more seriously. He checked Kate's ears and throat for jewellery, then her wrists; that's when he saw Jon's ring. 'Oh yes, kid.' His eyes lit up with avarice. 'That's for me.'

'No!' she dared to protest in spite of her fear. 'Please not that!'

Her plea left him quite unmoved in either direction. He tried to pull the ring from her finger, but this had become too tight in the last few months. He was unable to remove it though he twisted and pulled until she cried out in pain. She could see him seething with frustration.

'We'll go and get some grease on it,' he finally said. 'And if that don't work, I'll cut your finger off. I'm having that ring if it takes all night. Then he added in his mock gentle tone, 'Don't worry 'bout the pain, darlin'. These two boys will do lotsa nice things to you while I'm removing it. They'll take your mind off it real good. Won't you fellas?'

They both affirmed eagerly with lustful grins.

'And they're just as good as Bobby,' Ringman continued, 'I promise you won't feel a thing when I cut your finger off.'

They all howled with laughter, and Kate just carried on crying. She wasn't sure they'd really do the things they said, but she knew she'd want to die anyway if she lost Jon's ring. To her mind, that was the worst thing that could possibly happen. She felt very close to despair at that moment. 'Please help me Jon,' she whispered, irrationally.

They began to march her along, her two captors still holding her firmly, forcing her to walk with them, stumbling through the rubble of a bommie, following Ringman who led the way.

Then a shout rang through the night. 'Oi!' accompanied by fast running footsteps.

Kate looked up with just a glimmer of hope, and there was Bobby running full-pelt towards them. He was quite alone and unarmed but his face was a picture of avenging fury, and it was enough to strike a note of fear in the minds of those Hellcats.

'Christ – it's Atwell!' said the one on her right. He released her arm and took immediate flight. With sudden freedom to move, she gave an elbow to the ribs of her other captor, with her full weight behind it, causing him to release her also as he staggered back from this unexpected attack.

Bobby reached Ringman. Like a charging bull, he did not even slow his pace – just slammed into him, knocking him against a brick wall with the full impact of his speed. Ringman hit the wall like a sack of bricks with an awful wheezing sound as every ounce of breath was forced from his body. Then he sort of slid downwards.

'Run, kid!' Bobby told her, fiercely, and began to pound Ringman with his fists. Kate was about to do just that, but then she noticed the other bloke's hand slyly closing around a brick. She couldn't run off and leave Bobby with that! How could she? With visions of Joe Warner and Warren flashing through her mind, she didn't hesitate more than a split second – she stamped on that boy's hand, giving him full benefit of a small stiletto heel. He howled beautifully, and she was almost ashamed of the surge of savage triumph that swept through her – the cave-man.

Then a terrible, brain-shuddering pain hit the back of her head like a crack of thunder, and she knew nothing more...

Chapter Sixteen

There was drumming in her head.

It seemed to fill her mind. A fast double beat, as if someone were using both fists. Baboom – baboom – baboom. The drumming was good. "Drumming is soothing to a cave-man". How did she know that? Jon said so. Jon was here somewhere – she could feel his warmth. Where are you, Jon? She tried to wake up, but the pain was coming back. The drumming was better. Nice soothing drums...

'Kitty-cat!' The whisper was almost frantic. 'Please wake up.'

Strong arms were holding her – holding her tightly against his chest. The drumming was his heartbeat – Bobby! Memory began to stir, and with it the raging headache. She tried to speak his name to reassure him, but her mouth hurt too. It sounded more like a moan.

'Kitty...' There was relief this time. 'Thank God you're all right.'

She opened her eyes, though it made her head spin. She forced them to stay open while the spinning slowed, then wobbled to a shaky stop. They were in Bobby's living room. He was sitting beside her on the old, beat-up settee, and she was instinctively clinging to him. 'Where's Jon?' she asked, still dazed.

'I dunno, love. Believe me, I'd fetch him right now if I could.' His eyes were tear-glinted and the left one was almost closed. It would be black tomorrow. His entire face was battered with several nasty-looking cuts and there was blood on his faded T-shirt. It could have been his or hers. Full realisation dawned. Bobby had saved her; he was hurt because of her, but how had he known?

Tears threatened. 'Bobby, look at you, mate.'

'I'm okay,' he assured, 'just a few scratches. Adam came to help finish 'em off. They won't bovver you no more.'

Kate tried to get up, but the room spun crazily. He restrained her gently. 'Stay here 'til you feel better. I brought you home to fix you up a bit, so you won't be too much of a shock for your mum.'

That was so thoughtful. She was reminded just how deeply Bobby cared, and again she hated herself for the times she'd hurt him – but she loved Jon. There was nothing she could do about Bobby; nothing at all.

She noticed the bowl of water on the table, which smelled of antiseptic. By stretching up a little, she could see the tinge of blood in it. He'd obviously done his best already to make her look presentable. Kate dared to feel her throbbing lip.

'That don't look too bad,' his voice soothed. 'Ringman never hit you very hard.'

'Didn't he?' (It had felt like a collision with an express train.)

'Nah. You wouldn't have been still conscious if he had, and I wouldn't have left him still breathing. It's your head I'm worried about. That Sandy bloke came back and brained you with a brick – but Adam made him eat iron, I tell you kid.'

Kate shuddered. This meant Adam had used a metal chain, with which he had great skill. She had never seen such a weapon used, and had no desire to. But she knew he only used it in the direst circumstances; his fists were hard enough for most. The Alley-cats never looked for trouble; they simply defended their own. But trouble had a way of showing up. 'Is Adam all right?' She voiced her concern.

'Yeah, not a scratch.' He grinned reassurance. 'He looks a lot prettier than Sandy does. Tia's looking after him over his house.' He grinned wider. 'Though he don't need it – he still loves it.'

'I bet,' she agreed with mild amusement.

Bobby got up and went to the sideboard. She noticed he was a little unsteady on his feet. He brought out a bottle of brandy and a small glass, then poured out a tiny measure which he offered to her.

She shook her head, which was a mistake; her brain started ringing in protest. 'I don't drink,' she said, feebly.

'I know kid, but this is diff'rent. It'll make you feel better. Please take it.'

'My dad will smell that stuff on me,' was her next worry.

'I'll tell him my mum gave it to you. It is hers. I'll tell him she fixed you up – someone had to.'

'You'll tell him?' She was amazed that he was prepared to face her dad.

He nodded. 'I'm taking you right home and putting you right inside your door. Your parents will have to accept that this was an emergency.'

'Yeah, they might think better of you in future.' She took the glass from his hand and noticed the dried blood on his knuckles. Bobby – superhero – one mean fight machine. He grew to almost god-like proportions in her mind. She was so glad to have the best on her side.

She tasted the brandy and almost died of shock as the liquid fire filled her mouth and throat. 'You trying to poison me, Bob?' she gasped.

He grinned. 'Drink it all, kid. Show me what I know you're made of.'

With this encouraging challenge, she did so. She threw it all back, then breathed hard as the fire ran down to her stomach, then spread all through her.

He was still grinning. 'Better?' he asked.

'Yeah, it feels sorta strange.'

He took the glass from her and filled it almost to the brim. He downed this himself in a few swallows while she watched in disbelief. Then he gave a great shuddering sigh and resolutely screwed the top back on the bottle. 'My mum'll kill me,' he said, smiling.

Kate tried to smile back, but didn't quite manage it with her painful lip. She couldn't imagine Bobby's mum killing him. She was a small, pretty woman who thought the world of her fine, strapping son, and her daughter Tia. Their dad had run off with another woman while they were still babies. Kate couldn't understand why he had wanted to. But Bobby's mum had coped very well bringing up her two kids alone. Kate thought them a real credit to her. Unfortunately, her parents did not share this opinion.

'But I'll buy her another bottle,' he said. 'I can, now I'm working.'

'I'm ever-so glad, Bobby,' she told him, honestly.

'It's great to be earning,' he enthused. 'I feel like a man at last. I'm saving up for a motorbike and some new leathers.'

'Go, man!' she encouraged.

He took a packet of cigarettes from the mantelpiece and offered one to her which she declined. He lit one himself with a taper from the coal fire, and inhaled deeply, seeming lost in thought.

'You never come swimming any more,' he finally said. 'I don't hardly see you these days.'

Kate knew what was on his mind and her heart ached for him, but she wasn't going to give him any false hopes in that direction. 'I just don't wanna go nowhere, Bobby,' she told him. 'I'm waiting for Jon. I'm engaged to him, remember?'

'To an invisible man?' His expression was pained. 'I wish that bloke could see what he's doing to you.'

She was silent, battling with tears.

He threw his half-smoked fag in the fire, then came and sat down beside her again. He took both her hands in his and looked straight into her eyes. 'I know you ain't even allowed to date yet,' he said, quietly, 'but if he don't show up when you're fourteen, will you come out with me?'

'No, Bobby – I mean I dunno. I ain't sure what I'll do then.'

'Then at least say you'll come out in the evenings, so's I can see you. Jon asked me to look after you. How can I do that if I don't even see you?'

'You're already doing a fine job, Bob – and don't think I don't appreciate that. I will come to see you. It's nice talking to you.'

He smiled at this admission and gripped her hands tighter. It suddenly occurred to Kate that she'd never seen Bobby date any special girl, and she wondered why. Any one of the Alley-cat girls would have given her right arm to be his – yet here she was, refusing him. It was sort of crazy. Maybe she was just nuts.

'You just get prettier all the time.' He was still gazing at her like a love-sick puppy.

'With a fat lip?' she asked, flippantly.

'Yeah, fat lip or not.' He picked up a handful of her hair and held it to his face, breathing the scent of it. 'Look at this barnet,' he enthused, 'glorious!' Then he released her hair, seeing she looked uncomfortable.

'Bobby...' another thought struck her. 'How did you know to come running when you did? I never screamed or nothing.'

'I dunno.' He looked thoughtful. 'It was weird really. I was already worried – you'd been gone a long time. I had half a mind to walk down and meet you. Then suddenly I got this terrified feeling. I knew I had to find you quick. I just knew, kid.'

'Like a premonition?' She stared at him in wonder.

'Yeah, sorta like that.' His eyes were wide and serious. 'Then Adam too.'

'Adam?'

'Yeah, he felt it too. He wasn't nowhere near me at the start – he just appeared when Sandy bricked you. But then Adam usually knows these things.'

'The Shadow knows,' she agreed, still with a tinge of awe.

Bobby's eyes filled with tenderness, though his tone was fierce. 'You ain't going nowhere else alone in the dark. If you won't let me walk by your side, then I'll follow you. That's a promise, kid.'

Kate tried to smile, but it was too painful.

'Head feeling better?' he enquired.

She nodded, carefully.

He kissed her cheek, gently avoiding her damaged mouth. 'Let's get you home now, darlin'. It's too nice being here alone with you – I might lose my head.'

She needed no further reminding.

As it turned out, there was no need for Bobby to put shades on Kate. She simply wasn't allowed out after dark for the rest of that winter. Her dad wasn't particularly polite either, when Bobby brought her home that night. He told the lad in no uncertain terms to keep away from his daughter in future. You'd have thought Bobby had attacked her himself, the way her dad carried on, when in fact he'd saved her from God-knows-what kind of horror-show.

'Someone had to help,' Bobby mumbled just before her dad shut the door on him. Her mum might have been more sympathetic, but she was at work. Kate almost cried with shame for her dad. What made him think she was any better than Bobby? They were both working-class kids – the same kind, and she knew very well that Bob was a very fine young man, almost as fine as Jon. But there was nothing she could do to convince her parents. Even her mum would believe her dad's version. Maybe they would understand some day. She took to visiting the library on Saturdays, in daylight, and hardly saw Bobby or the gang all through the spring, for she didn't bother going anywhere else at all.

She continued to pine and fret for Jon, even though she had convinced herself he would turn up on her birthday. She literally counted the days, marking them off on the calendar. She read his cards and love-letters again and again, and those loving words made it seem impossible that Jon could ever desert her. She gazed at his picture. This had been taken when he was about five years old and didn't even look much like him – but it was the only one she had. Jon had always promised her a better one, but it had somehow been overlooked.

Her school grades began to slide again. Teachers began to look at her despairingly. 'I know you can do better than this, Katharine.' That was the kind of thing they said. One well-meaning teacher looked at her hollow eyes and asked if there was anything wrong at home. Kate denied this firmly. There was nothing wrong at home – at least, nothing new. The trouble was inside her.

Her mum thought she was going through another moody phase. 'Teenagers!' she would sigh in exasperation.

There were a lot of sad songs in the charts around that time, and every one seemed especially written for her. Elvis sang "I Feel so Bad" and "Stuck on You". Roy Orbison was equally morbid with "Blue Angel". At home, Kate continued to play a few old favourite tortures: "Poor Me" by Adam Faith, and "Only the Lonely": another Orbison tearjerker.

Rock 'n roll seemed to have taken a melancholy twist, as if in sympathy.

She thought of writing Jon a letter, but was afraid of what his mum might think if she should read it. She thought of simply going to his house and confronting him, but somehow she couldn't bring herself to do that. In those days, girls didn't chase after boys – it was a bad, unethical thing to do; and she was also afraid – afraid of what she might find. It was better to cling to the hope.

Hope was all she had.

Chapter Seventeen

Kate's fourteenth birthday finally arrived, and she left the house deliberately early to catch Bobby before he went to work.

'Happy birthday, kid!' He greeted her with a bright smile which didn't quite reach his eyes, and she knew at once that there'd been no news from Jon. She almost broke down and cried right there in front of Bobby. One whole year since she'd seen her Jon – one whole year she'd been wearing his ring, and she'd set her heart on this day. He'd promised this would be their first real date.

"Don't never forget that you are mine" he had said.

She had not forgotten, but it seemed like Jon had.

Bobby looked as distraught as she felt. 'Maybe he meant the weekend,' he suggested, 'he knows you couldn't have gone nowhere today – it's a school day.'

Kate nodded dumbly, but she didn't see why Jon couldn't have sent a card. She began to seriously think that he'd just given up on her. So why hadn't he asked for his ring back? She just didn't understand. Nothing made sense any more.

'Tell me where he lives,' Bobby suddenly said.

'No!' she responded fiercely, 'I told you before, Bobcat – you don't give him no hassle!'

He put his arm around her. 'I won't, I promise. I'll just put shades on him. He won't even know we're around. You gotta find out what he's doing, kid. This ain't no good for you – all this fretting. You gotta know.'

She knew that he was right. 'You promise not to touch him?'

'I swear.'

'Okay then. Wait 'til this weekend's over. He might show up then.'

'Right on, Kitty-cat.' He looked at her, hopefully. 'Will I see you this evening?'

'Yeah,' she nodded absently, 'I can wait for Jon down the alley as good as anywhere.'

'Seeya later then.' He looked much happier.

But Kate walked on to school with the cannonball still heavy in her chest.

On the way home, she was half hoping Jon would miraculously turn up to meet her from school. Every time she saw a dark-haired boy in a white shirt, her heart almost stopped beating. But none of them were him. She finally turned into the south alley, sick to her soul.

That evening, Kate dressed casually, but carefully, in a pale blue denim skirt and a white cotton blouse. She dared to use a little mascara and a subtle shade of lipstick. She hoped she was old enough by now that her dad wouldn't tell her to go and wash that shit off her face. Then she combed her hair loose. She still hoped that Jon might turn up – she just couldn't relinquish that hope.

'Going anywhere nice, dear?' her mum asked.

'Only to Mary's,' she lied.

'Make sure you're in by ten,' her dad sullenly reminded. Kate was sure he'd have kept her locked up in a tower and thrown the key away, if he could have thought of a good excuse.

She walked down the alley, idly thinking of all the times she'd run down to meet Jon – one year before; before the loneliness began.

She was quickly joined by a group of girls – Alley-cats, who surrounded her with friendly, sort-of knowing smiles. Bobby's sister Tia was there too, but she stood to one side in a doorway with Adam at her back, holding her. Kate noticed, with a shock, that she was rather pregnant. He had his arms right around her swollen belly, possessively – it had to be his. Everyone knew they had quite a thing going. She just hadn't realised how much of a thing. They both smiled at her, and Adam gave her a special "good to seeya" wink. They seemed quite happy about it, and Kate felt almost envious. They didn't have to sneak and hide the way Jon and she'd had to. Tia wasn't even old enough to get married. She wondered what Tia's mum thought about it. Even worse, what did Adam's parents think? They had to know by this time.

But that was not the worst shock she got that night. Brenda was smiling wickedly. 'So you're old enough to be 'llowed out evenings?'

'Yeah.' Kate wondered if the girl was ragging her, but decided it didn't matter. She could take it. She was used to teasing at school, and she never let it bother her.

'You know what you gotta do to join the Alley-cats?' This came from Maureen, dark-haired and plumpish.

'No.' Kate was intrigued. 'What you gotta do?'

They all laughed delightedly. All five of those girls were really enjoying this.

'Leave her alone!' Tia warned. 'Bobby won't like it.'

'She should be prepared,' Janey argued. (She was blonde and petite.)

Adam's eyes were trying to soothe. Kate didn't know how she knew that, but they were calling hers to his, and they spelled dark, secret peace. They were trying to tell her not to worry. She dragged her eyes from his with an effort, and looked back to the girls. 'Tell me what?' She was madly curious by this time.

There was an imminent hush, like the pause in the whine of a doodlebug just before it strikes. Brenda was still smiling gleefully as she dropped her bombshell. 'You gotta fuck with Bobby,' she said.

Those terrible words rang and echoed in Kate's brain. She could hardly believe what she'd just heard. Her senses reeled with the shockwaves. It couldn't be true. Bobby wasn't like that – not her Bobcat. He just couldn't be! She was still terribly naive, and in her mind she'd built him up to some kind of glorified being. This knowledge was unbearable.

They were all looking at her, still smiling. 'All of you?' she asked, miserably.

They affirmed enthusiastically. 'Only once,' Maureen said, regretfully.

'Speak for yourself!' Brenda exulted.

'Don't worry, square-baby, you'll love it!' Anne assured her. 'Bobby's fantastic!'

Kate looked at Tia, hoping for some kind of denial.

'Not her.' Ruth misinterpreted Kate's look. 'She's his sister. She had to make do with Adam.'

They all giggled, and Adam's dark eyes glowered briefly, then caught Kate's again with his plea for serenity, which she was quite unable to take.

Tia fiercely defended her man. 'There ain't nothing wrong with Adam!' And there obviously was not, judging by the size of her.

Kate knew then it had to be true. There had been no denial from Tia. She felt strangely desolate – disillusioned. She just wanted to run, and began to back away from those grinning girls, feeling almost sick.

Then Bobby appeared, strolling casually up the alley. His eyes lit when they first saw her, then darkened as he guessed from her face what those girls had told her. His pace quickened. 'Scat, you kids!' he yelled at them, and they did, like sparrows in the cat's path. Bobby hurried right up to Kate and gripped her wrist, firmly.

She immediately took this as further proof of his guilt. 'Let me go!' she almost spat at him. 'You're disgusting, Atwell!'

Rage superseded pain in his eyes. 'Come with me,' he said, gruffly, 'I gotta talk to you.'

'I ain't going NO-where with you!' She struggled vainly to escape his hold.

'You listened to them,' he accused. 'Won't you give me a chance to speak for myself?'

Kate breathed fast while conflicting emotions battled in her head. Her natural fondness for Bobby finally overcame the revulsion. 'Okay mate, but you better make it good.'

He led her, still by the wrist, to his own front door. She knew his mum worked evenings, and was suddenly wary. 'How do I know I can trust you, Bobby?'

He sighed with exasperation. 'My God, Kitty! How can you ask that after all these years? You've been alone with me before,' he reminded. 'You've been unconscious in my arms, for Chris'sake. I coulda done anything I liked to you if that's all I wanted.'

She bit her lip to stop herself from saying, "How do I know you didn't?" That would have been unfair – she knew he hadn't. 'All right, Bobby.' She forcibly calmed herself. 'I'm ready to listen to you. I ain't gonna run away. You don't have to hold my wrist so damn tight.'

'Sorry, love.' He let go at once, and she followed him down the hall and into his mum's living room. She sat down on the lumpy settee and he poured brandy for both of them. This time she took it without hesitation.

He began, awkwardly. 'This is difficult for me, Kitty. I never realised before just how very innocent you are...' He paused to swig his brandy. 'You've been seeing a boy for more than three years – I know you're both very young, but ain't you ever wanted to do more than kiss and cuddle him?'

'Yeah,' she was forced to admit, 'but that's diff'rent. I love Jon.'

He looked downcast and twirled his drink around the glass for a few moments. 'Kitty,' he began again, 'I dunno exactly what them birds told you, but I reckon it was something near the truth, and I dunno what to say to you – except you're the only one I really want, and you won't come near me. I wouldn't be able to control my feelings for you if I never...'

His helpless confusion was reaching her heart. He looked like a kid caught raiding the biscuit tin. 'Hell, Kitty! I'm just a man. I never pretended to be an angel, and this ain't cloud-cuckoo land. This is the real world and it's time you got used to it. Those girls – I never forced 'em, you know. Every one of them was more than willing. I ain't never forced a girl in my life, and I certainly ain't gonna start with you. You're diff'rent from them. You're sorta special to me. I thought you knew that.' He drained his brandy and put the glass down. She noticed his shaking hand.

Kate was impressed by his honesty. He'd made no attempt to lie or excuse himself. Lots of blokes would have. She understood at last why Bobby never dated any particular girl. He had no need to – every one was his for the asking. Besides, he wasn't her fella. What did it matter to her? What was that nasty, sick feeling in the pit of her stomach? What was she getting so worked up about? He was still Bobby, still her friend, her protector, still Bobcat.

She managed a smile. 'You said that very well,' she told him. 'I'm sorry I reared at you. I think I understand.'

His return smile was pure relief, and he moved to sit beside her on the settee. He put his arms around her, hesitant that she might shrug him off, but she did not.

His arms tightened. 'Please don't hate me,' he begged. 'And don't ever say I'm disgustin'. I'm only a man, and I need those sorta things.'

'I know, Bobby.' Her voice reassured, but in her mind something was struggling to surface which she couldn't quite comprehend – a niggle of resentment that made her want to hurt him. She quelled this firmly. It was selfish, whatever it was. His distress was more important. She stroked the long hair at the nape of his neck to soothe her mind along with his.

He sighed contentedly, loving this attention, and tried to draw her closer, which wasn't possible unless she sat on his lap, and she certainly wasn't going to do that. Kate pushed him away, suddenly guilt-ridden. Here was she, engaged to Jon, cuddling another man and enjoying it. What was the matter with her?

Soft grey eyes gazed into hers. 'That was good while it lasted,' he said with a resigned smile. Then he lowered his eyes. 'Y'know, Kitty, I'd never do anything you don't want. You can trust me. D'you believe me?'

This boy really knew how to melt her heart. Every time she got the least bit annoyed or angry with him – he never failed. She wondered how he did it. 'Course I do, you big dope! D'you think I'd be sitting here alone with you, if I never trusted you? D'you think I'm nuts or something?'

'No, darlin', I think you're beautiful.' He stroked her cheek with one finger. 'Y'know what I like most about you, Kitty?'

'No, what?' She couldn't help being curious.

'It ain't your pretty face or your lovely body, or even your sweet and fiery nature – though all of them things are fine...' He paused for effect.

Her face flamed at this string of compliments, but she still wanted to know. 'What then?'

'It's the way you always say exactly what you think. There ain't no pretence about you, like most girls. You don't play games. You're so honest, and sometimes that hurts, but a man knows exactly where he stands with you.'

Funny, that matched her earlier thoughts about him, but she wasn't so sure it was good for girls to be that way. 'You think that's good?' she asked him. 'You like that?' She'd always thought it was quite a disadvantage.

'Yeah, I love it, and that's what I want – let me take you out?' he suddenly entreated. 'Please be my girl, Kitty-cat. I promise you'll never regret it. I'd never even look at another girl if I had you.'

'No, Bobby,' she said, firmly.

'I'll come and ask your mum and dad properly,' he continued. 'I'm working now. I ain't such a bad deal. I'll put my best whistle 'n flute on. I'll even get my hair cut.'

'No, Bobby,' she repeated, though she had to smile at his earnestness.

'I ain't never said "please" to a girl before,' he protested, valiantly.

'No, Bobby,' she said, determinedly. 'I'm Jon's girl.'

'I wish you was mine,' he said, wretchedly, then he covered her face with fervent kisses.

'I think I'd better go home.' Kate was disturbed at the wild feeling he was rousing.

'Stay with me a bit longer,' he begged.

'No, Bobby.' She was beginning to sound like the needle was stuck.

'Okay, sweetness,' he said, hoarsely.

She went home and (yeah, you guessed it) she cried. Not only because Jon hadn't turned up. For some mysterious reason, she found herself crying for Bobby.

Kate didn't bother going out evenings any more for a while, not even down the alley. She knew that Bobby missed her and took her absence as further rejection, but she couldn't help it. She just didn't want to go anywhere without Jon. She wondered when the misery would ever end.

After a while, she noticed that Bobby seemed remote, the times when she did see him, as if he were afraid to speak to her. She thought this was because she'd hurt him and she was deeply sorry. She knew that his family was moving soon, and she hoped he'd meet a nice girl then and forget about her – she was no use to him. He still hadn't brought her any news of Jon, and she thought this strange. Bobby's shades were good. He would surely have sent Adam on such a special assignment, and Adam was the best. Maybe he hadn't bothered. Why should he after the way she'd treated him? She still cried at night.

She thought her mum was worried that she didn't seem interested in boys or even going out with friends, after she'd looked forward to it for years. All she did was shut herself in her bedroom and play sad records. Her mum must have thought she had the most miserable teenager in the world.

If she did, she was exactly right.

Chapter Eighteen

One Saturday afternoon in August, it was pouring buckets of English rain and Kate was trudging home down the north alley. She was laden with Mum's shopping and an umbrella, and was soaked to the skin except for her head and shoulders.

She didn't see Adam until she almost walked into him. He suddenly appeared in front of her as if he'd dropped from the sky along with the rain.

'Jesus!' she exclaimed in fright.

'Fraid not,' he said, humorously. 'S'only me. My name's Adam. Hope you ain't too disappointed.'

'Course I ain't,' she told him, gladly. 'But you shouldn't sneak up on me like that. I nearly took your eyes out with this brolly.'

He just grinned and took her arm, gently steering her into a deep factory doorway to shelter from the rain, taking her heavy shopping bag in one dextrous movement.

'I can't stop,' she protested. 'I gotta get home.' Yet it was so good to see him – a real pleasure. They hadn't really talked since that day on Tower Bridge, a year before, and she had unconsciously missed him.

'Loneliness inside the Lady,' he said. 'Too much sadness. I can't just stand by watching forever. Please talk to your brother.'

His sweet words brought tears to her eyes. She folded down the umbrella to hide her confusion, and they both stood there, making a spreading ring of puddles on the stone floor. He was even more drenched than she was. Water trickled down his face and dripped from his hair to his leather jacket in an endless patter. His jeans looked like he'd been sitting in the bath to shrink them. He'd grown a bit – managed to top her by an inch, and he seemed broader too. Clean-shaven now, except for baby-fine sideburns, but they were coming along nicely. The silver Star of David glinted at his throat, just visible with the front of his jacket not quite zipped. He looked very fine to Kate – like a gift of comfort from heaven. But she said,

'Shadow, I don't think I can talk without crying. I don't wanna cry all over you.'

'I don't mind,' he insisted. 'Cry all you want. Drown me if it makes you feel better. You won't talk to Bobby. I think you will to me. It's diff'rent with a brother. But I don't mean now – this ain't a good place. Come out with me tomorrow night. We'll go somewhere quiet and talk.'

His eyes were deep black wells of sympathy – so easy to drown in. Kate closed hers briefly, trying to deny his magic, but he looked just as good when she opened them. 'Adam, how can I go out with you? You're almost a married man. What would Tia and Bobby think?'

'Tia will understand,' he assured. 'I'll tell her. She knows about you and me.' (She knows more than I do, Kate thought.) 'And Bobby don't need to know. He might not understand 'cos you won't go out with him. But we know it ain't wrong, don't we, Kate? You know I just wanna help you and him 'cos I'm your friend and his.'

His face was so earnest, almost pleading. She couldn't resist the comfort he offered. He was right. It wasn't like being afraid to hurt Bobby who was madly in love with her. It was different with Adam. 'Okay, mate. Thanks for caring. You're one sweet brother. Make sure you bring a great big hanky.' She tried a smile which seemed strangely unfamiliar these days.

He had no trouble at all with his own beautiful smile, though she noticed he'd lost half a tooth at the front – fighting no doubt. 'I'm so glad, love. I'll meet you right here around 7:30. You won't regret it. The Shadow will take care of the Lady.' He kissed her cheek with this fond assurance, then picked up the shopping bag while she unfurled the umbrella. They walked to her door, sharing it in ungainly fashion. While she fumbled for her door key, he put the shopping down in the porch, then kissed her again, very briefly. 'Seeya tomorrow,' he said.

Kate watched him stride away with his head down against the driving rain, and realised with dawning shock that she'd finally agreed to go out with a boy – alone, in the evening. That was a date, there was no other word for it, even though they didn't mean it that way. So her first date would be with Adam. Tears welled up as she thought how it should have been with Jon. But Adam might have some news of him. Maybe that's what he really wanted to talk about. She cheered up with this thought.

And had no inkling of the danger...

Sunday evening, cool and clear, with lingering sunshine from a bright day. A raging storm the previous night had cleared up the weather. Adam was waiting in the north alley as promised. He didn't look much different from usual, except he was wearing his best black jeans and his boots were clean, but he was a very fine sight to Kate. She was glad she'd opted for jeans herself, and a soft, loose sweater. She didn't possess any smart, fashionable clothes anyway, and she'd have been floored if he'd turned up in a suit. His smile of welcome was all the adornment he needed.

'You look beautiful,' he said. 'I was scared you'd change your mind.'

'So was I for a while,' she admitted.

His arm slid around her waist in the protective way she remembered so well, and they walked. Kate realised with a pang just how much she'd missed walking with a fella in the last year, since Jon had gone. It was so good just to be in the company of a man you liked and trusted, and that was without being in love. She knew then just how much a girl needed a boy.

They walked to a tiny pub in Shadwell which was called "Turpin's Retreat". Kate thought that was rather appropriate as it was on The Highway. There were benches and tables outside and it would have been nice to sit there, but Adam said they'd better not in case any of the gang passed by and saw them. That was unlikely – they were far enough from home, but they didn't want to take any chances.

She'd never been inside a pub before and was utterly fascinated with this one. They'd preserved the Old English atmosphere perfectly. Low, oaken beams on the ceiling, bright copper jugs and tankards hanging on the walls, a great fireplace that you could have stepped inside, though this contained only dry logs in warm weather. A picture of Dick Turpin, riding Black Bess, hung over the mantel, wearing his eye mask and a sly grin. Only the juke box loomed grotesquely out of place, like a lost time machine.

'You like it here?' Adam had noticed her wandering appraisal.

'Yeah, it's sorta cute.'

'Perfect for you then, Lady.'

They selected a cosy corner seat, close to the fireplace. The pub was surprisingly deserted, but then it was Sunday evening, and most people preferred the livelier places. 'I don't drink, y'know,' she told Adam. 'I don't like beer.'

'Beer ain't the only drink in the world,' he informed, 'but you won't want your dad to smell spirits on you neither. Try a shandy – that won't do you no harm.'

'Okay.' She didn't want to be a complete killjoy. She watched his fine muscular form as he walked to the bar. Jon must be starting to look like that, she thought sadly, then tried to dismiss the thought. She mustn't cry already.

The landlord was exactly suitable for the pub's atmosphere. Middle-aged and balding, with a ruddy complexion; fairly corpulent, with braces holding up his trousers, and rolled-up shirt sleeves – a typical square person. He looked a little askance at Adam's long hair and leather jacket, obviously wary of young toughs in his pub. Then he looked at Kate and must have decided it was a safe bet. A boy alone with a girl usually has anything but trouble on his mind.

Adam returned to the table with a pint of bitter for himself, and shandy in a smaller glass. He seated himself close beside Kate, so that his thigh touched hers. She was startled at the tingling warmth which surged through her. She had noticed this before with Adam; this boy really got to her. She wasn't sure what it was about him – something very special that whispered to her senses in the same way that Jon did. Maybe it was just that his dark looks reminded her of Jon. Whatever it was, she felt ashamed and guilty. Even Bobby didn't affect her this much, but then he always held himself in check with her – she knew he did, and dreaded to think what might happen if he didn't. She was getting older all the time, and could no longer deny to herself that her body needed a man. She hoped Adam wouldn't try anything. Of course he wouldn't! He cared too much about Bobby and Tia, and he knew she was only for Jon. Kate tasted the golden liquid in front of her. It was much sweeter than beer alone – quite pleasant.

'Is that okay?' he asked worriedly.

'Yeah, smashing,' she assured.

He was looking at her with sudden sadness. She wondered why. Then he picked up her left hand and looked at Jon's ring. 'Mind if I touch this?' he asked.

A strange request, she thought. 'No, I don't mind. Why d'you want to?'

'Sometimes I get feelings,' he tried to explain. 'That ring belonged to Jon – was touched by him.'

Kate stared at him with mixed feelings of dread and wonder. The Prophet Isaiah was back. He might tell her something about Jon. 'Go on then, Shadow,' she urged.

He closed his eyes as he touched the ring, stroking his thumb across the tiny, raised diamonds. Kate watched his face carefully, and noticed his slightly sharper intake of breath. Then his eyes opened and, just for the barest instant, she thought she saw the brightness of tears. He released her hand and closed his eyes again, seeming to struggle with some inner emotion.

'What did you feel?' She was desperate to know.

He opened his eyes and they were depthless pools of dark sorrow. 'Nothing,' he said, determinedly. 'It don't always work.'

But Kate got the feeling he was lying to spare her the truth. She couldn't hide her disappointment. She was going to cry.

'I'm sorry, love,' he said, contritely. 'I've upset you. I shouldn't have done that.' He put his arm around her and nuzzled her ear while she fished in her pocket for a hanky.

The bloke at the bar was wearing a knowing smirk. Kate dabbed fiercely at her tears; she wasn't putting on a sob-show for him. 'You been shading Jon?' She asked Adam what she'd been dying to know.

'Yeah, every spare minute,' he said without meeting her eyes, 'but I ain't seen him, Kate. I ain't seen a sign of him.' He looked at her this time, wide-eyed and honest, and she knew he spoke the truth. Well at least Jon didn't have another girl. She knew Adam would have told her that. She watched him down half his pint, as if to steady his nerves, and she drank a little more of hers.

Then he said, 'Bobby misses you something rotten. You don't come out evenings like you said you would. You're 'llowed out now. You're breaking his heart.'

'I know,' she said sadly, 'but I think it'd be worse if I did see him. I don't think about nothing but Jon. I can't talk about nothing else. What would that do for Bobby?'

'You're a fool to yourself,' he said, frankly. 'Bobby knows all that. He's prepared to give you love anyway. That's what you need. You gotta give up on Jon, Kate. Bobby will help you, and so will I.'

This brought an uncontrollable burst of tears, and he pulled her close and held her while she cried. 'Go on, darlin',' he whispered, 'cry all you want. That's good for you.' He patted her back like she was a baby, and his arms were good and strong around her. But she couldn't ignore what he'd said about forgetting Jon. How could she? Kate pushed him away with an effort, and went to the ladies' to repair her ruined mascara. She saw him put his head in his hands as she glanced back, and felt sorry she was causing him such concern. Why did he worry about her anyway? But Adam was a really good bloke and she was honoured that he felt something special for her. Kate resolved to brighten up. That would make him feel good.

When she returned, he'd got two more drinks, though hers was only half gone. 'Sorry about that,' she told him. 'Tell me all the news about you and Tia.'

He smiled and looked relieved. 'Well you know I'm gonna be a dad soon. The nipper's due next month. I'm dead proud.'

'I know, Adam. I'm glad for you and Tia. But what about your parents?'

His face darkened. 'They wasn't too pleased at first. Tried to tell me it wasn't mine and all that kinda shit. I told 'em where to go, and they've accepted it now.'

Kate nodded approval. It must be great to be a strong man and stand up to your parents. She wished she could. She looked at him wonderingly as a thought struck her. 'Did you do that on purpose, Adam? Get her pregnant I mean?'

'Nah...' He grinned roguishly. 'I just got carried away one night. It happens real easy you know.'

'I know.' She sadly reflected on the last time she'd been with Jon. How easily it could have happened then. Kate almost wished it had. At least she would have had the memory. She gulped back the threatening sob. 'But ain't Tia moving soon? What you gonna do, Adam?'

'I'm going with her,' he said at once. 'Her mum will have room in the new place for all of us 'til we can afford our own. We're gonna get rich. Me and Bobby got great plans.'

'Go, man!' she said, but suddenly felt strangely lonely. The Alley-cats would fall apart without Bobby and Adam – and Tia was the nicest girl of the lot. She wouldn't have any friends left. Maybe she should start seeing them before they went. There wasn't long to go – only about six weeks. But then Bobby might start getting hopeful about her, even possessive. And what would she do if Jon showed up?

Adam was watching her thoughtfulness with dark, knowing eyes. 'You could be part of the family,' he reminded. 'Bobby would marry you tomorrow if you was old enough.'

There he went again, back down the same well-worn track. 'There's no way I can even think about Bobby 'til I know what's happened to Jon,' she told him, firmly. 'You can't expect me to.'

His eyes deserted hers, and she sensed his inner conflict again. Did Adam know something she didn't? Why wouldn't he tell her? Surely he realised it would be better if she knew.

Just then, three young men walked into the pub. Kate froze with shock as she recognised Steve Ringman and the same two Hellcats who'd attacked her last winter in The Highway.

'Well, well—' Ringman eyed the couple with obvious glee. 'Look who's here, boys.'

The other two grinned, fiendishly.

'It's little Jewfucker with Atwell's bird.' Ringman gave a low, mocking whistle. 'Does the King know, Jewcat?'

Adam's eyes blazed hellfire as he looked at Ringman. 'Shut your filthy trap!' was all he said.

The landlord interrupted these pleasantries. 'I don't want no trouble in here. You three can get out before you start.'

'S'okay, Dad.' Ringman spoke in his mock-soothing way. 'We're only kidding – we're all old mates.' He gave his best innocent smile as he spoke.

To Kate, that was part of his evil. He looked just the kind of young man you would gladly take home to meet your mum (that's if you removed his leather jacket). Dark brown, curly hair, wide hazel eyes, and the flush of extreme youth on his cheek, which was only belied by the size of his body – very well-developed for eighteen or so. But Ringman was totally evil beneath this choirboy exterior. Kate knew it from her own experience, but the landlord did not.

The other two still grinned. She noticed the sandy-haired boy had several missing teeth. That was courtesy of Adam. He would be hell-bent on revenge for one.

The trio moved to the bar to order their drinks while the landlord still looked undecided. He said, 'I got the phone right behind this bar. I can have the coppers here in two minutes if you lot start.'

'S'okay, Grandad,' Ringman further assured, 'we'll get together with our friends later.' He gave Adam and Kate a meaningful glance, and she knew he meant it didn't matter how long they stayed in the pub – the trio would get them outside. Her blood ran cold at the thought. Adam could fight. He was the Alley-cats' best. But there were three of them; they were probably armed – and he wasn't Superman.

He put his arm around her and whispered, 'Sorry I got you into this. It's the last place I ever expected to find Hellcats.'

'I know, mate. It ain't your fault.' She tried to sound calm, clinging to his shoulder with instinctive need for male protection.

'I gotta get you out. Let's think...' He whispered this almost to himself.

The Hellcats had got their drinks and moved to a table in the centre. Kate was glad they weren't sitting too close. They all had pints and whiskey chasers – obviously hard drinkers. This did nothing to allay her fears.

Still in a whisper, Adam said, 'When you've finished your drink, I'll get up and go to the bar. I'll get another one for you. You slip out then, as if you're going to the ladies', and then run home. They won't suspect if they see me getting you a drink.'

'I ain't leaving you, Shad,' Kate said at once.

'Kitty, you must.' His whisper was frantic.

'I ain't leaving you with them, and that's that.'

His eyes were dark desolation. 'They won't go easy on you 'cos you're a girl, y'know. In fact, it'll be worse for you. If anything happens to you, darlin', I'll be doing time for murder.'

'I still ain't leaving you. There must be another way. Think again.'

He was silent, thoughtfully nibbling her ear in the most delightful way. He couldn't seem to stop these little displays of affection under any circumstances. He was a truly lovable man. Kate knew she would blame herself forever if he got hurt.

'Ain't that sweet?' Ringman yelled across. 'Look at 'em cuddling in the corner, kids.'

'Sooo romantic...' Sandy-head enthused, mockingly.

'Lemme know when they get down to the int'resting bits,' said the third boy. He was dark and greasy-haired with an ugly jagged scar across his nose. This was the man whose hand she'd stamped on. Kate knew he had not forgotten by the evil glance he gave her, and was unable to repress a shudder.

Adam ignored these inane comments. He took out his packet of cigarettes and offered one to Kate, which she declined.

'Don't forget your friends, Jewboy!' Ringman yelled again.

'Fuck off!' Adam told him shortly, then lit his fag.

'Typical Jewpig,' said Sandy-head.

Kate felt Adam tense at this painful reminder of Nazism, but he controlled himself. She knew he was doing it for her sake.

'Yeah, tight as a duck's arse,' added Scarface.

'So bestiality's your thing,' Adam retorted with scathing wit.

It took several moments for the full implication of this remark to hit Scarface. Then he reddened, angrily, while the other two laughed at his expense.

'I'm warning you lot—' the landlord reminded.

Jon's ring tingled Kate's finger. It did that a lot lately. She thought because it was too tight, it might be causing bad circulation or something. She twisted it around a little to ease it. Ringman noticed her action. 'Still wearing Atwell's ring,' he commented, 'and going out with Jewcat.' He tutted with feigned disapproval. 'If you was my bird, you'd be dead.'

'If I was yours, I'd rather be,' she retorted.

He scowled as the other two sniggered, then glared at them until they stopped.

'Nice one, darlin'.' Adam grinned at her.

'You might get your wish before the night's over,' Ringman threw at her, and Kate felt herself pale.

Adam said, 'You lay one finger on her and you'll be wishing you was dead.'

'Oh yeah?' Ringman sneered. 'You and the whole fucking Israeli army, I s'pose.'

They all laughed loudly, and left it there for the moment. Sandy-head got up to the bar for refills. Scarface went to the juke box and made a selection. Moments later, the strident chords of Duane Eddy filled the small bar.

Under cover of the music, Adam said, 'They're gonna fire themselves with booze. I gotta act soon. I'm gonna give you my mum's phone number. When I go up to the bar, you sneak out like I said before, and nip in the other bar – there's a phone in there. Tell my mum to tell Bobby where we are, and we need the boys. Don't tell her too much, or she'll worry.'

'Okay Shadow, but then Bobby'll know I'm with you.'

'I'll just have to own up to it, love. Your safety's more important than Bobby busting my head.'

'He won't really, will he?'

'I reckon he will, Lady.'

'You won't let him?'

'I'll let him.' He took her hand and retrieved a biro from his pocket. Under the table, he wrote the number on the palm of her hand. 'Off you go, kid. Good luck.' Then he got up and went to the bar.

Nervously, Kate moved towards the door. She had to pass fairly close to the Hellcats' table. Sandy-head reached for her with wild, groping hands, and she shied away from him.

'Hurry back, darlin',' Ringman said. 'We ain't seen enough of you yet.' He leered evilly and, with this innuendo ringing in her ears, Kate hurried out.

Luckily, there was a connecting corridor between the two bars with the toilets situated along it. The second bar was not visible from the one she'd just left. This was occupied by a few older, square people, blissfully ignorant of the impending war next door. A middle-aged woman and a young girl were serving in here – possibly the landlord's family. She could understand his not wanting to involve them. They wouldn't have been much help in any case. Kate walked straight to the phone in the corner. With trembling hands, she inserted four pennies and dialled the number. The ringing tone seemed to last forever. Suppose his mum was out? What would she do then? She didn't know anyone else nearby with a phone. Not many people could afford them. She could have phoned the police, but Adam wouldn't like that. None of them liked police involvement. Once they knew your face, you were marked. The Alley-cats had so far managed to stay out of trouble with the law.

At last, the receiver was picked up at the other end and a pleasant female voice stated the number, then "Hello".

'Hello,' Kate replied. 'I've got a message for Bob Atwell. It's very important – from Adam (she'd almost forgotten to mention him).

'Who's speaking?' enquired the voice.

'My name is Katharine, and I'm with Adam in Turpin's Retreat. Please tell Bobby to come and bring the Alleycats.'

'Which cats?' The voice was puzzled.

'I mean kids – fellas – young men.' Kate realised desperately that Adam's mum might misunderstand teenage slang, though she should be well used to it with him for a son. Maybe he didn't talk like that at home; she knew she never did. Her mum was always going on about "talking proper", which was quite funny when you thought about it.

The older woman's voice became concerned. 'You sound scared, dear. Is Adam in trouble? Shall I phone the police?'

'No.' Kate forced a laugh. 'It's only for a snooker game.' She said the first thing she could think of.

'Where did you say?'

'Turpin's Re-treat,' she said, slowly and distinctly.

'Is that a public house?' She sounded disapproving.

'Yes – please hurry.'

'All right, dear. I'll tell him.'

She seemed sceptical. Kate wondered if she'd seen through her frenzied explanation. She heard the click of the dropped receiver, then the buzz of disconnection. Oh well, she'd done her best. She had to get back to Adam.

Once again she had to pass the Hellcats' table; her face flamed at their crude remarks: 'That was a long one, darlin'.'

'Been playing with yourself?'

'Jewcat won't like that. He wantsa do it.'

'Leave her alone!' Adam growled, seeing her discomfort.

Kate reached him gratefully, and huddled close to him again.

'Okay?' he enquired in a whisper.

'Yeah, she's gonna tell him,' Kate assured.

'Good girl!'

'Whaddo we do now?'

'We don't hafta do nothing. They're on their third round already – they'll start soon.'

'I'm scared, Adam,' she admitted.

'I know, darlin'. I asked you to go.'

'I just can't leave you.'

He cuddled her in silence while she watched the Hellcats, nervously. They were just talking amongst themselves; they knew they had the two of them cornered. Loud rock music continued to blare from the juke box, and the landlord eyed them all, suspiciously. Kate reckoned he felt as frightened as she did. She prayed that Bobby and the gang would arrive before anything happened.

Adam's hands were fondling her back through the soft sweater. 'You feel gorgeous in this woolly thing,' he whispered, appreciatively.

'This ain't no time to get fruity,' she told him.

'Might be my only chance,' he said wickedly, though his eyes said something deeper.

Kate didn't argue further, because she suddenly understood his deeper meaning. Adam might die tonight. The Hellcats were thoroughly vicious bastards. They wouldn't care if they killed him, or her either. She was so scared.

He said, 'Under my jacket, at the back, slide your hand down. Don't make it obvious.'

She knew by his tone this was some important ploy; he wasn't just getting fruity. She did as he said, until her hand was on his waistband. She noticed he wasn't wearing a belt, and the feel of him reminded her so much of Jon, she almost cried.

'There's a metal catch on one belt loop,' he instructed. 'Undo it and put it in my back pocket.'

Kate found the catch, which was the squeeze and spring kind. This was attached to a fairly thick chain – the type you'd use to restrain a dog. The rest of the chain length was already in his pocket. She knew what he meant then. He wanted the weapon easily accessible, just in case. Adam wouldn't use it unless it became imperative. He was no mindless butcher. She undid the catch and slipped it into his pocket.

'Good girl!' he said again. 'Now I'm ready for anything. Gimme a kiss.'

This last request was so unexpected, she looked wide-eyed into his face. 'In front of them? You must be joking.'

'I ain't joking, love.' His eyes confirmed it. 'I need that small thing from you – I need to know you trust me.'

'Course I trust you. What am I still doing here? – but I can't kiss you, Adam. Not with them watching.' Her face burned with guilt. The truth was that she was afraid to kiss him because of the way he might make her feel. Kate couldn't trust herself with him. Somehow, she thought he knew this.

'Please, just a little one,' he begged with dark, imploring eyes.

She thought again that he might die, or get badly hurt – all for her. She thought of the extreme danger they were in. And she relented. 'Okay Shad, just a little on—.'

His mouth was on hers before she'd hardly finished speaking, and his arms tightened around her. His tongue searched, hungrily, but she couldn't yield to it. Fear held her back. Fear that she would hate herself, that she would betray Jon, that she would want Adam too much, and guilt about Bobby and Tia. He finally contented himself with nibbling gently on her lower lip.

The Hellcats whistled and cheered, and her face coloured up again as she tried to hide behind Adam.

'Go, girl! You can do better'n that!' Scarface yelled.

'I'm really gonna enjoy telling Atwell about you two,' Ringman added.

'Come here and give me some,' Sandy-head invited Kate.

'Get fucked!' Adam told him, venomously.

'You off'ring shares?' Sandy asked, delightedly.

'I think it's time you did.' Ringman stood up, challenge in his cold eyes. All pretence at innocence was gone. He looked every inch the dangerous animal he really was. He moved out from his table and towards the couple. One hand remained in his pocket, the other a little way from his hip. This was it. He'd made his move. He stopped halfway between his table and theirs.

Adam stood up to meet him. He moved around the table and placed himself squarely between Ringman and Kate. She knew he would fight himself out of sight to save her. Her heart pounded with frantic fear.

The other two Hellcats took up their positions, knowing the weak spots from long experience. Sandy-head covered the doorway to block retreat. Scarface leaped right over the bartop with a single bound, and caught the landlord around the throat before he could move to the phone. Kate noticed with horror the six-inch blade wielded before the poor man's terrified eyes.

Ringman issued his ultimatum. 'You gonna hand her over? Or die first? Your choice, man. We'll get her anyway.'

Adam answered not a word. Though his back was to Kate, she knew he was giving Ringman the cold, dark eye of Satan. She'd seen him do it before. His right hand inched like slow motion in a dream towards his back pocket. She hardly dared to move or breathe.

Ringman was taller than Adam by at least three inches, and was well-built like Bobby, yet somehow he didn't make Adam look the least bit small. He snarled with rage when he realised Kate's defender wasn't going to back down. Then his hand whipped from his pocket and she heard the deadly click as he released the death blade. She could just see it from where she sat – six inches of naked steel glinting in the soft light. She put both hands over her mouth to stop herself from screaming, afraid to distract Adam in any way.

'Get outa my way, Jewpig!' Then Ringman slashed at Adam with the blade, aiming low at the belly. What happened next was so fast, Kate hardly believed it. Adam stepped back sharply to avoid the knife which swished through empty air. Then the dog-chain was in his hand, and he used it like a whiplash. She saw the bright flash of metal, and heard the ring of chain links, then the awful thwacking sound as heavy iron hit the bones of Ringman's hand. He dropped the knife with an anguished yelp, and his features contorted with a grimace of mingled hatred and pain.

There was no man faster than the Shadowcat, and Adam proved it to Kate beyond belief that night.

The next instant, Ringman dropped to a crouch to retrieve his weapon, and Adam's boot was on his hand. With a swift flick of his wrist, he somehow got the chain around his opponent's neck, twisted and pulling tight from behind. Then he had him. Ringman made a terrible choking sound, and wisely remained still.

Sandy-head was halfway across the room with his own flick-knife, a steely glint of menace. But he stopped dead when he saw his leader's predicament.

'Drop that knife, and back off!' Adam ordered. 'Or he's dead.' He increased the pressure on the chain with an extra half twist, and Ringman whimpered.

Sandy obeyed. The knife hit the polished floor with a clatter.

'And you!' Adam told Scarface. 'Let him go!'

Scarface released the near-fainting landlord, but threw his knife towards Adam with obvious malicious intent. The Shadow turned Ringman slightly to shield himself, and the flying weapon narrowly missed the captive's nose. 'Stupid fucker!' Ringman managed to gasp.

The landlord had recovered enough to disappear into the back recess, and could be heard dialling the phone. Ringman tried an elbow back into Adam's groin, but this was effectively blocked by a deft twist of the hip. The Shadow retaliated with a hefty knee in the back, which painfully increased the pressure on Ringman's throat. He made frantic gasping sounds; his face was turning a funny colour.

'Now Kitty,' Adam addressed her, 'come and pick up all these knives, love.'

Kate was naturally glad to be of some help, but approached each weapon cautiously, expecting Sandy in particular to jump on her. But he did not. His loyalty to Ringman was more than the creature deserved. Adam took his foot off the Hellcat's hand as soon as the weapon was gone. She thought this rather over-generous of him. She moved back to the corner, holding all three of the ghastly things.

'Now, you two get out!' Adam told the henchmen. 'You've got your chance to run before the coppers get here. He's staying.'

Sandy and Scarface needed no further encouragement. Scarface was over the bar and out of the door almost as fast as Sandy was.

'Bastards!' Ringman wheezed at them.

'They won't get far,' Adam told him. 'They'll run straight into Bobby. They'll wish they'd stayed.' He encouraged Ringman to his feet by yanking on the chain, and pulled him towards an oak pillar with coat hooks. The captive's hands frantically scrabbled at his throat in an effort to save himself from throttling; he was powerless to resist. Adam wound the extra length of the chain up and around the coat hooks, finally looping the ringed ends over the highest, so that Ringman could hardly move without choking himself. Then Adam said, 'I owe you this from the Lady. You hit her last time, didn't you?' And he gave his captive a hard fist to the body, which caused Ringman almost to double up, and strangle himself in the process. Kate closed her eyes as the agonised sound escaped him. She just couldn't bear to watch that much pain, much as she knew he deserved it. When she opened them, Adam had produced a length of rope from somewhere about his person, just like a conjurer. He used this to tie Ringman's hands back behind the pillar. There was no escape for him.

The landlord had watched all this with open-mouthed disbelief. Adam moved towards Kate and took the knives. He returned to the bar and laid these on the top. 'All yours, mate,' he said to gaping man. 'Ready for the coppers. We'd be grateful if you never give a very good description of us.' He added a confidential wink.

'Good work, son,' the man finally managed. 'Me lips are sealed.' He returned the wink.

Ringman had recovered slightly. 'I'll get you one day, Jewpig!' he hissed.

Adam turned towards him. 'Yeah, when you get your speed up, little mate.' He patted Ringman's cheek, mockingly. 'Seeya when you get outa nick.' Then he grabbed Kate's hand and they left the pub.

The Shadow was true to his word. He took care of the Lady, didn't he?

Didn't he just?

Chapter Nineteen

It was about nine-ish and just growing dark. Adam furtively glanced about before they set off, his eyes still fierce, the warrior still evident. His arm went around Kate's shoulders and he pulled her close to his side. She put her arm around his waist to complete the close feeling. This pleased him and he smiled. Then they began to walk and he said, 'I'm sorry our date was such a mess. I wanted to give you a pleasant memory, and all you got was horror from Ringman.'

'It wasn't your fault, Adam. You was brilliant. I still don't believe how you done it. I'll never forget it.'

His eyes were darting everywhere. Kate knew he was worried that those Hellcats might still be somewhere about, lying in wait. He said, 'We was dead lucky, that's all.'

'How d'you mean, Shadow?'

'It's lucky that Ringman came for me himself. If it'd been one of the others, he'd have called my bluff. He'd have known I couldn't really kill a man. He'd have kept right on coming. Then we'd have been dead, love.'

Kate shivered, knowing he was right.

'Besides,' he couldn't resist crowing a bit, 'it takes a man to step on the Shadow, not them three goons.' He grinned. 'Wonder what happened to Bobby? You needn't have bothered phoning. I got in big trouble for nothing.'

'Maybe he thought "Serves 'em right" and left us to it?'

'Nah,' he said with conviction. 'Bobby wouldn't do that. He might murder me himself, but he'd never let anyone else do it – and he'd certainly never desert you, darlin'.'

Her arm tightened around him, almost of its own accord. 'Don't let him hurt you, Adam. Explain to him, or I will – or Tia will. I'd hate to cause trouble between you and Bobby. I know how close you are – like brothers.'

His arm tightened in return. 'The best of friends fight sometimes,' he said. 'Just like brothers do; just like lovers do. You can't have a really close relationship without lousing it up now and again. It's human nature. The closer you are – the fiercer you fight.'

Kate remembered that awful time when she'd rowed with Jon on the beach, and she knew what he meant. They'd both said terrible things they didn't mean, and it had hurt so bad. Tears tried to surface with the memory. 'What makes you so wise?' she asked him.

His eyes had softened, as if sensing her sadness. 'The Shadow knows,' he reminded.

Kate understood then that Adam couldn't explain the things he knew. He just knew them. He really was a prophet. Or what was he? Telepath? Imp of Satan? Or dark-eyed angel? She knew which one she thought.

Suddenly, he pulled her into the darkened doorway of a bommie, well back into the shadows. 'What–?' she asked in a fright.

'Shhh – listen!' he told her.

She did and, out of the growing darkness, she heard the sound of many running feet.

'It might not be our boys,' he warned in a whisper. 'It could be Hellcats looking for us.'

Kate nodded as she clung to him. If she'd been on her own, she might have walked straight into them. But Adam had heard – all his fine senses ever alert. The warrior never really relaxed. He peered out of the doorway while she stood behind him. Then he chuckled. 'Guess what? Here comes Sandy and Scarface with the Alley-cats chasing 'em. Boy, are they shitting themselves! Come and see, love.'

Kate looked over his shoulder and, sure enough, there were the two Hellcats running like the devil. Sandy was limping a bit, sort of hopping, and begging Scarface to wait for him. He was sobbing like a scared kid. They passed their doorway. Seconds later came the Alley-cats – five of them, strung out across the road, whooping and howling bloodlust by this time – they were that close and sure of their prey. Bobby was in the middle of the line.

'I gotta warn him about the coppers,' Adam said. 'Stay here a minute, Kitty.' Then he ran out to meet Bobby who stopped when he saw him. The rest of the gang ran on.

They were close enough that she could hear what they said. 'Don't go near Turpin's,' Adam warned. 'The landlord phoned the police, and I left Ringman wrapped up as a present for 'em.'

'S'okay.' Bobby's eyes were cold as he looked at Adam. 'We don't hafta go there – we got 'em already.' This was confirmed by howls and shrieks coming from further down the road. 'Where is she?' Bobby then demanded, fiercely.

'Here,' Kate said, and walked out to stand by Adam's side.

He looked from her to Adam, then back to her, and she'd never seen Bobby's eyes so cold – like silver flashes in his head. 'Well...' he finally said, 'I hope you two are proud.'

'Bobby, it ain't like you think–' Adam began.

Bobby ignored him. 'I don't blame you, Kitty.' (She'd never have guessed that from his expression. He was looking right through her with eyes of stone.) 'You got the right to go out with anyone you want. I ain't got no claim on you. But this little shit–!' He pulled Adam up by his collar and shook him, '–is s'posed to be marrying my sister. She's gonna have his kid any minute – and he's s'posed to be my friend!' He lifted Adam right off his feet, then dropped him. The smaller man only just managed to stay upright, staggering a bit.

Kate stared at Bobby with horror; she'd never seen him like this before, a cold-eyed stranger – a bully. 'Bobby, please don't,' she begged.

Adam tried again. 'I just wanted to talk – I thought she'd talk to me. I was gonna tell her–'

Bobby's backhander across his mouth effectively stopped whatever he would have told her. Adam reeled backwards, and his lip bled a little. 'You don't tell her nothing!' Bobby almost snarled. 'Unless I say so.'

Adam cast his eyes down and looked like a little kid who was going to cry. Kate couldn't believe this was happening. Where was the warrior? How could he take that from Bobby? She knew he wouldn't take it from anyone else alive. She couldn't stand it one moment longer; she threw herself between them, and slapped Bobby's face hard. 'He was trying to help me!' she ranted at him.

'He's been telling me all night to listen to you – but I'll never listen to you again. You're just a great big self-centred bully, and I don't even like you any more!' She tried to slap him again, but he caught her wrists in his iron, gripping hands. Shock and anger showed in his eyes, but at least the coldness was gone. He was shaking with suppressed rage. 'You'd better take her home, Adam,' was all he said.

'Maybe you'd better,' Adam argued.

'NO!' Bobby almost threw Kate to Adam who caught her in his arms. 'YOU took her out – so YOU take her home! She's YOUR date!' Then he turned and ran after the other kids.

Kate dabbed at Adam's bleeding lip with her hanky. Then he took it from her and wiped her tears with a clean corner. 'I feel so terrible, Adam. How could you let him treat you like that? I just bring grief and pain to everyone. No wonder I don't wanna go nowhere.'

'Don't say that,' he chided gently. 'I hope you'll see me again.'

'What?' She was thunderstruck. 'After all that with Bobby?'

'He'll get over it,' he assured. 'When he's got all the rage outa him, he'll calm down, then he'll listen. I'll make him understand that you and me are diff'rent – and it's not like he thinks.'

They were walking on, and had almost reached the end of the south alley. His arm was around her again, like he didn't even care if any of the gang saw them, and his eyes were starry-bright in the lamplight. 'Ringman spoiled everything,' he continued. 'There was so much I was gonna say to you – so much to explain. You still don't understand something I've known for a long time. I know you feel confused and guilty about me.'

He was absolutely right. 'How do you know?' she asked.

'The Shadow knows,' he replied, as she should have expected. 'There ain't much time to explain to you now, but I'll try a bit. I don't wanna leave you all mixed up.'

'I'm listening, Shadow.'

He began, cautiously, 'You're in love with Jon, and I understand that 'cos I'm in love with Tia. But you think, because of that, it's wrong to love anyone else. That ain't so, kid. Love is essentially good. It can't never be wrong.'

'But–' she began to protest.

'I know you love Bobby.' He ignored her interruption. 'It's very clear to me, though you ain't admitted it yet to yourself – your mind won't let you. I also know you love me, same as I love you – but that's a bit diff'rent and even harder to accept.'

'I can't handle this...' She was almost in tears again.

'Being in love is the worst or the best kind.' He was determined to make her understand. 'That's the kind that tears out your heart and eats you up – the painful kind – the possessive kind. That's what's wrong with Bobby. That's what's wrong with you. The Shadow knows. But the other kind of love is more gentle on you – 'cos it's love without pain, like you and me, Kitty. You can talk your head off about Jon or Bobby, and I'll never mind a bit 'cos I only care about you. Myself don't come into it.'

He was beginning to make sense. She stared into those brilliant dark eyes, hanging onto his words.

'You're worried that your feelings for me are bad. You think it's just animal lust, or something. That ain't true, love. A girl like you don't feel that way without something deeper. We're more than close friends – more than brothers. You sense that and you feel guilty. In a way, we're even more than lovers, 'cos you and me are on the same plane. I'll explain that next.'

They'd reached her door and stood in the shadowed porch. His eyes were black as the starry night. She was reminded of Jon and the tears threatened again. 'I'm still listening, Shadow,' she said.

'I can almost feel your mind,' he continued, 'I can nearly guess what you're thinking. When I look in your eyes, I can feel how you feel – and I know you can feel it from me too.'

Kate thought about that. It did seem like his eyes spoke his thoughts. They could say a thousand things in silence – she'd often noticed. She'd thought that was his own special magic. Was it her?

He went on. 'I'm receiving you like a radio transmission, and you're receiving me. Ain't that beautiful? That's the only way I can explain it, darlin'.'

She was filled with wonder. 'Yes, Adam. It is beautiful. I'm so glad you told me.' She held him by the shoulders, reluctant to let him go. He pulled her close and held her tight.

'Don't forget I'm your Shadow,' he said. 'And I'm your soul-brother, part of you that can't be denied. When this cloud of misery is gone, you'll be with Bobby, and with me and Tia. Whatever happens, I'll always be with you.' He gently kissed her forehead. 'And I hope – someday you won't be afraid to kiss me.' He looked into her eyes and the sparkle of mischief was back in his.

Emotion welled up in Kate's throat, fit to choke her. 'Shadowcat,' she told him, quite inadequately, 'thank you, brother.'

Kate's mum and dad were naturally surprised when she walked in at only 9:30. It was the first evening she'd been out for weeks – in fact, since her birthday, and she was sure they worried that she wasn't normal.

'You're early, dear.' Mum stated the obvious.

'Yeah, I got fed-up,' Kate lied (that must have been the most exciting evening of her life). 'I've got a headache – I'm going to bed,' she then announced.

She caught the glance they exchanged as she left the room. "She just gets nuttier" the glance said. But she wanted to go to bed, so she could be alone and think. She was so worried about Adam. Would Bobby really beat him? And would Adam let him? She couldn't bear to think so. She should have gone to see Tia. Together they might have calmed Bobby. Kate decided to go straight round there in the morning...

She dreamed of Jon that night, as she often did.

This time, they were standing on Waterloo Bridge, and the sunset flamed his hair. He turned gentle brown eyes towards her, though he didn't touch her. He said, 'I'm right here. I'll always be with you. Please don't be afraid. The Shadow knows.'

Kate tried to reach her arms to him, but they refused to obey her. He shook his head sadly, then began to walk away from her. His footsteps made a ringing sound on the silent bridge. She desperately tried to follow, but in the fickle way of dreams, her limbs were leaden and unable to move. 'JON!' she called to him, frantically. He turned once and called back, 'Drumming is soothing!' And his voice echoed on and on in her mind. She woke up, sobbing his name, with tears wet on her cheeks.

This was only one of many similar dreams she had of Jon around that time, every one painfully realistic. She thought these to be the product of turbulent emotion – all the things she felt mixing up in her mind.

Much later, she wondered about that.

Chapter Twenty

In the morning, Kate got up exceptionally early, considering it was school holidays, and went straight to Bobby's house. She didn't expect to see him; he would be gone to work by this time, but she wanted to see his sister. Tia would tell her what had happened.

She was dismayed when Bobby answered the door. It was past nine and he should have been gone. He looked equally disconcerted to see her. 'Kitty?' He couldn't hide the question in his voice, nor the hope.

'I've come to see Tia,' she said coldly. 'Is she in?'

'Yeah.' He lowered his eyes from her accusing stare. Guilt was written all over him. Kate feared the worst for Adam. 'She's in the kitchen,' he finished awkwardly. 'Go right in.'

Kate firmly quelled her unreasoning desire to comfort him – to tell him she understood how he felt, and everything was all right. First she had to know what he'd done to Adam. She walked right past him, down the hall and into the kitchen. He didn't follow.

Tia was busy with a load of washing-up. Kate noticed a blood-stained T-shirt soaking in a bucket by the sink. It looked suspiciously like the one Adam had been wearing. 'Hello, Kitty,' Tia said, brightly. 'Long time, no see.' She looked cool and pretty in a cotton smock-dress. Kate eyed her maternal bulge with something like envy.

'Is Adam all right?' was her first helpless question. 'Are you angry with me, Tia?' was the second.

Her calm grey eyes were just like Bobby's. 'No, I ain't angry with you, Kitty. I know all about you and Adam. I knew before you did. He told me the very first time I went out with him, and I had to accept it. He tells me everything. There ain't no secrets between us. I was angry with Bobby last night, but I'm over it now. Adam's okay, 'cept for a fat nose and a few bruises.' She smiled sweetly, showing her exquisite dimples. Tia was a beautiful girl.

'Please tell me what happened,' Kate begged.

'Sit down then.' She pulled a chair out from the kitchen table. 'There's still tea in the pot.'

Kate sat down gratefully, while the other girl poured tea for them both. Then Tia sat down with her, abandoning the washing-up for the moment. 'I don't know all of it,' she began. 'I woke up and came downstairs when I heard them. Bobby must've just hit him in the face. There was blood everywhere, Kitty.'

'My God!' Kate's voice hushed with horror.

Tia explained. 'No-one knew this before except me, but Adam's got a very sensitive nose. One little tap and it bleeds like mad. Course, Bobby wasn't exactly holding back, and Adam was barely defending himself – didn't seem to want to hit Bobby. But he was bleeding gallons. I had to clout Bobby with the broom to make him stop.'

At the time, Kate was outraged, but when she thought about this later, she had to laugh. Tia – eight months pregnant – laying into her big brother with a broom. It was hilarious.

'What then, Tia?'

'Bobby got scared when he realised how much blood Adam was losing. It was just pumping out. We laid him back, but he started choking on it, so we had to sit him up. I put cold, wet cloths on him 'til it stopped. Then we gave him a stiff drink. Bobby was so relieved, he had tears in his eyes. He really thought Adam was gonna die.'

Kate was close to tears herself. 'Did it hurt him a lot?'

'I reckon so, Kitty. But you know what a soldier he is – he never complained once.'

'Yeah I know.'

'We got him cleaned up and put him to bed here. Bobby went to tell Adam's mum he was stopping over. Then we had a right old time clearing up the living room before Mum got home. After that, me and Bobby had a good natter. I talked some sense into him.'

Kate was impressed. 'What did you tell him?'

She took several sips of tea before she replied, and Kate did likewise.

'I told him this: "Bobby," I said, "Jon has always known how you feel about Kitty. Ain't that true?"

"Yeah," he said.

"But he don't try busting your nose. He trusts you to look after her. Why d'you reckon that is, Bobby?"

"I dunno" he said.

"It's 'cos he knows that your feelings for her are so fine, you would never take advantage – you'd never do nothing she don't want. Can't you see, Bobby? Don't you trust Adam that much? I do. It ain't just a flame or a fancy, y'know – Adam really cares about Kitty, just like you do. But you ain't got nothing to worry about, 'cos he's already committed to me. And that's the way the world turns, brother."

'He looked so pissed-off then, I nearly cried. He said, "But she'll never forgive me now, and neither will he."

'I just hugged him then, Kitty – my sweet big brother. I love him, you know.'

'Course you do,' Kate said in a choked voice.

'Anyway, this morning, Adam came wandering downstairs in a bit of a daze. He looked so funny, Kate, with his fat nose, and nearly tripping over Bobby's jarmers – much too long for him. So cute and funny – I never loved him so much before as I did right then. Know what I mean?'

'I know, mate,' Kate told her, gently. She really did.

'Bobby told him, "Sorry Shad." Adam was so surprised he just sat down on the end of the stairs. Bobby said he understood now, and Adam could take you out and talk any time, 'cos he would do the same, even if Jon knew.'

'Tia, you're an amazing girl,' Kate said.

'I gotta be, if I wanna keep that amazing man.' And just for a moment, Kate caught the barest betrayal of pain. She swore to herself right then, that Tia would never have cause to worry about her and Adam. He was Tia's fella – not hers.

'Go out and see him if you want,' she then said. 'I know you must be dying to. He's in the back yard recuperating. Then I hope you'll talk to Bobby. He's suffering, Kitty.'

'I will. Thanks, Tia. Thanks for everything.' Kate walked through the back door and out to the sunlit yard.

Bobby's back yard hadn't changed since she was knee-high. It was still littered with bicycle bits and pieces of engine that he was always tinkering with. It looked like the same relentless weeds bravely struggled through the cracked flagstones; the same array of socks and T-shirts flapped on the washing line, though somewhat bigger, and even the same wasps droned around the dustbin. That's how it seemed – a place immune to time.

Adam was sprawled in a deck-chair, wearing nothing but shorts and his Star of David. His eyes were closed and he seemed to be asleep. For several moments, Kate didn't even notice his damaged nose – she just feasted her eyes on the rest of him. The bruises did not diminish his physical perfection. Though small, he was well-muscled and beautifully shaped. She longed to touch him, but didn't dare; just gazed at him with a deal of girlish wonder and helpless delight. She thought again of Jon, and battled with tears.

Then he reached for her hand without opening his eyes. 'The Lady likes to look at her Shadow,' he said, as if it were the most natural thing in the world. He'd caught her hand with unerring precision. She gripped his tightly, then looked closely at the black silk lashes. 'You peeking, mate?'

'No way.' He opened his eyes and gazed into hers. Only then, she noticed his swollen, misshapen nose. She knelt down beside him. 'Does it hurt much?' she enquired.

'Only when I breathe,' he replied, humorously. 'It's real nice to see you, Kitty.' He squeezed her hand and told her love with his eyes. There was no discernible fierceness now.

'What did Bobby say to you last night?' She just had to know this. 'I can see what he did, but what did he say?'

The eyes were darkly serious. 'Darlin', it's better you don't know that. You gotta remember he was running high on pain – he never meant it.'

'I understand that, Shadow. Please tell me.'

'Well – he called me a lotta names, which I'd rather not repeat to you. But the worst was "Judas". That really hurt, love.'

'Oh Adam...'

'But it's all right now. He understands – I told you he would. You seen him yet?'

'Only for a minute. He looked upset.'

'You'll tell him it's okay – I know you will.' He squeezed her hand again and smiled. 'Ain't it good? Everything's all right now.'

'Not quite everything,' she reminded, 'I still don't know where Jon is.'

Once again those dark eyes troubled over and guarded against her. She didn't like that. 'Shadow, remember I know your mind. There's something you ain't telling me.'

His deep regret was obvious. 'Kitty, it ain't me – it's Bobby. He don't want me to tell, and I can't betray him. I wouldn't even tell you that 'cept I can't lie to you now. It was hard enough before!'

'S'okay, Shad. I don't expect you to betray him.' She stroked the dark hair on his arm, finding this suddenly irresistible, feeling the muscle tense under her touch, fiercely reminding herself he wasn't hers to touch. She thought of Jon again, with a stab of pain. 'I'll see Bobby myself. Take care of your fat nose. 'She stood up and gazed at him once more. The Star of David mirrored the sun and momentarily dazzled her.

He suddenly reached around behind his neck and unclasped the silver chain. 'I know you like this,' he said. 'Take it. Wear it for me.'

'Adam!' She was a bit shocked. 'I know that's important to you – you always wear it.'

'I got another one at home,' he assured, 'and Tia's got one, and there's one for my boy.'

She admired the little etched star in the palm of her hand, already loving it. Then she fastened the chain around her neck. Kate knew she would wear it with pride. 'How d'you know it's a boy?' she asked, unnecessarily.

'The Shadow knows,' he replied as expected.

'Course he does.' She bent to kiss his funny face, 'He knows it all.'

Bobby was sitting on the front doorstep. As Kate walked down the narrow hallway, his dejection was apparent even from the back view, and there was no way she could avoid him. She felt apprehensive, unsure if she could honestly forgive him. She would have liked a little time to think about it first – to rehearse what she would say; but it couldn't be helped. She sat down beside him, where she had sat countless times before, and waited for him to speak first. It seemed right that he should. To her mind, he was the guiltier party.

In those few moments, flashed through her mind the long years she had known him. Bobby had always been there; always part of her life – ever since she'd been a tiny five-year-old kid who had first been allowed out to play alone. He had taken her under his wing at once, at an age when he regarded most girls with natural, nine-year-old, masculine disdain. He had let her ride with him in his home-made go-cart, a ramshackle assembly of planks and pram wheels. Then later, on the crossbar of his cranky old bike which he had put together himself with bits from the rubbish dump. Bobby had rescued her on more than one occasion from bullying/ragging sessions from other kids. He had climbed a lamp-post to retrieve her new school scarf, after Tommy Dixon had thrown it up there, in a devilish mood. Then he had slapped Tommy's head and sent him howling home to his mother. Bobby had almost taught her to swim, before it became compulsory in school at the age of eight. He'd taken her with him to the local swimming baths, and even paid for her as she was too young to warrant pocket money. He would swim with her on his back, then suddenly dive away from her; but he was always there if she began to flounder. Bobby had taught her to climb the bommies without fear. The roof-riding which she'd flaunted at Shelagh Durran had all been down to him. He could kick a football right up to the sky, or so it seemed to her; but when he'd accidentally broken a neighbour's window, he'd remembered to grab her hand and pull her into a bommie to hide with him, so that she would not be blamed. And if ever she fell and grazed her knees, it was always Bobby who picked her up and kissed her better. He'd named her Kitty-cat right from the start, and she'd always looked up to him and adored with a kind of helpless hero-worship. That might have sparked off his feelings for her, or maybe they'd been there all along. "I'm gonna marry you when I grow up" had been his constant childish promise. If she had never met Jon, there would never have been any question about Bobby and her. She wondered if he knew that too. Soon he would be gone from the alley, and Adam and Tia with him. She might never see them again. It really would seem like losing her family. How would she feel then?

Kate felt the sudden rise of tears and blinked them back with annoyance. Why was she always crying? She must be the world's biggest cry-baby.

He was looking at her sadly. His arm went straight around her when he saw the tears, all reserve forgotten in his concern. He held her head against his shoulder. 'Kitty-cat,' he said softly, 'forgive me?'

It was exactly the right thing to say. Her heart melted at once and she cuddled him close. He heaved a great sigh of relief, then lifted her chin to look into her eyes. 'I don't deserve it,' he said. 'I don't deserve you ever to speak to me again – I wouldn't blame you.'

'I was just as bad – saying rotten things to you. I swear I never meant 'em. Sometimes I can't control my temper. I'm sorry Bob.'

'Your temper? What about mine? I might've killed Adam if Tia hadn't stopped me.'

'I understand how you felt. It was pain reflex. When something hurts so bad, you just lash out against it.'

He looked amazed. 'That's exactly right. How d'you know those sorta things?'

'I'm learning all the time,' she told him. 'Besides, I learned that one a long time ago.'

His fingertips were making love to her face, caressing every contour. His eyes were warm with gladness. She wanted to keep it there. She was pleased with the way things were going so far – much better than she'd expected. Her feelings for Bobby were very confused at that time. She couldn't possibly be in love with him, because she loved Jon, and you can't be in love with two people at once, can you? Yet she cared very deeply for Bobby. She didn't like to see him unhappy, and it made her feel good to see him smile. Those were the only things she knew for sure. 'Bobby,' she said, 'do you remember the first day I met you?'

'Funny you should say that,' he replied thoughtfully, 'I was thinking about it earlier.'

'What d'you remember?' she encouraged.

'I was nine and you was much younger – tiny. You musta been all of five.'

'That's right.'

'I found you all alone in the middle of a bommie. You was playing some kinda 'maginary game – sitting on a slab of brickwork, throwing flowers.'

'Yeah, go on.' (His memory was perfect so far.)

'I musta scared you, 'cos you looked up at me with them big, frightened eyes – dark blue – almost navy-blue.'

'Airforce,' she corrected.

'You sorta froze with terror, and your eyes were so big...'

'I was scared of boys, and you seemed enormous to me.'

His eyes softened. 'All that dark, fluffy hair, tied with a pink ribbon; those big eyes, and your cute little face. You reminded me of a kitten. I knew right then that I would rather die than ever hurt you – or let anyone else.'

She gripped his hand while emotion rose in her throat. 'D'you remember what you said?'

A tiny frown puckered his brow for an instant, then cleared. 'Something like, "Hello, I ain't seen you before. My name's Bobby."'

'How do you remember so well?'

'I dunno. I reckon it must be important to me.' His hand tightened around hers. 'Tell me what you remember.'

She too, recalled the occasion with bright clarity. She smiled as she began her version. 'I looked up and there you were – Prince Charming straight from a story-book, except...'

'Except what?'

'It never seemed right for you to have such a lovely face. You was one of them big, rough people – a boy.'

They both chuckled. It was good to see him looking happy. 'How did you know at that age?' he asked next.

Kate reflected a moment. 'Y'know that is strange. How do little kids know? It wasn't just clothes, 'cos girls often wear shorts or dungarees too, and even then your hair was quite long. I reckon it must be instinct – or just a certain aura which each sex has for the other.'

'S'too early to throw dictionaries at me,' he complained, humorously.

'You know what I mean,' she chided. 'Aura's just something you can't explain. You feel it, but you don't see it.'

'Yeah, I know, kid. Please carry on. I'm enjoying this.' His smile proved it.

'You had the handsomest face I'd ever seen.'

'Come off it! At nine I was a scrawny little git,' he argued.

'You dunno how you looked to me. Your hair was pure gold in the sunshine – it ain't so bright now – more like straw-blond.'

'Old age caught up with me.' He grinned with mock ruefulness.

'And your face was tanned like a film star. Your eyes looked smoky coloured to me, and even then I noticed your lashes was too dark for your hair.'

'My mum always said that was a sign of beauty.' He was still grinning.

'You looked like an angel, but I was still scared – you were a boy. I felt better when you smiled and told me your name. I told you mine, and went all red. D'you remember?'

'Yeah, you blushed like a rose. Why?'

''Cos Katharine is such a cissy name. I was sure you'd laugh.'

'But I never did.'

'No, you didn't. Then you said...' She paused to giggle. 'Then you said, "I'm gonna call you Kitty-cat. D'you wanna play with me?"'

They both laughed at this memory of innocence.

'I'd run a mile if you asked me that now,' she added, wickedly.

'I know you would, darlin'. Ain't that a pity?' His eyes sparkled humour. 'What Then?'

'Well, I was intrigued with the idea of playing with a boy.'

'You naughty girl!' They both laughed helplessly again, while she slapped his shoulder playfully. It was so good to see him in his natural jovial mood. This was the Bobby she knew and loved.

She continued when they had recovered: 'I said "yeah", still a bit nervous, and you grabbed my hand and said, "Come and see my go-cart."'

'Yeah, that's right. I remember that old contraption.'

'You told me you made it yourself – you had to do things yourself 'cos your dad had gone away. I thought you must be amazingly clever.'

'You was dead right, love.' He still grinned, disarmingly.

'You said I could be Bo-dee-seeya, and you would be Caesar. I'd never heard of either of them.' She giggled again. 'I never knew you had your historic partners a bit confused.'

'Did I?'

'Yeah, they was enemies. But who cares when you're five?'

His eyes were growing tender again.

'You sat me in front of you, between your knees—'

'Wow!' He closed his eyes to let his imagination run riot.

'—And you called Adam to give us a push-start down the alley. It was fast and bumpy. I was scared, but thrilled. I held onto your legs real tight.'

'Y'know, this conversation is doing great things for my morale, and I'm getting all fired up.' He pulled her closer.

Kate wound up her narrative. 'From that day on – I adored you.'

His voice softened again. 'You was the cutest little thing I ever saw. Something about you made me want to look after you. You grew into the most beautiful girl in the world, and then you grew away from me. I always thought you was my girl – on and on forever. But Kitty-cat don't want her Bobcat no more.'

'Bobby please – don't get upset again. Y'know I think the world of you.' She held him tighter.

'Then come back where you belong. Let me take you out, Kitty. I've waited so long.'

'No, Bobby.' Automatic response, even though she hated herself.

Hurt appeared in his eyes. 'I don't understand, love. You went out with Adam the very first time he ever asked you, and I've begged you loadsa times. How d'you think that makes me feel? I know you care – I know you feel something for me. So why won't you ever say "yes" to me? Why, Kitty-cat?'

Everything he'd said was perfectly right. She was running out of excuses and beginning to think she was nuts, herself. She tried hard to explain, choosing words carefully. 'I never went out with Adam for the usual reasons. I thought you understood that. He offered me sympathy...'

'You think I ain't got sympathy?'

'Don't int'rupt when I'm trying to explain!' she told him, sharply. 'I knew I could talk freely to Adam about Jon. I can't do that to you no more, Bobby – not now I know it hurts you.'

'I don't care.' His voice was firm, but his eyes betrayed him. Of course he cared.

Kate continued: 'I also hoped he might tell me something about Jon, but he never did. He knows something, but he ain't telling. I can read Adam – I 'spect he's told you that. Then last night, you slapped his mouth to stop him telling. I know that you know it too. What is it, Bobby? You once said you'd never hold out on me. Why are you doing it now?'

He looked stunned. Worse than that, he looked cornered. His eyes were wildly fearful like those of a trapped animal. She sensed his inner conflict. He seemed to struggle with speech for several moments – then came the lies. 'You're wrong, Kitty. We don't know nothing. No-one's seen Jon. He's left you, love. You gotta give up on him.'

All her pent-up misery and frustration broke loose with a vengeance, and she yelled at him, 'You expect me to TRUST YOU?'

Her brain felt like a live coal, spitting sparks. 'You expect me to go out with YOU! – when you tell me bare-faced LIES? D'you think I'm FUCKING STUPID?' She slapped his face just as hard as she had the night before, then stood up and fled the length of the alley; tears streaming – hating herself – hating Bobby – hating the entire rotten, cruel, hateful world – filled with blind, savage, useless hate.

She didn't see the way he laid his head on his knees in despair, nor if he really cried.

Chapter Twenty-One

Kate stayed at home for a whole week. Rage and resentment against Bobby warring with her concern for him. Even while emotions battled, she knew she would have to make her peace with him before he left. She couldn't let him move away without trying to patch things up. She might never see him again – then she would always regret her childish tantrum. The secret he kept from her would still cloud their friendship, but at least he knew she wouldn't go out with him until he told. In that way, they were even and an uneasy truce could be maintained.

It didn't take long for Mum to notice Adam's Star of David, and she was more than a little disturbed. She looked at Kate as if she'd suddenly announced she was turning pagan, or taking up devil-worship or something. 'You shouldn't be wearing that Jewish thing,' she scolded. 'You're a Catholic.'

'I ain't a very good Catholic,' Kate told her, 'but I am a good Christian, which is more than a lot of Catholics are. Do you think Jesus hates Jews? He chose to be a Jew 'cos he knew they were fine people, and he was no bad judge.'

'The Jews crucified Jesus,' she justifiably argued.

'They acted in ignorance,' Kate informed. 'Are we any better? If Jesus lived next door to you right now, and told you he was God, would you believe him? Would you accept?'

Mum was silent. Kate knew she had her thinking.

She pursued her advantage. 'They was just normal people like you and me. You and me would dismiss Jesus as a nutcase if he showed up today. That's all the Jews did. He forgave them, even as he died, 'cos he understood that. So why can't you?'

'That's quite enough cheek, young lady!' But she said nothing further, though Kate knew she was still worried. She thought her daughter might be getting involved with a Jewish boy. Well actually, she was right, but not in the way that she feared. There would never be anything sexual between Adam and Kate, even though there easily could have been. They both instinctively knew it would somehow spoil the special relationship they had – and besides, there were too many other people to consider. She thought of Adam's parents; they were just as bad as hers in reverse – horrified because he loved Tia who was Christian. She was sure Jesus never intended things to be this way. He said that all men were brothers – all children of God, and Kate knew that He was right. She continued to wear her precious Star of David, and her mum never complained again.

She felt she had won a small victory.

On Saturday, Adam waylaid her again in the north alley. As usual, she was laden with Mum's shopping which he took from her at once. At least it wasn't raining this time. In fact, it was unbearably hot. He was wearing shorts, vest and plimsolls. The warrior was not in evidence; he looked like any other young man taking the sun. Kate was pleased to note his nose was almost back to normal – Bobby hadn't broken it – and he was wearing another Star of David which glittered against his sun-bronzed throat. She couldn't help her admiring appraisal of his fluid, muscular movements.

He grinned with full appreciation, and looked her over in the same fashion. Her attire was very similar to his, with the exception of flipflops instead of plimsolls. 'You've got great legs,' he complimented. 'You shouldn't hide 'em away in jeans all the time.'

'I get quite enough of wearing dresses at school,' she told him.

He put the shopping down and hugged her impulsively. 'Lady, I've been missing you all week. You're hibernating again.'

Several passers-by were giving them amused glances, but Kate didn't care. She hugged him right back. Her little soul brother; he was so good for her – the greatest comfort in the world.

'I've come to give you the word about Bobby,' he went on. 'I reckoned you might be a bit scared to approach him after your little explosion on Monday.' He chuckled.

'The Shadow knows,' she affirmed.

Dark eyes searched hers relentlessly. 'I persuaded him to stay home tonight. He's been down the boozer every night this week, drinking himself stupid. That ain't good, Kitty. I know he's pretty skint. I told him I'll buy the beers tonight if he stops home. I ain't told him you're coming – but I know you will. We'll be playing cards at number five. Don't be scared. Just walk right in. Me and Tia will be there, and some of the gang – you won't have to face him alone. But I tell you, kid, he'll be over the moon just to see you.' He had placed a hand either side of her neck and was absently caressing her ears. His eyes were full of trust. Kate really wanted to kiss him at that moment, but she controlled the urge – still felt that wouldn't be right.

She stroked his wrists with both hands. 'You're wonderful, Shadow,' she told him. 'Ain't you the Angel of Deliv'rance?'

He grinned, happily.

Number five, South Alley was a bombed house – uninhabitable of course, except for the living room which had escaped destruction by a miracle. The kids often used this as a meeting place, away from the prying eyes of parents, neighbours or police. The dining table and chairs were still there, and were used for card games or night beer parties. In winter, they even lit a fire in the old black hearth, although smoke from the half-crumbled chimney belched all over the alley through the upper floor of the ruined house.

That evening, Kate entered number five, hesitantly, unsure of her reception, yet longing to make peace with Bobby after her fiery outburst earlier in the week.

Tommy Dixon caught her in his arms, as she trod carefully down the rotted hallway. He was tall and lean, tow-headed and spotty, with a cheeky elfish grin. 'I am the tollcat,' he informed. 'The entry fee is a quick grope and a kiss.'

'Get knotted!' Kate struggled in his hold, thinking to run right out of there.

'Let her in, Tomcat!' Bobby's voice sharply ordered from the dimly-lit room.

Tommy released her at once and she walked in. There were about six Alley-cats present, mostly involved in the card game. Candles in bottles sputtered on the table and on the mantelpiece. A haze of blue cigarette smoke drifted above their heads, moving continuously with the heat from the candles – like a spectral presence. There were plenty of beer bottles in evidence, especially around Bobby. Adam and Tia both gave her welcome smiles, and Adam added a wink of approval. The atmosphere was a bit spooky, but warmed by the faces of friends. A tranny radio was playing pop music from Luxembourg. Ruth and Janey were draped all over Bobby, and Kate's first resentful thought was that he seemed just fine without her. She did not even recognise this as jealousy until very much later. But his stern expression dissolved into a helpless smile at seeing her, and he dismissed the two girls at once with a gentle nudge to each. Ruth moved to sit with Jim, and Janey joined Tommy by the door. Bobby then motioned Kate to sit beside him. She did so gladly, floored by his easy forgiveness. He flicked the top off a beer by banging it on the edge of the table, helping it along with the heel of his hand. A waft of vapour escaped from the bottleneck. This he handed to her without a word of reproach. She took it, too dazed to remember she didn't like beer. Then his arm went right around her and she leaned against him. Adam blew her a kiss across the table while his eyes sparkled happily. Kate knew he meant, "We are yours and we love you".

She returned his silent message.

Not a word had been spoken. She watched the card play and sipped the beer. Harpie had been right – it wasn't bad when you got used to it. She was dealt in at the next game. It was Pontoon, she later learned.

And Kate felt that she had come home.

Adam had taken Tia home early. She got tired easily these days. Ruth and Jim had abandoned the cards and were getting down to some heavy petting in the corner, with complete disregard for anyone who cared to watch, though actually no-one did. Tom and Janey had replaced them at the table. But Kate thought it was about time she went, and stood up, a little shakily. She'd drunk three or four beers which she wasn't used to. Bobby stood up with her. He'd drunk an awful lot more than she had. Adam had said he drank far too much these days. Kate was worried a lot about that, thinking it might be her fault. She'd enjoyed a quiet evening with him, without any fights or upsets, and she didn't want to spoil it. She could still feel resentment grumbling away in the corner of her mind; it wouldn't take much to make it rear up again.

He pulled her close to him, possessively. Fiery passion smouldered in his eyes. That was dangerous too. It wouldn't take much from Kate to fan the flames. He said, 'It's early yet. Come home for coffee. My mum don't get in 'til eleven.'

Tia would be in bed by now. He wanted her all to himself. And God help her, she knew how he felt. With all that beer racing through her veins, she was seriously tempted. But she said, 'Bobby, I don't think that's wise. I don't wanna upset you. I wanna keep the peace between us. I don't think we should be alone together. Please understand.'

She thought he did. Disappointment clouded his eyes. He knew the rift between them was only shakily bridged; it could not be closed until he told his grim secret. His arms tightened around her, and she could feel the wild beating of his heart.

Drumming is soothing...

No! She refused to listen to that gentle, insistent memory. It was too painful.

'Thanks for coming, anyway,' Bobby said, huskily. 'I'll walk you up the alley.'

'No!' That startled him a bit. 'I'll walk alone. I'm sorry, Bob. I think it's best. Don't get angry.'

His eyes searched hers, shouting love at her, which she was forced to ignore. 'Okay, darlin'.' He was accepting her terms with reluctance. 'I'm not angry. I hope you'll come out again. We've only got a few weeks left. But you ain't walking home alone. Tomcat will take you.' His lips touched hers, undemanding as a petal in a breeze.

Tommy stood and stretched himself lazily, just like his feline namesake. Janey gave a peevish little pout at his desertion. 'At your service, darlin'.' He gave Kate the Alley-cat salute with the back of his hand flat against his forehead.

'And keep your hands to yerself,' Bobby told him, 'or I'll cut 'em off!'

'Yessir, Bobcat,' Tommy said.

And so Kate walked up the alley with Tommy Dixon. He gave her his arm to hold at once, in chivalrous fashion, and his elfish grin to go with it. She smiled back. All of the Alley-cats were nice kids. They had to be or Bobby wouldn't have them.

He said, conversationally, 'What happened to that little friend of yours who used to come round in the holidays – the one with big blue eyes?'

'You mean Mary?' Kate knew he did. 'I still see her every few weeks, but she's courting now. Besides, this is a long way for her to come, then walk home alone. She lives in Stepney Green.'

'I'd walk her home,' he said at once, with an impish gleam in his eye.

'I'll tell her that,' Kate offered, 'but I doubt if her boyfriend will approve.'

'Thanks anyway.' He grinned again. He really did remind her of an elf. Green eyes and a cloud of fair hair that sprouted in all directions like a storm-tossed haystack. She stored away his picture in her mind for future reference.

Then he looked more serious. 'Y'know, Kitty, all the kids think it's a real shame about you, getting jilted an' all.'

Anger surged through her as fierce as the pain. So that's what they all thought. Maybe they all knew the truth and she didn't. But Tomcat might be willing to tell her. This could be her chance to unearth the facts. She controlled the anger with an effort and decided to sound him out; he was obviously sympathetic. 'Tomcat,' she began, 'd'you know the thing that Bobby won't tell me? I've gotta right to know. If you tell me, I'll never let on who told – I promise.'

He looked scared then and sort of helpless. 'I only know what everyone does – that Jon's left you and he ain't coming back. I dunno how or why.'

Kate was silent, furiously fighting back the tears. They were all so convinced about that. It must be true – it must. Maybe Jon had been around and told that to Bobby, and that's what he couldn't bring himself to tell her. Poor Bobby – how she'd made him suffer! But she had to know for sure. Why wouldn't he tell her? Did he think she was that much of a baby?

Tom was not insensitive to her unspoken misery. He stopped and turned to face her. A streetlamp shed light on his fair hair, giving him a haloed look. Crazy moths flitted through the halo. 'Look, Kate,' he began awkwardly, 'I know it ain't none of my business but, if you want, I'll tell you what I think you should do.'

'Okay mate, tell,' she encouraged. Anything might help. She was desperate.

'I think you should take off that ring and send it back to him through the post.'

'No...' She was horrified.

He continued, unperturbed. 'If he's suff'ring from amnesia or something, then that'll jog his mem'ry. And if he's just undecided, then that should force his decision. Send a letter with the ring, saying if he still wants you, to get his arse round here, and if he don't – then at least you'll know for sure. If I was him, that would definitely provoke some kind of action.'

Elfin green eyes glittered in the lamplight, perfectly serious for once. Tom was genuinely concerned, and he was trying to help by giving the male point of view. At least it was constructive advice, and she believed him that he didn't know Bobby's secret. He could never have been so sincere if he had. Probably no-one knew except Bobby and Adam. 'Thanks, Tomcat,' she said, gratefully. 'I'll think about what you said.'

He smiled and gave her his arm again. They walked on to her door. 'Don't tell Bobby what I said.' He looked worried. 'He does his nut if anyone upsets you about Jon.'

'I won't say nothing,' she promised.

'Remember all us kids are with you,' he reminded. 'Even when Bobby's gone, we'll still be with you.'

'Thanks, Tomcat.'

'I'm gonna scarper back to Janey now, before she changes her mind. I think I'm on a promise.' He left with a knowing wink and another elfish grin.

Thoughts buzzed like a bombardment of kamikaze bees in Kate's brain as she climbed the endless stairs.

She stayed awake a long time, thinking about Tom's advice. She knew it was good and sound, and probably more sensible than Mary's. She also knew she couldn't take it – not yet. She couldn't bear to part with Jon's ring: the only tangible part of him she had left. Suppose she sent it back and heard nothing more? She would still never know what had happened. At least while she had the ring, she had hope. Someday he would come for it – or her – or both. She decided to wait until Christmas. Jon might write then. He knew he could write freely now. She was over fourteen. Her parents wouldn't think it was bad if she got letters or cards from boys. They probably wondered why she didn't.

Kate finally slept with that thought – wait until Christmas...

As it turned out, she didn't have to.

Chapter Twenty-two

School resumed the following week, and mates began to tell Kate about the new youth club which was run by St. Michael's Church. It was groovy, they said. Loads of talent (boys) and good music, and the Pepsi was cheap. It was time she started going out and dating, they said. She couldn't sit around moping forever.

The youth club was close to the old school, and therefore close to where Jon lived. Kate thought she might see him there; that was the only reason she agreed to go. Her mum seemed quite pleased that she was going somewhere at last (apart from down Mary's which was where she thought Kate usually went when she was with the gang). Even her dad was quite amenable so long as she was still home by 10:30.

But Bobby didn't seem too keen when she told him about it.

'What d'you wanna go there for? I could take you somewhere much better'n that.'

She was a bit snappy with him. 'Like down the pub? Oh yeah, my dad would love that. And before you say I never minded going to a pub with Adam – I'm afraid that put me off pubs for a bit. And anyway, I told you I ain't going out with you 'til you come clean with me. When you talk – we date. You know the score, mate.'

The way he looked at her made her feel like the world's prize bitch, but she was determined not to give in first. No way would she go out with a bloke who told her lies. His stubborn secret was a cold, dark wedge between them – and he knew it.

'Well I'm coming with you,' he finally said. 'You ain't walking that Highway alone. And if I can't make it, I'll send Adam. The Hellcats would love to get hold of you.'

She was disturbed by this reminder. 'But Ringman's in the nick now. Why would they be int'rested in me?'

His eyes were deeply serious. 'Don't you understand yet? It's me they really want. They think you're mine. They think they can get at me through you – and they're right about that. I hope I don't have to spell it out for you, darlin', what they'd do to you. And if that happened, I'd never rest 'til I'd killed every last one of them.'

Kate turned cold with fear. She knew then, she would have to stick with the Alley-cats after he'd gone. She also knew his concern was very real; he wasn't just being jealous and possessive. She felt ashamed of her earlier annoyance. 'Okay, Bobby,' she said in a gentler tone, 'but don't forget, we ain't dating. You walk me there and back – that's all.'

'I won't bovver you while we're there,' he promised.

The club was held on Wednesday and Friday evenings, and they fell into a sort of routine. Bobby walked her there and back on Wednesday – Adam on Fridays. Bobby was true to his word. He usually got involved in a snooker game, and never bothered her in the club except to buy her an occasional drink. Adam, on the other hand, stayed right by her side all evening, and she was glad of his wonderful company, and proud to be seen with him.

On the first occasion, when she turned up at the door with Adam, Father O'Brien was there, checking membership cards. He looked Adam all up and down with obvious wariness. Leathered and studded, as usual – the warrior was showing. Adam looked the typical young villain. Then the Father's eye caught the gleam of the Star of David. 'You're Jewish, son?' came the inevitable question.

'Right on, Dad,' followed at once. Adam was fiercely proud of his origin, and rightly so, Kate thought.

'This is a Catholic youth club,' Father announced, coldly.

'Come off it, Father,' Kate interposed, 'you don't even ask no-one else if they're Catholic. Half of them ain't. And anyway, Christians are s'posed to be loving and giving. Ain't that what it's all about?'

The priest looked a little ashamed then. He wrote out a membership card for Adam without another word, giving him the pen to fill in his name. Kate was interested to note that his middle name was David. Then Father copied his full name into the book. 'Shalom, Adam David.' He looked up and smiled.

'Shalom, Father,' Adam returned with his easy grin.

'Don't forget, son, this is place of peace. It's designed to keep kids out of the pubs and off the streets.'

'That's cool,' Adam told him, sincerely.

'What does that word mean – Shalom?' Kate asked Adam as they walked up the stairs.

'I'm surprised you don't know that,' he said. 'It means more than "Hi" or "Hello".' He looked thoughtful. 'The old, square meaning is "Peace be with you", but these days it's more like, "Hope you're doing fine. It's real nice to seeya".'

She repeated the word, savouring the sound of it, rolling from lips to tongue and back again. 'Sha-lom. It's a nice word,' she approved.

He smiled like an angel. 'Sure you don't need an extra man in your life?' he joked, lovingly.

She slapped his wrist with playful admonishment. 'You're marrying Tia. Don't be greedy!'

'I'm a real glutton,' he admitted with a grin.

They entered the hall and girls from her school quickly surrounded them, ogling Adam with unashamed interest. 'Kate – where d'you find 'em all?'

'Is this one your fella? Ain't he cute?'

'Let me know when you're fed-up with him!'

'Nah,' she answered the most relevant question, 'he ain't mine. He's just borrored.'

'I'm her brother,' he announced, matter-of-factly.

'Yeah? Pull the other one. You look just like her.'

'Where's the big, blond brother you had on Wednesday, Kate?'

'Got any more going spare?'

Giggles all round.

Kate looked at Adam, worried he might be overwhelmed by all this female silliness. But he seemed to be lapping it up contentedly. He winked at her, then moved to the bar to buy drinks for them.

She had to admit she enjoyed those few evenings with Adam. The easy-loving affection between them was refreshing – relaxing after the strain of being with Bobby. It was love without anxiety, without pain. If only every human relationship could be like that, the world would be a much happier place. Everyone should have a soul brother. There ain't nothing else like it.

The club wasn't bad. There was snooker, table tennis, darts or chess, and dancing if you felt like it. They played all the latest pop records and quite a few old favourites. Kids took turns at being DJ for the evening. It was good to see old faces from primary school. Kate saw quite a few kids from her old class, but she did not see Jon. She kept right on going every Wednesday and Friday, always hoping.

It was a Wednesday night when she met Joe Warner, and that's how it happened that Bobby was nowhere near her at the time.

Kate knew that Joe was a good mate of Jon's, and decided to sound him out. He had slimmed down a lot since his primary school days and she hardly recognised him. He bought her a cola, and they chatted amiably about school and careers – stuff like that; but she thought he seemed a little guarded, almost nervous. This was strange – they'd once been desk-mates, and had gotten along so well, but he kept avoiding her eyes.

She knew he went to the same school as Jon, but he just didn't mention him. Finally, she couldn't stand it any longer – she came right out and asked, 'How's Jon these days?'

Poor Joe. He choked on his cola, then looked at her with a sick kind of horror. He'd never dreamed that he would have to be the one to tell her. 'You don't know?' His voice hardly made whispering level. 'You really don't know?' He was visibly shaking.

'Know what, Joe? TELL me!' Nameless fear clawed at her heart. Kate knew she had gone deathly pale.

He was struggling to form the terrible words. He knew he had to tell her now. 'Jon died,' he finally managed, 'last August. He – he got a virus— then pneumonia.' Joe was almost in tears. 'A load of us from school went to the funeral. His mum found a picture of you in his wallet. She wanted to let you know, but none of us knew where you lived. He called your name...'

So that was how the world shattered around her ears. The room just reeled, and Joe's face shimmered through a wave of tears. She was vaguely aware of the poor boy asking if she was all right, as if from a great distance; putting out his hands to steady her. Then her face crumpled up along with her dreams, and she ran. She forgot all about Bobby, and she ran from that place of horror never to return. She ran to the loneliest place she knew: the infamous Highway, and there she just cried and cried as if her eyes were fountains.

Under the fuzzy, yellow streetlamps, her agony raged.

Jon could not be dead – not her Jon. He was not even fourteen years old! He was young, strong and healthy – he should not be dead. But he is! How could you allow that, God? What kind of God are you?

Her tortured mind continued to rave...

Over a year ago – only weeks after she'd last seen him. All this time, she'd been thinking all those wrong things – that hurt most of all. How long was he ill? Why didn't he ask his mum to come and get her? She knew why. He wouldn't have wanted to get her in trouble with her dad. Even while he was dying, Jon would have cared that much.

You had a lucky escape, Dad! Jon's never gonna beat you now! He'll never be man enough. But he was already more man than you, Daddio! though he was only fourteen. Jon would never beat a girl! Am I screaming in my head? Or out of my mouth? And why am I laughing?

She was crazy with grief – almost out of her mind.

Oh my darling, my little Hero – you were the best boy in the world. You would have been the finest man – you would have been mine. How could you die? How could you leave me?

Then she cried all over again for Jon's mum. She had lost her husband and her wonderful son, in the space of a few years. How can life hit some so hard and others not at all?

Don't worry, my love. You'll still live. You'll live forever in my heart, and in every one of my stories. You are now, and will always be – my Hero. I will never forget that you are mine...

Kate didn't remember how she got home that night, but she learned this later from Tia:

Bobby followed her from the youth club when he realised what had happened. He caught up with her after her desperate flight, and found her in the middle of the road, screaming her head off. Unable to quiet her hysterics, he eventually carried her home in his arms, knocked her door, and tried to hand her over to her dad. He explained that she was very upset because a friend had died. But as soon as she'd seen her dad, she'd clung to Bobby, frantically begging him not to leave her – they'd had to prise her away from him. Bobby had gone home and he'd cried, because he hadn't wanted to leave her with her dad. He hadn't wanted to leave her ever – he'd had no other choice.

That's what Tia told Kate. She came to see her a few days later. Kate's mum actually let her in, even though she strongly disapproved of a fifteen-year-old girl who was so obviously pregnant. She let her in when Tia begged that it was very important, and Kate knew her mum was at her wits' end about her.

Kate was still in bed. She hadn't moved from it in three days. Tia stood by her bedside, and her belly was enormous. Kate knew she was about to have her baby any time. Lucky Tia! She had a wonderful boy like Adam, and his child. Whatever happened, she had part of her love to keep forever. How she envied her. She wished she could have had Jon's baby.

'I've brought a letter from Bobby,' Tia said. 'Please read it, Kitty. He's so upset.'

'Okay, Tia.' Kate was rational for the first time in days. It was good to see her – someone who really understood about love. She unfolded the sheet of notepaper with trembling hands. Bobby's writing and spelling were pretty awful, not because he was stupid, but he'd never bothered much in school.

So here's a swift translation:

Dear Kitty-cat,

Please believe I know how you feel, for I feel the same about you. I must confess to you, at last, that I knew about Jon a few months ago; that was the thing I couldn't tell you. I just couldn't be the one to destroy your world. I was scared you'd hate me forever if I did. I hit that kid in the youth club – the one who told you. I know it was wrong – someone had to tell you. But at the time, I just couldn't stand the pain he'd caused you. I got barred from the youth club, but I don't care – I know you won't never go there again. You know we're gonna move next week. I gotta stay with my mum 'til she gets settled in the new house – she needs a man around 'til then. But I'll never give up on you, darlin'. Jon asked me to look after you, but he never had to ask. I'da done it anyway. Please come to see me in a few days, when you feel better. Please see me before I go.

I love you, my Kitty-cat. I always did.

Love forever

Bobby. xxxxx

Kate was moved to the depths of her soul as she looked up at Tia, fighting the inevitable tears.

'I ain't never seen my brother cry before,' Tia said. 'Even when we was little kids, he was always the tough guy. Please see him, Kitty.'

'Tell Bobby I will,' she promised, 'but tell him not to hope for nothing more. There ain't nothing left inside me, Tia – nothing left.'

Her eyes filled up with tears. They were the same grey as Bobby's. She gripped Kate's hand briefly, then she left. Kate cried again. Her heart ached for Bobby as well as herself. He deserved better than her – he really did.

She just walled up in her room for almost a week, mostly staring at nothing. She didn't eat, hardly slept, nor heard a word anyone said to her. In her mind, she relived over and over every precious moment she'd ever spent with Jon. That's probably how she remembered it all so well – she just fixed him in her mind forever.

During that time, she wrote some of the wildest poetry she'd ever written – real primitive stuff – the kind Jon would have liked.

> The time has come for tears to start again
> Those faithful tears that always ease the pain.
> Release the raging rivers of my soul!
> Let me drown and then rise up again.
>
> Let me drown until the river dries
> Until the numbing coldness settles in
> See the world once more with empty eyes
> No spark of warmth can penetrate the skin.
> Crash the thunder! Howl the wind!
> Freeze my heart and beat the driving rain!
> Let me know these dreams are empty lies
> Let me die and come to life again.
>
> In the silent darkness of my mind
> Let me wonder who you really are
> Let me feel that you were just a dream
> That fades on waking, like the morning star.

Kate might have eventually died if she hadn't remembered her promise to Bobby. He was hurting too. That boy had done so much for her; she couldn't just ignore his pain. She had to see him before he went away. Sometimes it takes the grief of another to overcome your own.

His mum let her in and gave her a warm, sympathetic smile. Bobby must have told her everything. She led Kate to the living room, and he was just standing there, staring out of the window. She tactfully left them alone.

He turned and looked at her with desolate eyes. 'Look at you, kid!' he said. 'What have you done to yourself?'

She knew she must have looked a mess – all hollow-eyed and getting thin, like she was fading out of sight. Then he held out his arms, and she ran to him, instinctively. He held her tighter than he ever had before and whispered into her hair, 'You held me like this the other night when I brought you home, and I never wanted to let you go – not never. Please let me look after you, Kitty. I told Jon I would.'

It was good to be held like that. She couldn't deny it. Here were strength and comfort, the two things she needed most. But she knew that was selfish. Bobby loved her. It would hurt him too much to know she loved someone else. Sooner or later, it would hurt him more than he could bear. She just couldn't do that to Bobby; she thought much too highly of him, and she had to let him go. 'No, Bobby,' she said, for what must have been the thousandth time.

He looked despairingly into her eyes, and must have seen the emptiness there, for he sighed defeatedly. 'I told you once love, that I'd never give up on you, and I meant it. I'll keep trying 'til I reach you. We're moving tomorrow, but I'll keep in touch. I'll write and, if you give the word, I'll be round here like a shot. I'll have wheels soon – I'll be getting my new bike. Distance will be no problem. And I know Adam will still see you.'

She noticed the glint of golden stubble on his face where he hadn't shaved, and touched this with a tinge of wonder, liking the rough, raspy feel of it. Bobby was a full-grown man, she suddenly realised.

'I know I'm a scruffy sod.' He kissed the palm of her hand.

'Cave-man.' She smiled through fast-welling tears which she couldn't explain. 'I'll look forward to your letters.'

And that was the only promise she gave him.

Adam was waiting in the alley.

Suddenly stricken with guilt, she thought of running past him, but this impulse died as she looked at him and sensed his knowing. He stood in a casual man-stance, hands in the pockets of his faded jeans, wearing his "Ban the Bomb" T-shirt. Side-swept, black hair lifted a little from his forehead in the autumn breeze, and she was fixed by the intensity of his gaze. Dark as midnight, bright as a galaxy, each eye contained a perfect mirror image of herself, haloed in starlight, as if he had captured her soul. Adam David – eyes of the prophet.

He knew very well the outcome of her visit to Bobby, and she knew he was disappointed. But he also understood – probably better than she did. This was the only admonition he gave: 'How can you deny what you both need so bad? You make me wanna stay and look after you myself. But I can't do that. Tia needs me.'

'I wouldn't want you to,' she told him, sadly.

'I won't never give up either,' he continued. 'I'll be back to see you without invite, and I know you won't refuse to see me.'

'The Shadow knows,' she agreed.

'I'll even bring my boy to see you in a little while, when I bring him to see Mum and Dad – but I hope that won't be ness. I hope you'll be coming to see us by then.'

'Adam...' Kate was unable to express her emotion.

He hugged her tightly, and did it for her. 'The Lady's trying to say that she loves her soul brother, and she always will. Ain't that right, darlin'?'

Still unable to speak, she just clung to him.

'And this man loves the Lady – on and on forever,' he finished his fond assurance. Then he walked her back up the alley with his arm firmly around her.

She finally found her voice as they reached her door. 'Shadow, I've just decided – someday I'm gonna write your story.'

He gave his beautiful smile. 'No-one would believe it, love.'

And the Shadow was her only star of brightness in the dark, empty years that followed.

Kate sent Jon's ring back to his mother, when she'd managed to remove it with a great deal of Vaseline. It broke her heart all over again to do so, but it seemed the right thing to do at the time. Later, she was not so sure it was. Jon had given it to her – his special girl. She enclosed a short letter with the ring, simply telling Jon's mum how much she had loved him, and how deeply she shared her grief. She was careful to put no return address at the top of the page. She didn't think she could have faced meeting her. That would only have sharpened the pain for both of them.

She saw Mary for the last time when she was sixteen. Mary still lived in the same block of flats in Stepney Green. Kate had just left school, having somehow managed to scrape through five GCEs, and had finally landed her good job in a city bank (the one that was supposed to have helped Jon through his apprenticeship). In the daytime, she was a smart, slick, city chick – all skirt suits and trim, white blouses, with her hair neatly coiled up on her head. But in leisure time, she became her real self: leather jacket, jeans and long, swinging hair – the look that Jon would have liked (Long hair and animal skins – cave-man stuff.) Kate still didn't go out with boys, with the occasional exception of Adam. She spent most evenings with the Alley-cats, or at least their veterans. Most of them were married with babies, and street gangs were out of fashion. Everyone was "doing their own thing". The rest of the time, she spent hanging around the Ace Café on the North Circular, or motor-cycle joints with other "oldies", the leather crew.

Mary looked fine. In fact, she looked smashing. She was getting ready for a date. Her hair was tinted chestnut and worn in a flattering "flick-up" style. Her eyes looked bluer than ever, accentuated with eyeliner.

They chatted in friendly fashion while Mary painted her nails, filling in the missing years. Eventually, she noticed the absence of Jon's ring. 'What happened to him?' she asked innocently, though Kate knew she thought they had simply outgrown each other.

All the old pain welled up with a sharp shock. That's when Kate knew for sure that she'd never really get over it. She told her – hardly able to control the rise of tears. Mary was sympathetic, but Kate could tell she didn't know what to say. What can you say? What is there to say to someone who's died inside?

'Remember that puckfig Shelagh?' Kate asked to change the subject.

She caught slight disapproval in Mary's eyes at her choice of language, although she had invented the word. Kate realised then that Mary had changed. She had fulfilled all her parents' dreams and become the young lady they wanted their daughter to be. She was no longer a rough, Cockney kid, and they weren't twins any more. They were years and worlds apart. She wondered then if Jon would have changed, if he would have become the man he promised to be, or if the world and time would have spoiled him. Somehow she didn't think so.

Nothing else ever stayed the same, she decided. That was the greatest thing she had learned in her life. Times changed and people changed, and you could never go back to the way things were and find them to be the same. They wouldn't be.

Maybe that's what was wrong with her; she lacked the ability to change. Inside, she was still the rough, Cockney kid and she was still Jon's special girl.

"Never forget that you are mine" he had said.

And Kate had never been able to.

Dear Jon, she thought, I'll see you in heaven.

Excerpt from Katharine Keegan's diary c:1962

They say that time is the greatest healer.

But let me tell you this:

There are some things that can never be healed. They can only be locked away inside you. Sometimes you think these things are gone and can never hurt you again – like a snake in a basket – quite safe, until you take off the lid.

Some day, I know I will take the lid off the basket, just to take a peek – like some day I'm gonna write all of this down.

Doing that might finally lay the ghost...

Epilogue

1963

Sunday evening – wintertime. London was shaded in grey. Bleak and bereft, a ghost city, stretching away in all directions. Kate, the sole survivor on a dead planet. Tower blocks had risen to torture the ashen skyline, where once the dome of St. Paul's had dominated. The dying sun on the other side was a globe of muted redness: glory defeated, forsaking the desolation.

An arctic wind had whipped her hair to a wild frenzy. The feral growth almost reached her waist by this time (Jon would have liked that; he always loved her hair). Why did she agree to come here – to this place – this special place? The memories were too painful. It was her own fault; she was early. She should have come late, so she wouldn't have to stand here and remember.

Kate was alone on Waterloo Bridge, watching the winter sunset reflect in the black, swirling river. The water seemed tinged with blood – like life flowing away. She could actually hear the heedless rush, the only sound apart from the keening wind. She could not help thinking of the last time she had stood there, in that exact spot. Was it three years ago, or four? It had been summer then, and Jon had stood by her side. "This place will always be special to me" he had said, "sort of magical". Except "always" hadn't been very long for him – only for her, left to endure forever without him. Tears sprang unbidden, as they usually did. When would the pain ever stop? Would she hurt forever?

She shivered, in spite of her leather jacket. The wind blew harder in this exposed position. The icy gusts seemed to tear through her as if she were an empty shell, a hollow thing. Big Ben struck five, echoing across the deserted city: a sonorous reminder of the passage of time. That was it; he was late. She wouldn't wait any longer, standing here – and remembering.

'Kitty-cat!'

She whirled to the sound of that barely-remembered pet name. She hadn't even heard the car pull up. A dark green Cortina: brand-new and gleaming – the latest Ford model. She stared without true recognition at the tall young man who got out of the driver's side and smiled at her. He must have been more than six feet tall and was well-built, as far as she could tell, in his bulky, leather flying jacket. The straw-blond hair was still a little too long for the current trend, and sideburns fuzzed out his cheeks. His smile was radiant as he moved towards her, and his eyes were just as she remembered: gentle and sparkling delight – grey eyes.

'Bobby...' she whispered with disbelief. He looked so fine; he looked gorgeous.

'I hope you wasn't expecting no-one else,' he said, jovially. He stood looking down at her with his hands on her shoulders. 'You're beautiful as ever,' he said fondly, 'but your eyes are sad. It's so good to see you, Kitty. Why didn't you turn up all them other times? Why didn't you answer my letters?'

Kate just shook her head, not knowing how to reply. She hadn't seen Bobby since his family had moved from the alley, though he'd written and begged her to meet him many times.

Another Siberian gust of wind hit her, and she shivered.

'You're cold.' The old concern was back in his voice. 'I shouldn't have asked you to wait here.' He unzipped his airman's jacket and snuggled her inside it with his arms around her. His warmth enveloped her, and it was good. She huddled with relief against the soft, cashmere sweater he wore.

'Where's the bike, Bobby?' she asked. Kate knew from his letters that he owned a Norton Dominator (a Dommie). She'd expected him to arrive on that.

'It's too cold tonight to make you ride pillion,' he explained. 'I'll take you biking in fair weather. D'you like the motor, kid?'

Kate refrained from reminding him that she'd agreed to meet him just this once. This wasn't the moment to shoot him down again. She didn't know one end of a car from the other, but even she could see that was some smart dream machine. 'Yeah, It's t'riffic,' she said.

Bobby was doing all right. He and Adam had gone into the scrap metal business, and it was booming. Adam's financial wizardry and

Bobby's natural leadership qualities had finally paid off. Two snot-nosed alley kids, but they'd made it good. Bobby would make a fine catch for some lucky girl. Adam already had.

'Let's get you in,' he said, 'outa this wind.' He opened the passenger door for her and she got in gratefully, leaving the winter behind. He got in himself at the driver's side, then looked at her as if he still couldn't believe she was real.

The sound of the wind was cut off and remote in the warm haven of the car's interior. The radio was playing a mixture of chart singles and oldies. Kate felt better just being there with Bobby, her old street-mate. She realised with a painful twinge just how much she had missed him. She said, 'You've come a long way since the days of Caesar and Bodicea.'

He grinned at the fond memory. 'Yeah, now I'm Mark Anthony and you're Cleopatra.'

'That's more like it.' She smiled back. He'd got his history right this time.

Then he looked serious. 'Y'know, I asked you to come so early 'cos I gotta talk to you first.'

'Go on then, Bobby.' She began to comb her windswept hair, as if she had not a care in the world.

'I've been hearing things from Adam that I don't like, Kitty.'

'What d'you mean?' She stopped combing and stared at him. 'I ain't never done nothing wrong with Adam!'

'I don't mean like that,' he said hastily. 'I don't mean bad things – I mean sad things – things that really freak me out.'

'I ain't your concern, Bobby.' She began to comb her hair again.

'Hell—no, I forgot.' His tone was mildly sarcastic. 'You wasn't my concern the night you ran from that Warren kid, or the night Steve Ringman nearly got you, or all the times your dad hit you and it nearly screwed up my mind. You ain't never been my concern, love.'

'Sorry, Bob.' How did he always manage to make her say that? Her voice was as small as she felt. 'But you really shouldn't worry about me.'

'Listen to this.' He turned the radio up slightly. 'This song says it all...'

Johnny Burnett was singing:

> You're my baby. You're my pet
> You got love that you ain't used yet...

'That's what I mean,' Bobby continued. 'Adam says you ain't been out with a single bloke 'cept him since Jon died. That's bad, kid. You're sixteen for Chris'sake.'

Johnny Burnett sang on:

> You walked outa my dreams into my arms – now you're my angel divine.
> You're sixteen, you're beautiful and you're mine.

'I wish you was,' Bobby said, wistfully.

He was making her cry again.

'I can't help it Bobby,' she told him, tearfully. 'I don't wanna go out 'cos I'm just a drag on other people. I make them miserable. I just keep seeing Jon everywhere I go – hearing him in every sad song. I don't want no-one else – not NEVER!' The tears flowed fast by this time. 'S'diff'rent with Adam,' she finished lamely.

'That's crap!' he said with unexpected vehemence. 'I never heard such a loada bollocks! You'll end up going loopy – you know that?'

'I don't hafta stay here and listen to you!' Kate raged as she fumbled for the door handle; almost blinded with tears, she had trouble locating it.

Then his arms were around her, holding her back with impossible strength. 'I'm sorry, Kitty-cat,' his gentle tone soothed. 'Please don't go. Please stay and listen. I know I started off badly – I ain't no good with words, but I've got something very important to say.' His voice pleaded, but there was no way she could have escaped his hold in any case. She realised his desperation, and turned back to him in silent acquiescence.

He drew her close and put his cheek next to hers. She felt a pulse throbbing in his temple, and the soft, tickly feel of his sideburn against her face. His aftershave was expensive and heady. Then he whispered into her ear, 'I never meant to upset you. It kills me to see you like this, and I just wanna help.'

'There's nothing you can do, Bob.' She was calmer now and the tears had stopped.

'But I've always wanted so much to help. Please let me try.'

'Okay, Bobcat,' she said weakly, using the old nickname that he had loved so well. His closeness was having some effect, a bit like an injured butterfly fluttering on the ground, vainly trying to take flight, going around in circles.

He released her and the spell was broken – the butterfly died. But then he looked into her eyes and she saw the expression there. She'd seen that same look before; she'd seen it in Jon's eyes, and in her own when she'd looked in the mirror. It was the look of aching loneliness, of unspeakable longing for something impossible. It was the look of love denied.

The lamps on the bridge had begun to glow, and spilled soft silvery light across his face. That was when she first became aware of something strange...

'Kit, you gotta start living...'

What had made him call her that? He never had before; only one boy had ever called her that. She was suddenly gripped by a feeling of unreality and a wonderful sense of peace. She stared into his eyes and paid close attention to his words.

'D'you think Jon would like to see you like this? If he could see you now, with your young life in ruins, d'you think he would be happy?'

'No, Jon.' (Why did she call him that?) She noticed the way his hair fell across his forehead, and the trick of light on his cheek that almost looked like a curved scar, and she was mesmerised.

'I think Kit, that he cries every time you do, and he won't never rest in peace 'til you are better...'

For someone who was no good with words, he was doing magnificently, with long pauses between sentences, as if he were being prompted. She didn't interrupt – it seemed important that she should not. His eyes looked darker now, shadowed under his hair, and his voice seemed softer – too youthful for a twenty-year-old.

'I think he would like me to take care of you. He asked me to, remember? If ever he couldn't be around. I think that sorta means now, darlin' – he knows you need someone.' Bobby put his hands on her shoulders and moved a little closer. 'Please let me, Kit. I can make you better. Maybe not completely, but better than you are now – better than this living hell you got.'

Kate just couldn't shake the feeling that Jon was with her – with them. She had that warm glow inside her which she hadn't felt since the last time she'd seen him – or almost felt that night she'd been unconscious in Bobby's arms, the night she'd heard the soothing drums. Was Jon trying to reach her – through Bobby? She hardly dared to believe such a thing.

'I know you've had a rough time, Kit. I'll make it up to you – I swear. Somehow I will...'

Almost Jon's exact words. Kate was convinced. Jon was trying to tell her that this was the only way he could keep all his promises. Bobby hardly seemed aware of what he was saying. He was gazing at her like someone entranced.

The radio had been eerily silent during Bobby's speech, but suddenly flared into life, as if an invisible hand had touched the dial. Brian Hyland sang:

> I'll see you in the sunlight
> I'll hear your voice everywhere...

Bobby said, 'I love you, Kit.'

'I love you too Hero,' she replied automatically, as if that magical name were the key to her heart, as indeed she thought it was.

Brian Hyland continued, mercilessly:

I'll run to tenderly hold you

But darling, you won't be there

I don't wanna say goodbye...

The tears welled again.

Bobby reached to turn off the radio.

'Thanks Jon,' Kate whispered to her lost love.

'What d'you say, kid?' Bobby was obviously himself again. 'Will you come out with me – give me a chance?'

'Yes, Bob. You persuaded me.'

He looked staggered. 'You really mean it? You finally said "yes" to me? I can hardly believe it!'

'You better believe it, boy. I gotta a few things to make up to you as well. D'you really love me?'

'Yes I do, Kitty-cat. How did you know?'

'You just told me, crazy-man. And anyway, ain't you made it obvious all these years?'

'Oh darlin', I'm so happy.' He reached for her, and Kate knew he was going to kiss her, and that she was going to let him. She tensed a bit. Bobby had kissed her before, but always briefly and chastely. She knew this would be different, and she'd never been kissed properly by anyone but Jon.

But when his lips touched hers, she forgot her fears. Bobby kissed her just the way Jon had done – with love and deep passion, and a deal of care and restraint. He held her face between his hands, as if it were something infinitely precious, and her heart began to pound along with his. The butterfly revived and began to flutter again, gaining strength every moment, then finally lifting and dancing away on a warm summer breeze...

He smiled happily into her face. 'D'you know how long I wanted to do that?'

'I reckon I really do.'

His smile was ecstatic. Kate knew he was happier than he'd ever been, and it warmed her heart to see him that way. 'I'm gonna take care of you,' he said. 'Marry me, Kitty-cat. Let me do it properly.'

'Hold them reins!' she admonished gently. 'You only just swept me off my feet. Gimme a chance to get up again.'

'I'm gonna lift you up to the sky,' he promised. Then he took a packet of cigarettes from the glove compartment, flipped the lid and offered one to her, which she accepted. He looked surprised as he took one himself. 'You never used to,' he commented, retrieving a cigarette lighter from his jacket. This looked like it was pure gold.

'No,' she said, Jon wouldn't have liked it.'

'But now he understands,' he stated convincingly. 'I know he does.'

A small spear of golden flame spouted from the lighter as he gave her a light and lit his. She inhaled, contentedly, as she silently marvelled at what had just happened. There was no doubt in her mind that Jon had spoken to her through Bobby – had tried to speak to her before, but she hadn't understood. No way could it have been her imagination. The feeling of Jon's presence had been so strong, and it lingered still. She'd heard that contact with the spirit world was accompanied by a deathly chill – but she'd felt nothing like that, only a beautiful warmth. She felt more content than she had for three wretched years. Jon was dead. No power on earth could ever change that. But his love was still with her – still within her reach. Bobby was alive. He was real and warm and here and now, and he loved her. For the first time in her life, she knew that she could love him back – just as he'd always wanted – just as she always had, somewhere deep inside. Bobby was pure gold for her – just as nature intended, right from the start, and he was hers – all hers. It felt so good, just to love without guilt or shame.

'I asked you out,' he reminded. 'London town is yours for tonight. Where d'you wanna go, kid?'

'I dunno, Bobby. Anywhere with you.'

He smiled and glowed with delight.

'Leicester Square,' he suggested, 'theatre, Lyceum, posh-nosh in a restaurant. Nothing's too good for my girl.'

'I ain't dressed for nowhere like that.' She looked down at her leather and jeans in dismay. 'I was expecting you on your bike, remember?'

'Don't matter how you're dressed,' he assured. 'You'll still slay 'em, darlin'.' He stubbed out his fag in the dashboard ashtray. 'But I know you ain't used to the limelight. I know a nice little pub in Chelsea – some of the gang still get in there. And by the way—' He grinned. 'Adam reckons you still owe him a kiss.'

'Cheeky little devil!' she said, smiling. 'The pub sounds fine.'

'Drunken orgy it is then.' He winked enticingly. 'And that's just five minutes from my groovy pad, love.'

'You got your own flat now, Bobby?'

'Yeah, you'll love it.'

She must have looked a little wary.

He held her hand and she was amazed at the sheer size of his. 'I promise you right now, my darlin', that I'll never do anything you don't want. My name ain't Warren nor Ringman.' He squeezed her hand gently. 'But I hope you won't blame me for trying. I love you so bad, and you really fire me, anyway.'

She tried to give her best assurance. 'Bobby, I just hope I can please you. You're the finest man alive, and you deserve it.'

'Kitty, you please me up to the eyes just by being here.' He breathed hard and his eyes caressed. 'You're a virgin, ain't you? I think that's the sweetest thing in the world, and you know kid, I'd be honoured.'

'You'd be loved,' she told him.

He was giving her the cave-man look. She shivered with delight. Then he grabbed her and kissed her again; this time with wild abandon, hungrily seeking the love he craved, and she kissed him right back and gave him all he was worth.

He grinned wickedly at her breathless excitement. 'How d'you like your new cave-man, Kitty-cat?'

'I just love him, Mr Cool.'

They both chuckled happily.

'Y'know,' she reflected aloud, 'no-one hardly talks or dresses like us no more. The girls at work are starting to call me "rocker".'

'Then they must be proper little squares.'

'Yeah. Y'know they're all getting short haircuts and wearing long skirts and granny shoes.'

'Yuk!' he exclaimed. 'I hope you don't get like them, darlin'. I love you just fine the way you are – my little rocker.'

She squeezed his arm, savouring the feel of the hefty muscle. 'We won't never change, will we crazy-man? We won't never be square.'

'No way, not never, darlin'. We're gonna rock forever.'

'Rock 'n roll will never die!' Kate declared with jubilance.

'You said it, Kitty-cat.'

'I love you, Bobcat.'

'That's mighty cool, sweetness. That's t'riffic.'

They giggled inanely for several moments. Then he reached to turn on the radio again. Susan Maughan was singing "Bobby's Girl".

> When people ask of me
> What would you like to be
> Now that you're not a kid any more...

'I sorta like this song,' he said.

'So do I. Let's make it our song forever.'

'Did you buy the record?' he asked.

'You bet I did!'

'Me too. I wonder why.' He grinned suddenly. 'You wanna see this baby machine fly?'

'Roll them wheels,' she affirmed giddily.

Bobby let out one long whoop of joy which went sort of "Woo-wooo-eeee!" And she knew exactly how he felt. Then he turned the ignition on and that sweet old Ford engine thrummed into life, just like soothing drums – just like the heart of Katharine Mary Keegan.

And she flew...

Lightning Source UK Ltd.
Milton Keynes UK
22 September 2010

160213UK00001B/18/P